# The Public Works

# The Public Works

Clay Carpenter

**To order additional copies of this book, contact:**
Xlibris Corporation
1-888-795-4274
www.Xlibris.com
Orders@Xlibris.com
48034

To my wife Ann-Marie

# Introduction

Certainly February 1985 wasn't all that long ago. Though faced with today's growing torrent of headlines spewed forth with abandon by a mass media increasingly consumed by its own ego, many of us can still recall the names and places that dominated the news of this most recent time.

Ronald Reagan had begun a second term more or less by acclamation and the nation's economy continued its greatest surge in forty years. Around the world we grew familiar with such places as Afghanistan, El Salvador and Poland. Of course, Middle East issues continued to expand along their all too familiar course of religious and political violence. Amidst this backdrop of compelling human drama the events of a scant eighteen hour period which occurred in and around the town of Melonia, New Hampshire nevertheless swept these stories aside. At least for the moment. Maybe it was the general reluctance of a southerly based media to deal with a harsh New Hampshire winter, which had recently become a good deal nastier, that led them to center more on the tabloid potential of the story rather than take the time to accurately discern precisely what occurred and why. Then possibly they just screwed up in their all too familiar follow the leader fashion.

Therefore, bits and pieces of the story became fodder for the public's perceived insatiable thirst for the sensational and bizarre. As a result, the truth was predictably treated with little respect, at best glaringly distorted. As interesting, fun and downright profitable as this all was, when clothed in a clown suit it became pretty lightweight stuff. Though several people were now dead in connection with the New Hampshire incident, the story was quick to slither off the front page in favor of more commonplace tension and tragedy. During the next few days disagreement between the U.S. and the U.S.S.R. regarding nuclear arms control grew uglier and more threatening. Another airliner went down, this time in Spain. One hundred and forty-four people died. A drugged up high school senior somewhere in the Midwest went berserk and killed several of his classmates with a squirrel gun before jumping off the roof of a nearby grain elevator. The public psyche staggered on its weary way, its outward demeanor not unlike that of a small animal staring blankly at oncoming headlights.

So by silent agreement the Melonia story all but died. Oh, the yearly anniversary was well remembered at the local level, but if some thread of the real story threatened to make its way toward a wider audience, somehow it never seemed to arrive. After all, it was far too late to openly illustrate how inept the major media had been. Plus, it became obvious there were those that didn't want particular aspects touched with a ten foot pole.

Though I was in a position to know a great deal about what went on that stormy New Hampshire evening, with so many people involved, it was impossible to establish the whys and wherefores of what became almost a spontaneous action on the part of the Melonia faction. A couple years ago I began the task of fitting the many pieces of that eighteen hour period together into an accurate and complete account of those events. The Melonia participants were basically intact with only a couple having left town. Two others had since died.

Other principals were scattered about the country. I thought members of this latter group would be the hardest to approach, not because of their location, but due to the nature of their shaded existence or government responsibilities. I became pleasantly surprised for they were among the most cooperative. Although most were unwilling to be quoted or identified, they too seemed eager to set the record straight.

Also surprising was the fact that recordings still existed of the radio transmissions of that evening. Though many Melonia residents frequently listened to the Public Works Department frequency for its entertainment value alone, a few had switched on a recorder when they realized that something out of the ordinary was taking place. Little by little, this strange tale took shape in its entirety.

# chapter 1

Organized crime had suffered a series of setbacks during the past year. Federal investigations had resulted in several indictments, and even a few convictions of those once thought to be untouchable. State and local enforcement agencies that once tiptoed carefully in the midst of a dark and powerful foe had now joined the fray as a firm law and order stance again gained popular support.

What was once a well oiled criminal machine was now coming apart at the seams. To those of the old and respected guard, to those who had successfully nurtured their wicked domain in the midst of outwardly wholesome neighborhoods and cities, the sight of new and arrogant faces rising to wrest a bigger piece of the action proved a sobering reality. Such foreign factions didn't care much for appearances even if they had known how to appear in the first place. Ethnic communities whose criminal elements had historically fed mostly on their own kind were now looking to the American mainstream. In doing so they showed little respect and used even less finesse in accomplishing their ends. They were indeed giving crime a bad name. Increasingly, society's wrath was coming forcefully down on all.

The large metropolitan cities of the northeast particularly were the scene of rising turmoil. Such disagreements stemmed not only from attempts by more traditionally entrenched factions to wrest control of locally based revenues from groups recently dismantled by law enforcement, but also from those outside forces who would change the face of the entire organized crime establishment.

The term Mafia had been seldom heard in recent years and the old guard, made up of controlling families, had enjoyed the lack of attention. Now the term was coming back. Their approach was to burrow still deeper into the realm of legitimate investment while retaining friends in high places who could round off any sharp edges that might be encountered along the way. Many of the "older" old guard wanted to get out of the nickel and dime street action entirely. A shaky operation required constant care and bad publicity was not welcome in the corporate board room.

The younger generation viewed the situation quite differently. The organization would live or die by its grassroots connection, they said. To abandon the need for the illegal, the elicit and the forbidden would only force people to look elsewhere for their pleasure. Those who used, and in turn were used, had to be orchestrated and controlled for therein lived the power of "The Organization". To attempt to dry one's feet and rise above it all would only allow someone else to fill the void and then come snapping at your heels. If you climbed higher they would pursue until you had nowhere to go.

Such would not do at all. Drafting legislation from afar was fine, but real power belonged to those who would look it in the eye and liked feeling it with their hands. Hell, that's where the fun was. Of course, the "older" of the old guard remembered only too well. But a few of their kind were tired and only wanted their house of cards to last until they died a peaceful death.

However, short range problems were viewed by a united front of young and old alike. Of these, the drug situation was a prime example. Foreign sources were completing their own transactions on the streets of New York, Miami or anywhere else a deal could be made. And their operations! Free-lancers, one-timers, amateurs. Christ, what a mess! As law enforcement got a taste of blood on this sometimes easy prey they occasionally stepped on the toes of the old guard and they too took losses. It cost them money. It cost them security. They took more chances. The underworld just wasn't what it used to be.

Due to pressures from within and without, there filtered down word that there should be "A Meeting" of traditional family heads and assorted bosses to discuss a full agenda of topics and to establish the future course of "The Organization". Though attendance would be held to a minimum, several dozen top people and another hundred or so of their entourage would have to be present. The logistical nightmare of a gathering of such individuals, many of whom disliked each other intently, would be staggering.

Security was by far the biggest problem. The fiasco in up-state New York many years ago was still remembered by many of the "older" old guard and they were wary of a repeat performance. A few potential conferees who knew they were under constant surveillance laid elaborate but singular plans to allow an undetected dash to "The Meeting". Others preferred not to go, but feared policy would be made without them. Still others counted on exactly that. Most felt the need to coordinate certain future activities while arranging to cultivate substantial personal gains at someone else's expense if need be. However, all agreed to a list of rules which governed The Meeting for they knew their safety depended upon setting differences aside for the duration. The plans and preparations had somehow taken a life of their own and all soon found they were captive to a course of action that would control their immediate future.

*   *   *

Forty years ago the Hallingford farm was the largest for many miles around. Tragedy struck late one fall evening when the car carrying most of the Hallingford family home from a school play was struck broadside by a tractor trailer truck. Four were killed instantly. Sixty-eight year old George Hallingford, family head, lingered on for a week and a half. Beatrice, his daughter, survived, badly crippled. Three greatgrandchildren had remained at home, looked after by a long time neighbor. A few months later the large dairy herd was auctioned off and the property was sold.

J. Wallace Wakefield was the new owner. J. Wallace had chosen to retire from active participation in his huge New York publishing holdings and move to the country. He was not interested in farming, but rather wanted the sprawling network of sheds and barns to house his extensive collection of antique and classic automobiles. J.W. refurbished the twenty-seven room main house and installed gleaming hardwood floors in the outbuildings on which to rest his Auburns, Cords, Packards, Duesenbergs, etc. During the sixties and early seventies Hallingford Farm became the scene of many classic car gatherings open to the public. J.W. himself proved a friendly down-to-earth sort about the community and used one or more of his old cars on a daily basis.

At age 78 a rapidly deteriorating heart condition brought a sudden end to J.W.'s endeavors and shortly after his cars were seen being removed and shipped to scattered destinations. The property itself did not move quickly and remained on the market for several years. Besides the huge main house, which was built during the mid-nineteenth century as an inn and tavern, the carriage house, sheds and two barns, there was also more than five hundred acres of fields and woodlands, including nearly a mile of prime lakefront property. A price tag approaching seven million dollars was not seriously contemplated by many. In 1983 the weathered for sale signs were finally removed as it was learned that Hallingford Farm had been sold to something called ARABI Corporation based in New York City.

"Christ! The Arabs are in town." Such was the immediate reaction among the locals. However, it was soon learned that ARABI stood for Association Representing Approved Business Interests. Of course, this revelation provided no specific information at all. By way of defending their original pronouncement a couple people insisted that they could still be Arabs.

Almost over night, well dressed, smooth talking representatives of ARABI Corp. presented elaborate plans depicting a 560 unit condominium complex to town officials who almost fell over themselves trying to please these bearers of millions of projected property tax dollars. The project quickly got under way. During the next year the first seventy plus units appeared in attractively spaced groups along a new road leading down to the lake. Though many of these were now complete, sale closures had been delayed until every last landscaping detail was in place in this initial phase. ARABI's stated policy of not subjecting a new owner to the distraction and inconveniences of onstruction next door, or even down the street, was apparently being carried out.

By spring of 1984 the new common-use facilities that would ultimately serve the future condo community had been completed. A fully equipped health club and spa, racquetball courts, bowling alley, restaurant, lounge, and even a moderately sized convention center, had been opened to the public on a limited basis. The old main house and former tavern had been tastefully restored to its former glory, however, its lavishly appointed rooms afforded guests far more luxury than was granted any former patron.

Curiously, this complex had closed its doors in late fall for what was said to be further interior renovation. Construction proceeded on the condos for a while until this activity was halted and Phase I was closed for the winter. ARABI officials stated they did not wish to pour additional concrete in sub-freezing weather and that work would resume in the spring. Locals mused this decision with mild surprise. Though the rigorous conditions and subsequent miscues of "winter work" had long been accepted, ARABI was praised for their stated unwillingness to accept anything but the highest quality product they could build.

Following the Christmas-New Year holiday, activity once again descended on the Hallingford main complex. Company officials offered a series of real estate courses featuring the latest in market technology for qualified people in the area. The one night a week course would run all winter. Enrollment was enthusiastic. The tuition was nominal. In reopening its doors even further,

ARABI made available the remainder of its facilities on a limited basis to local club functions, reunions, etc. During periods when these activities were not scheduled, ARABI conducted private meetings involving its own personnel, at times collecting people from other company projects in the northeast. Thus, the pattern of an occasional large private gathering injected into Hallingford's good neighbor, public friendly policy was accepted without question. For those uninvolved, the goings on at Hallingford Farm produced only a protracted yawn.

In fact, for those past few months, every detail at Hallingford had been carefully orchestrated to produce exactly that perception. It was a big place. People came. People went. Some were familiar. Others were not. Very few of the inner ARABI circle actually knew of "The Plan". In early February another private meeting would take place amidst a business as usual setting. Commencing shortly after dark during normal workday homeward bound traffic, the cars would start arriving at the complex. The large common looking sedans would be parked either in the Carriage House garage or in the open parking lot to the rear of the Health Spa. By Sunday evening, as guests filtered south to mix with those heading home after a weekend on the ski slopes, decisions would have been made by some of the most powerful men in the country involving billions of dollars, all of it dirty, some of it bloody as well. Nobody in the Melonia area would be the wiser.

*     *     *

New England weather is unpredictable to say the least. Daniel Webster once said something to the effect that if you don't like it, just wait a minute and it will change. Meteorologists traditionally keep long hours and become notably thick skinned as they must ward off constant abuse from residents who hold them responsible for forecasts gone awry.

By early Friday afternoon, February ninth, 1985, snow had spread across the region from the west. By 3:00 PM weathermen became convinced that the low pressure mass had stalled just off the Atlantic coast and a second one was forming to the south. Only hours before, the forecast had been for two to four inches of accumulation. It became apparent that this might only be the beginning.

The Public Works Department of Melonia, a city of eighteen thousand nestled in the lakes and mountain region of central New Hampshire, had been getting ready for what could be a big storm. The Department had a somewhat colorful, though excellent reputation for keeping the city's streets and roads clear of snow during the harsh winter season and most of the men had been looking forward to a storm they could really sink their teeth into. Since early December snowfall amounts had been frustratingly small and the crew was tired of contending with a piddling two or three inches at a time. What's more, the storm's timing appeared to be perfect. Coming in as it was late Friday, the whole thing would be on overtime.

A big storm could be something of an adventure, dangerous even. As a plow truck driver on the road in the middle of the night, with only your trusty wingman at your side, one had to be ready for almost anything. There were, of course, those other trucks in other sections of town similarly engaged, but on a lonely road the only camaraderie was that which came over the two-way radio. However, it was enough for this squadron of snow fighters battling nature's wrath. Ridiculous? Even childish? Possibly. But fun? For these men? Definitely.

Then too, a fully loaded twenty ton dump truck equipped with its massive front plow and side mounted wing plow is a formidable vehicle and is absolute boss on the highway where even large tractor trailers willingly yield the right-of-way. Further, a city plow is historically granted release from obeying most traffic regulations. Stop signs, yellow lines, one way streets, and to some degree, traffic lights, are at the discretion of the driver of a city plow. Normal everyday traffic must scatter from its path for a city plow truck is unlikely to swerve from its chosen trajectory.

A city plow truck usually has little trouble going where it wants in the worst of conditions and this ability additionally fuels the air of superiority of winter maintenance crews. While most of the populace is sliding over the landscape, the plow has plenty of traction afforded by its massive rear wheels loaded down by several tons of sand in the truck body. If conditions warrant, tire chains can be added, but only if necessary as they may break and thrash about at speeds approaching 50 mph.

Here, a word concerning the second crew member in the plow truck, the Wingman. The wing plow is mounted to the right hand side of the truck cab. It can be raised or lowered hydraulically, or when not in use, be tucked up beside the cab door in a vertical position. When down, the wing significantly widens the path cleared as it pushes snow coming off the front plow farther away to form that endless pile along the side of the road called the windrow.

While the wing performs a valued function, it can also be utilized in mischievous ways by a driver or wingman out to settle a score, or just in a bad mood. In front of the wingman, mounted off the truck dash are five large levers. Three of them combine to operate the wing. The fourth raises and lowers the front plow and the fifth raises the truck dump body.

The streams of snow cascading from the front plow and wing can vary depending on the depth of snow being plowed, its consistency, and the speed of the truck. At its least, it may be nothing more than that emitted from ones own driveway snowblower. At its fiercest, a stream may project a ton of snow every second a distance of twenty or thirty feet away from the truck. Mailboxes, fences, or the other somewhat fragile objects within range of this onslaught can disappear forever. Pedestrians who unexpectedly find themselves in the path of a city plow are often gripped with terror as they attempt to flee, often becoming trapped in a high snowbank. They may fall down and have to crawl rapidly to safety. Such scenes often evoke smiles and sometimes loud guffaws from the plow truck crew. The wing itself, when operated expertly, can horrify the occupant of a parked car in its path as it is raised, narrowly clearing the car roof, and then is released to crash to the pavement in front of the vehicle as the plow goes on its way.

A driver and wingman must work as a highly coordinated team, each anticipating the other's actions. A mistake in close quarters can spell disaster. During the normal course of plowing snow, fire hydrants, telephone poles and other obstacles may be cleared by an inch or two by the speeding plow. It is the wingman's job to warn the driver if he is going to strike an object because usually the wing cannot be raised in time to avoid it. If an unyielding object is solidly hit the wing may rise violently into the air on its mounts and come crashing into the passenger side door, demolishing the large rear view mirror on its way to smashing the window, the resulting impact propelling the wingman's head toward the jagged hole. With the main wing supports mounted midway of the truck's wheel base such a collision may snap or disfigure the truck's frame. If the object struck happens to be a pole carrying high tension electrical lines and transformers, frigid temperatures may have rendered it extremely brittle. Such a pole, already under great strain, will usually fall on the plow truck as it slides to a stop. However, this seldom happens as any seasoned driver usually knows where the wing is at all times without notice from the wingman.

Guardrails, however, are viewed with somewhat minor concern. Being a continuous row of lesser obstacles, it is the rising crescendo of that steady rat-a-tat-tat-tat of the wing tip striking the cable turnbuckles that the driver depends upon to let him know if he is getting too close while the wingman may sit idly by picking his nose or taking a sip from his beer.

Smaller private plows that do driveways, parking lots and the like are historically viewed as scum by city plow crews unless operated by a close friend and drinking buddy. These vehicles usually perform their task long after the city crews have finished theirs, so they are rarely encountered. If they do meet, however, it is the duty of the latter to hinder and harass these smaller vermin. Private plows always plug up sidewalks and leave excess snow in the street thereby making the city's work look bad.

Homeowners along the drivers plow route are placed into one of three categories; prick, nice guy, or no opinion. Plow crews do not take kindly to unwarranted criticism, or that born of ignorance of the situation, particularly when directed over the driver's head, say to City Hall. Such complaints will surely land the offender on the "prick" list, retribution from which can be long and painful and probably just plain hopeless. Retribution for a first offense is usually several times that which caused the complaint in the first place. Calls to higher authorities complaining that, truck number such and such filled my driveway with snow after I spent three hours shoveling it, are greeted by "where did that stupid bastard think we were going to put it?" The next storm said complainant will be buried under a pile of snow he won't believe, even if it only snowed a couple inches and the city truck has to spend extra time scraping it up from way down the street and putting it there.

Most homeowners will learn their lesson after a dose or two of this punishment, but occasionally a stubborn soul may delude himself into thinking he can eventually come out on top. Such feuds may last for several winters, or until the homeowner sells his house and moves away, or dies. If the plow truck driver quits his job, retires or dies, the gauntlet is passed to whoever takes over his plow route for the honor of the entire department is at stake. The complaints, threats and retaliation continues. Occasionally, during a heavy storm trucks from other parts of the city are invited to join in wreaking additional devastation upon the offending homeowner.

The nice guy is one who usually shovels or uses a snowblower to clear his own driveway or walk and is out there slaving away whenever the city plow passes, day or night. The nice guy never throws snow in the street and understands that the city plow will naturally dump more snow in his driveway as it passes. Often he is bright enough to remove an amount of snow along the approaching windrow to his drive thereby lessening the volume that the plow will deposit in the open driveway. The plow truck crew is always quick to recognize such brilliantly applied principles of physics and will usually respond by varying the path of the truck ever so slightly so as to assist the nice guy.

The nice guy always smiles and waves as the truck goes by and as Christmas draws near may offer a bottle or two of holiday cheer to the city crew. This person may sometimes be shown some extra consideration and crews have been known to push heavy piles of snow away from the nice guy's driveway. At other times plows have been seen plowing the entire width of the street in that area to the opposite side of the road leaving the poor slob over there wondering the next day where all the snow cam from. If the nice guy lives in the country with no near neighbors, stories of monetary remuneration and driveways being plowed by city trucks have surfaced. Even cases of drivers and wingmen leaving their trucks and going inside a private home for refreshments, or whatever, have been hinted at.

Last on the list is the "no opinion". The home of the "no opinion" is owned by non persons and are those shadowy residents who are never seen or heard from at any time during the course of the entire winter though a properly cleared driveway indicates that something dwells within.

The image of the Public Works employee is greatly enhanced during the winter, as he sits high off the ground in his powerful city plow truck commanding all he surveys, over what it is during a hot summer day, when viewed from an air conditioned Cadillac, as he leans on a shovel beside an open sewer manhole. Though he may drive the same truck during the summer, it's just another vehicle. In the winter it's a City Plow and his personal power climbs one hundred fold. How else could he lay on his piercing air horn at 3 AM while stopped on a sleepy upscale residential street in order to wake up some scumbag who has left that familiar Cadillac parked in the street and be free from any recourse? What's more, if the asshole doesn't climb out of bed and wade through a foot or more of snow to move his car so the Public Works Department employee can do his job, the truck driver can simply turn down his FM stereo, pick up his two way radio mike, and initiate action which will summon a wrecker to come and tow the Cadillac away. How's that for power?

One of the few hazards feared by driver and wingman is the hidden solid object which can be squarely struck by the front plow while traveling at speed. A manhole, watergate, or railroad track may mysteriously elevate just enough to catch the leading edge of the front plow. The plow has passed safely over this iron dozens of times during the winter, but this time? Bang! The plow may decide not to trip over the object, in which case real damage can occur. The truck stops quite suddenly and its two passengers are thrown into the dash and windshield frequently causing facial cuts and abrasions which can bleed profusely. This is not all that funny except to those who may be at the city garage when the battered crew returns.

Many years ago, some faceless bureaucrat buried deep within a City Council study committee had generated a detailed list of do's and don'ts directed at the Public Works department to assist snow removal crews in the performance of their duty. Upon posting on the bulletin board at the City Garage the document was greeted with laughter and sneers. By the end of the day the list had disappeared. The survival rate of subsequent copies proved even less significant.

The following week a second list appeared, its authorship unknown. Though it too was finally removed from the board, days later it reappeared in the local newspaper. As its true origin continued to remain clouded, the brief by-the-numbers uproar that followed pitted an indignant city Government against a news editorial staff that yawned, smiled, then turned a deaf ear in the direction of City Hall.

Although the first "official" list was never seen again, the second list is alive and well and can still be resurrected through proper channels. Let the following serve as its most recent public airing.

Rules to Plow By

1.  All containers of partially consumed food stuffs open for more than one week shall be cleared from the City Plow truck cab prior to embarkation.
2.  Consumption of alcoholic beverages by those operating a City plow truck is strictly forbidden during daylight savings time.
3.  Compliance with traffic signaling devices, speed limits, one way streets, or other ordinances aimed at the general masses, shall be at the discretion of the City plow truck driver.
4.  Pedestrians found trapped in the street before an oncoming City Plow shall be shown reasonable courtesy—the first time.
5.  Small private snow clearing machines being operated in the chosen path of a City plow truck shall be rendered inoperable and summarily swept aside without regard.
6.  Garbage cans left for pick-up, reachable by either plow blade or projected snow are hereby declared to be within the active field of play.
7.  House coated elderly women found beating on the City Plow truck late at night with broom or shovel shall be treated with restraint—unless they give the finger to the crew.

8. Late night female guests in a City Plow truck shall supply their own gender orientated toiletries.

9. Homeowners found to have pushed snow back into the street after the City Plow has done its job shall be recipients of a tenfold amount of snow the next storm.

10. Habitual offenders or constant complainers shall be subject to various other departmental retribution forevermore and their families, generation after generation, shall remain targeted in timeless perpetuity.

By late Friday afternoon on February ninth, the city's fleet of three dump trucks equipped with salt spreaders had been cruising Melonia's main drags and hills loosening the new snow from the pavement and creating a salt brine that would allow more snow to be scraped from the highway without the danger of traffic having turned it into a sheet of packed ice. Most of the drivers and wingmen of the city's nine plow routes, as well as most of the remainder of the winter maintenance force, had left work at the usual 3:30 PM time fully expecting to be called back by six o'clock at the latest. Some were grabbing a bite to eat and perhaps a little sleep in anticipation of a long difficult night. Others settled into their usual after work routine, though within easy earshot of the telephone. To a few this meant retreating only as far as some nearby bar, the telephone numbers of which were written on the wall in the Melonia city garage office.

The snow continued to fall steadily.

# chapter 2

New York City could be the dreariest of places this time of year. The rain pelted down, each drop striking with some secret satisfaction as if proclaiming, "There's a lot more where that came from".

Lorenzo Denecy stood motionless before the seventh floor window, watching the small rivulets collect and build, then go streaming down the glass. In a couple months the rain would change, he thought. It would bring warmth and life. Now it was just wet and cold. Why did it take so long for a man to notice these small important things?

Behind him he could barely hear the words still tumbling forth. Somehow their fleeting reality didn't seem on par with the rain. Grudgingly, Lorenzo allowed their existence back into his mind.

"I don't like it," the voice said. "But I don't suppose we have a choice. We've lost a lot of ground in the last couple years. Hell, some of our operations are on a week to week basis. Three times in the past month I've been within ten feet of the guy tailing me. Christ, they ain't even being professional about it anymore. They don't care if we know or not. It's a damn insult!"

The voice paused, but only for a moment. "Look at Tornia and Sabace, both indicted. Hell, look what we had to go through to be half way sure nobody knows where we are right now. I'm telling you, they've lost respect for us and when that happens we're screwed. Christ, even in Sicily the Mafioso is hiding. Lorenzo, we've got to . . ."

"Shut up, Frank." The words came softly, but with a distinguished air of command. Denecy turned to survey the room. My God, this is all we are. We are all that's left, he thought. Gratefully, the sadness passed quickly.

The office, now darkened, save for a small lamp on a far table, exhibited a fine though dated taste. The now silent speaker, Frank Denecy, slumped in a large leather chair before the huge desk where Lorenzo now stood. Stephen

Langella, long time family confidant, accountant, occupied the room's only light source, his eyes cast downward to a stack of papers he was busily sorting into groups. A forth man, well groomed in his late twenties, leaned against a smaller desk toward the end of the room, his manner suggesting restrained impatience.

Frank Denecy shifted in his chair, glancing to each of his companions. "New Hampshire! This time of year. Of all the God awful places. It's cold as hell up there and the weather's going to be lousy. Christ!"

Lorenzo looked sternly at his nephew. "This respect you talk so much about, Frank. It starts in your own gut. If you don't have it there . . . you are, as you say, screwed." Lorenzo paused to turn back to the window as if gathering strength from the world outside. "Maybe you're spending too much time down on the street. You should go up in a tall building and open a window once in a while. And New Hampshire? It will do you good. The air doesn't stink up there. Besides, the arrangements have been made."

Frank straightened his long frame to a standing position. "That's right. All the planning which has taken too damn many people for my liking. And more than a few of them know it all. I'm just saying I don't like it."

"Think positive, Frank," Lorenzo countered. "Think opportunity. Think what we have to accomplish."

Frank looked to his uncle, hoping to find the source of his confidence. Lorenzo stepped to clasp an arm around his shoulder. "I know you were upstate with us . . . what was it? Twenty years ago? You were Vincent's age here. It was very embarrassing. But we have learned a lot in twenty years. We must be many things today. Tough is not enough." Lorenzo laughed momentarily. "I make a rhyme, a joke, huh? No? We have to be smart, Frank. That won't happen again. Look at this meeting as a chance to regain some of this respect you say we are losing."

The youngest man stepped away from the desk, glancing at the ornate old clock on the wall.

"I see you are getting impatient, Vincent," Lorenzo remarked.

"We should be leaving soon, Grandfather."

"Ah yes, we have Miss Talli waiting up there in the cold." Lorenzo smiled. "That was an excellent idea of yours to have her accompany us. She may well prove helpful as you suggested."

Lorenzo released his grasp of Frank, stepped to the side of his grandson and reinstated the arm around the shoulder gesture as though his physical contact might instill some measure of confidence, even enthusiasm. Vincent did not resist, but carefully appraised the older Denecy as if half expecting such a osmotic reaction.

"Come, I will introduce you to some important and powerful people," Lorenzo assured. "Some are on their way up. Some are on their way down. The trick is to tell the difference before it becomes obvious to everyone. You and I, however, are family, we shall always be here. Come, we shall do some business."

Only during the past couple years had it been made crystal clear to Vincent Denecy that he must take a more active interest in the business, family business.

After a patchwork education at some of the finest schools in the northeast, Vincent was allowed to continue his life of well financed overindulgence as a member of the so-called international jet set. Vincent, like others close to him, had reveled in this carefree existence, little knowing that much of it was orchestrated by his elders to provide a worldly view of yet controlled extremes, the occasional mess seemingly melting away before him. Vincent was never actually as free as he had thought. He had, of course, always known where the money came from, but those realities were far away, and besides, the undertone of a Mafia inheritor excited the endless line of notable females of fine background.

And then came that telephone call at 3:00 AM, Paris time. His father and cousin had all but disappeared in a tremendous blast precipitated by the turn of an ignition key. "Come home at once," his grandfather's voice had said.

So, all at once, a man that Vincent could remember speaking to perhaps a half dozen times in his life had suddenly become his chief guardian, his mentor. His mother had wholeheartedly approved of the arrangement, but then what choice did she have.

At first Vincent resented the expectations thrust upon him by "the family". Most of all he resented his grandfather. Lorenzo Denecy showed actual respect for few people and Vincent had felt he was not, nor would he ever be, one of these. But like it or not, he had learned much over the past two years and curiously, while under the watchful eye of his grandfather, Vincent grew to see the tools with which he might take control of his own life once again.

Vincent Denecy knew what was expected of him at "The Meeting". He was to present before the gathering a picture of youthful confidence and intelligent purpose as the heir to the Denecy name and all that it implied. He was to meet certain people. He was to watch and learn.

Vincent's frequent companion during the past few months had been one Carla Talli, daughter of wealthy southwest banking interest and one of New York's leading fashion models. Vincent knew very well that his grandfather was much impressed with Miss Talli and two days ago he had suggested that she accompany their party to "The Meeting". "You have seen her many times, grandfather," Vincent had said, carefully choosing his words. "Her presence may well disquiet those intent on more important matters."

Lorenzo had looked long and hard to his grandson. "Why don't you see if Miss Talli might visit us later this evening? I should like to speak with her."

Vincent Denecy had closed the study door softly behind him and smiled to himself in the hallway.

Lorenzo moved back behind his desk and fingered a couple buttons under its rim. Two T.V. screens on the opposite wall above the office door came to life. They showed opposing views of a parking garage housing several fine cars. A man in a dark suit wearing a chauffeur's cap could be seen sitting in a chair reading a newspaper. Lorenzo Denecy glanced to Langella who was inserting the last of his papers into a leather briefcase. "Are we ready, Stephen?"

Langella hefted the case and smiled. "Deals they can't refuse. I feel like Santa Claus."

The foursome moved through the anteroom and into the garage. Lorenzo nodded at the chauffeur who moved away toward a line of cars parked along one wall. There was a new black Cadillac limo, a Rolls Royce convertible, a Jaguar, a Pontiac, two Corvettes and a pale green mid-seventies Lincoln Town Car. The chauffeur moved toward the black Cad.

"The Lincoln is ready, I trust, Tony," Lorenzo said.

The chauffeur stopped and turned, mildly surprised. "Yes sir, Mister Denecy. The Lincoln is ready as always," he smiled.

"Then we shall take it. Transfer our luggage if you would, Tony."

"Yes sir! Yes sir, Mister Denecy." Tony seemed happy about the change.

"Why the Lincoln?" Frank wanted to know. "The Cadillac seems more comfortable and God knows we're going to be in it long enough." Lorenzo looked squarely at his nephew from close range. "Why not, Frank. Change for the sake of change. You don't seem to remember. We must spend more time together. Besides, we are sure no one knows we are here, right? But are we very sure?"

Frank thought for a second then nodded agreement. The group moved toward the car where Tony was just securing the last of the luggage in the huge trunk. The rear and side windows seemed darkly tinted. It was difficult to see into the car even at close range.

"I have been having Tony drive this car all over the city during the past month. They don't bother to follow him anymore. I think they believe I have given him the car." Lorenzo flashed a quick smile at the chauffeur. "And Tony, when we get back, it is yours."

Tony grinned broadly and opened the passenger side doors for the party to enter.

"Shall we?" Lorenzo offered.

Stephen Langella smiled to himself as he slid into the front seat. Even Vincent glanced with respect at his grandfather. Frank laughed briefly as the last to enter. Tony happily settled himself behind the wheel.

The garage seemed surprisingly bright through the clouded windows. Vincent looked about, inspecting his surroundings. "I've never been in this car. Very nice," he remarked.

"They started making them smaller after this," Lorenzo explained. "The last of its breed, you could say."

"I hope you're not dropping some additional meaning there." Frank hesitated only a moment for an answer. There wasn't one. "Never mind. I believe I am feeling better. I hope we have something to drink in here. I seem to recall a concealed bar somewhere."

The Lincoln moved silently across the floor to a large door which opened into an elevator. The car entered. The door clanked back to a closed position.

"At the third floor take the other elevator to the west side exit, Tony," Lorenzo ordered.

"Yes sir," Tony replied.

The rain now descended in heavy wind whipped sheets driving all but a few desperate pedestrians from the sidewalks. The pale green Lincoln unobtrusively poked its nose from an alley, hesitated a moment at the curb, and was then swallowed into the slow moving city traffic accompanied by its own symphony of tires on wet pavement, the clack, clack, clack of windshield wipers, and an occasional horn.

\*    \*    \*

A cloudless sun dripped warmth and brilliance over the Lear jet as it stood ready and waiting near the airport taxiway. Beside the craft, two men busily handed up several pieces of luggage plus a variety of sealed boxes to a third man in the plane. One of the two on the ground seemed intent on getting the job over and done with as the assembled pile in the open hatch soon overtaxed the ability of the on-board worker to contend with it in an orderly manner.

"For Christ sake, Brian, give me a chance to get some of this stuff behind me," he complained.

Brian Verrill straightened up from his work and glanced at Jeff Larazas beside him who just stood and returned his gaze. Brian finally nodded. "I'll go see if I can hurry Carl along."

Forcing himself to walk calmly away, Brian headed for a Mercedes limousine parked twenty yards distant. Approaching the drivers side door, Brian looked past the chauffeur, through the raised glass partition to his boss in the rear seat. Carl Endicott sat gazing off to the openness of the airstrip as he spoke steadily into a telephone, his lips ceasing their movement only for brief moments before continuing. Beside Endicott was seated an exquisitely beautiful woman, her manner one of composed patience. Brian turned back to the chauffeur and bent forward to his open window. "Any late news on the weather?"

"Yeah, all of it bad," was the reply.

"Damn!"

The chauffeur glanced quickly to the rear view mirror. "Should be finished in a minute."

Brian again silently nodded his acceptance of the situation and straightened up to wait.

Carl Endicott spoke a final word into the phone, brought it slowly down from his ear and turned to the woman beside him. The couple exchanged a brief, but warm kiss. Endicott opened the door and stepped out of the car. "Well, Brian," Endicott smiled. "Shall we proceed to the frozen north?"

Brian raised an eyebrow at the remark, but said nothing. The pair walked towards the plane as the Mercedes swung a wide arc and moved away. The woman turned her head close to the window to catch a last glimpse at Endicott, but his attention was centered on the plane before him.

Carl Philip Endicott was born on January twenty-first, 1938, in a third floor tenement in New York's lower east side. In this diverse and congested neighborhood Carl learned, while still a youngster, that there were easier ways to make money than by exercising the American ethic of hard work. Let others concern themselves with earning the money. It was a simpler task to take it from them or make them give it to you.

By the mid-fifties Carl's abilities along these lines became noticed by those engaged in much grander schemes. Carl's father had disappeared early on and in 1956 his mother had passed away after a short illness. Carl allowed himself only a brief moment of regret before plunging ahead and upward, although at that time he had no clear cut goals. His ambitions for wealth and the things money could buy could be simply translated to the word "more".

Endicott's infrequent brushes with the law taught him a respect for the consequences of his actions, a lesson seldom learned by one so young. A few of Carl's friends and associates were doing hard time in prison. A few others were dead by various hands. Such would not be the fate of Carl Philip Endicott.

Carl's activities became very selective, cautiously planned, and immensely more profitable. A move up town was the next step where he purchased a fine men's clothing store. Carl took particular interest in this new legitimate enterprise, and although he left the store's management and staff intact, he found himself increasingly fascinated by the business itself, its trends, and fashion in general. Carl also spent a great deal of time meeting and talking with many of his wealthy customers who immediately took to this good looking, intelligent young man. Quickly, Carl Endicott moved into New York society, soaking up the necessary culture and polish as he did so. The year was 1964. He was twenty-six.

One night at a cocktail party following a Broadway play opening, a man in his early fifties introduced himself to Carl. "My name is Julian Denecy," he said smiling. After a brief exchange of pleasantries, the older man asked, "have you ever been to Europe?"

During the next twenty years Carl Endicott spent much of his time in Europe, as well as the Near East, the Far East, South America, or anywhere else that the intricate workings of the international underworld community needed tending to. In a short time Carl's personal wealth reached a point where the word "more" had shed any tangible meaning it once had. Most of this money was invested in additional clothing stores, and under the care of one of Madison Avenue's most prestigious advertising agencies, the Endicott chain had spread up and down the east and west coast of the United States and was more recently forming a solid link between the two in the Chicago Midwest area. As the Endicott name became synonymous with contemporary men's fashion, the man behind the name graced the covers of the day's magazines. The playboy image was carefully cultivated.

It was shortly after Julian Denecy's death that the east coast families knew that they had lost all practical control of Carl Philip Endicott. He had served them and himself too well for far too long until now the thought of who was more powerful was best not considered.

Although Carl's actions and dealings had affected the deaths of many people around the world over the years, Carl had personally killed but three men and one woman and these in self defense, either immediate or perceived. His ever present caution had led him to become an expert of disguise and his person represented a dozen different people, each with the ability to further the cause of Endicott himself. Although few knew of Carl Endicott's real nature, fewer still knew of the entirety of his true scope. Only Carl knew how powerful he really was and he knew it only too well.

But for the first time he was afraid, or rather fearful. It was not a personal fear of life and limb, or even exposure or imprisonment. It was an uneasy awareness of the future's course. Few people had become as knowledgeable of world politics at its basic gut level as had Carl Endicott. The U.S. State Department could well have used his services if such had been possible. And maybe they had.

Endicott was one of the few people eagerly looking forward to "The Meeting" in Melonia. In fact, it was he who was largely responsible for bringing it about. But this was not known. Carl would appear as himself before a select group at the conference, this a first in such a capacity for many years. Furthermore, what he would say would also be a first. Carl Endicott was sure everyone present would pay strict attention.

Jeff Miles fingered a series of controls from the co-pilots seat. The Lear's engines came to life. The third crewman busily secured both luggage and cargo at the rear of the plane. Carl Endicott reached to undo his necktie. "Those details at our destination, Brian?"

Brian nodded. "They've been taken care of. It's the weather I'm beginning to worry about. In three hours it could be very bad."

Endicott pulled the tie from around his neck and started unbuttoning his shirt. "Get an update as soon as we're in the air. I've got to change and then check some of our cargo. I'll be up later." Brian nodded and made his way forward to the pilot's seat. Endicott sat down and removed his shoes.

The Lear gathered speed as it moved down the taxiway. Pausing for only a moment at the end of the runway, the plane pointed itself down the long strip of asphalt. Again, it accelerated amidst the roar of its engines, this time its purpose urgent, even predatory, as if some distant prey had been sighted. At once the craft was airborne and in less than a minute was hardly a speck in the clear blue sky.

*   *   *

By late afternoon it was already dark in Melonia. Ordinarily, the day's fading light would have hung on a little longer, but the falling snow from darkened clouds had taken care of that. Two or three inches of the virgin white covered the ground. Traffic was light and careful as most people seemed intent on completing their after work errands and heading home to possibly reassess any planned weekend activities.

On Jefferson Street, lined with its large old trees and even larger and older houses, the scene was just another heartbeat of seasonal evolution to be enjoyed or endured as one's mood dictated. On the street a car slowed, then turned, its lights sweeping the wintery front lawn of a towering Victorian home. The dark colored and somewhat battered old Buick finally came to a stop near the porched rear entrance of the house. The creaking of the driver's door as it opened seemed to match the overall character of the car though its occupant would certainly have angered had one pushed the association any further. Walton Conover, Public Works Director of Melonia, got out and slammed the car door as though knowing it needed this extra little push in order to close properly. Conover looked around, sniffed the air, and headed up the few wooden steps to the house.

Inside, he stomped the remaining snow from his feet onto a thick mat by the door and tossed his coat and gloves onto a chair near the kitchen table. The sounds of a television newscast could be heard from an interior room and light, presumably from the same source, spilled from the hallway onto the kitchen floor. Conover switched on the kitchen light and stepped to a wall hung telephone.

"Walt?" came the female voice from the interior.

"Yeah."

"Will you have to go out again tonight?"

Conover paused in his reach for the phone and pursed his lips. "I imagine so. They're saying we could be getting quite a bit. I'll probably have to go see how things are shaping up."

Conover paused an additional second to allow for another remark from the living room. None was forthcoming. He reached for the phone receiver and methodically dialed a number on the old style instrument. "Marion? . . . Walt Conover. Is Charlie there? . . . Oh, Okay, I'll call him there." There was a longer pause as Conover smiled slightly. "Oh, I hadn't heard . . . . Well, we'll see how it goes. Goodbye, Marion."

Walton had turned sixty-eight in December and many wondered why he didn't just retire. The day to day workings of the department hadn't held his interest over the past couple of years and much of his time had been spent at the state capital where his input had a marked effect on larger state projects encompassing several communities in the Central Lakes Region District.

However, dealing with the political infighting of the largest state legislature in the country had taken its toll also and Conover frequently arrived back at his Melonia desk in a bad mood, frustrated by the inability of these minor bureaucrats to comprehend the simplest of concepts. "Goddamned fools," he would snarl at no one in particular as he attacked his rising pile of paperwork. At these times his voice would boom over the Public Works radio frequency and foremen and crews alike were aware that Conover's personal battered old Buick might show up at any job site at any time.

Furthermore, Walton Conover's life had been made considerably more complicated by the city's implementation of an inclusive computer system involving all departments. Installed at great expense to simplify municipal operations, the system had, of course, done just the opposite. Information once at his fingertips was now resurrected with great difficulty and his operating budget had become an elusive figure of rapidly shrinking proportions. Conover suspected that his department had financed a good share of the damned computer and this, plus the fact that Public Works always seemed to get the short end of the stick when the city tightened its belt, grated on his nerves.

A retired colonel in the Marine Corps, Walton Conover had seen active service dating from World War II through the Vietnam war. But even though the armed forces had been known for an occasional circuitous route to a logical solution, dealing with state and local governments had been particularly maddening at times.

It was common knowledge that Walt and his wife, Grace, were not wondering where their next dollar was coming from and Conover's thirty-five thousand dollar a year salary plus his service retirement was not vital to their existence. Blue chip investments years ago, in addition to Grace's more recent real estate dealings, had provided a tidy nest egg that would continue to afford them a comfortable living, and in time, a sizeable inheritance for their son and three daughters.

With two exceptions, the Conover's tastes were not expensive. The first was their beautiful Victorian home and the second was Grace's Cadillac, which unlike her husband's car, was rarely allowed to age more than two or three years before it was replaced with a new one.

Conover's activities as a member of a certain community service organization had decreased of late in favor of a renewed interest in model World War II aircraft. He had an extensive collection of these finely crafted replicas, most of which he had built himself. Although many were fully powered, none had seen the light of day. Very few people knew they existed.

Until a few years ago, Conover had been an avid golfer whose scores were good enough to warrant serious attention from those who devoted a much larger portion of their existence to the sport. However, a fall from a ladder while repairing a shutter on his home had left him with a back problem from which he still suffered from time to time. Result, little or no golf.

So once again, people asked why didn't he retire to enjoy some leisure time and perhaps travel a bit to see more of his children and grandchildren scattered across the country. Those few who asked in the role of a caring friend got a polite but evasive reply. The answer, however, was not all that complex or unique. Grace knew it very well and she had never had to ask.

Walton Conover realized only too well that his active participation in life was winding down to a close. He was no longer a young, or even a middle aged man. While others seemed able to accept and somehow look forward to these years, Conover couldn't and didn't. Possibly his active military career of more than thirty years was part of the reason, but Conover knew it was more than that. Walton Conover longed for another challenge, a cause, or yes, even a good fight from which he might again feel that rush of excitement, that moral commitment, the strain of pumping blood through his veins. And if it wasn't too much to ask, maybe even a chance of victory. A fresh memory to smile at in the dark and place above those that had grown so dim would be a prize worth almost anything.

Conover picked up the phone receiver a second time and dialed another number. "Charlie? . . . I guess we might's well get moving." Conover replaced the receiver and walked slowly out of the room.

Grace Conover, an attractive woman of a few less years than her husband, looked up from her chair as he entered the room. "Marion thinks this is a big one," Walt remarked with a slight smile. "Of course, she always thinks its going to be a big one."

# chapter 3

Twenty miles to the north, the fresh falling snow had the advantage of settling on a more substantial base of that which had come down in weeks past. Across an open field from a little used secondary road a lone street lamp highlighted the undulating surface made smooth by the virgin white. The dark shapes of a half dozen condominium structures could be seen a hundred yards distant, their windows lifeless except for three at the lower left of the farthest building where light from these tried vainly to stretch toward the road and meet with that of the street lamp. At the center window the shape of a man paused briefly, then turned away to the interior of the room.

Bradford Nevis walked behind the bar of the large luxuriously appointed living room and began to mix himself a drink.

It was hard to tell how long Nevis and his companions might have been in residence. A couple open suitcases on the floor indicated they could have just arrived, however, an assortment of empty food containers and beverage cans strewn about testified to it being a bit longer.

John Elvio, slouched in the softness of an overstuffed recliner, displayed an acute concentration in manipulating the attached pieces of a metal puzzle.

Stanley Fagner stood before a coffee table on which were two handguns. Reaching to pick up one of the guns, a small .25 caliber automatic, he inserted the loaded ammunition clip and shoved the firearm down the front of his pants in the area of his crotch.

"One of these days you're going to shoot your balls off," remarked Ellie, glancing up from his puzzle.

"One of these days this piece is going to come in handy," retorted Stanley. "Not many guys are going to frisk your crotch. Not mine, anyway."

At the bar, Bradford Nevis had finished assembling his drink. Walking to the center of the room, he hefted the glass toward the windows and the swirling snow outside. "Gentlemen. A toast to Mother Nature. This snow is the best thing that could have happened."

Stanley looked up from tucking in his shirt. "Wha do ya mean? We could have trouble getting out'a here."

Nevis smiled. "Tell him Ellie."

John Elvio separated the puzzle pieces with a sudden flourish and tossed them on the table. Standing, he picked up the other handgun, inspected it and stuffed it in his shoulder holster. "What the boss means is that we're already here, or close to it. Most of the others are coming in right about now and they'd be the ones having the trouble. Some probably won't make it at all which will be all the better for those that do."

Nevis nodded. "Very well put, Ellie."

"Oh," said Stanley.

Nevis took a long sip of his drink. "I'll bet the L.A. group is flying into some smaller airport in the southern part of the state, maybe even Massachusetts. Ranklin hates the big ones ever since some guy came out of a crowd and stuck a shiv in his ass a few years ago." The threesome chuckled at the amusing recollection.

Nevis continued. "Most of them small airports will be closing soon if they ain't already and anything coming in now is going to stick out like a sore thumb. What's more, I'll bet Ranklin's got at least a half dozen people with him." Nevis paused and squinted into his drink. "The bunch from Miami has probably holed up in Atlantic City for the past few days. They'll make it in somehow. Denecy will drive up from New York. He hates planes. Chicago? Hell, they're coming into Logan in Boston and that may close anytime if this stuff don't turn to rain down there. Them other groups from the south have got to drive in this shit once they get here . . ." Nevis began to smile as he consumed the thought.

"This whole damn thing sounds crazy," offered Ellie.

"Yeah, it is and it isn't," Nevis nodded. "The one person I want to finally see is this Endicott guy. Him and his faggoty clothing stores . . . Which is a crock, of course. Anytime you try to find out anything, all you hear is he's big, very big. He does cover his tracks, though. Like he's not even there. But he's here . . . somewhere. Bet on it. And I want to find out what his angle is."

"Hell, maybe he'll come right out and tell us," Ellie offered.

"Maybe. But I want to come away knowing all the things he doesn't say," Nevis added.

"Who owns this place we're going to, anyway?" Stanley asked, filling the pause following Nevis' last remark. Both Ellie and Nevis looked at Stanley in mild surprise.

"A damn good question, Stanley," said Nevis.

Stanley seemed embarrassed by his boss's look which bordered on respect.

"I had Denning fill me in before we left," Nevis continued. "The papers say ARABI Corp. Don't matter what it stands for. What it is is just another dumping place for eastern money. A lot of the contractors are out of Philly, so that . . ."

At that moment the telephone on the bar started to ring. Stanley jumped visibly, his eyes wide. Ellie's look at Nevis, though less animated, showed considerable concern.

"Well, go ahead and answer it!" Nevis ordered, his own eyes narrow. "Its either a wrong number or its Stevenson."

Ellie stepped to the bar and snapped up the phone. "Hello? . . . Yeah." Ellie turned and held the receiver out to Nevis, his expression grim.

Nevis swore and grabbed the phone. "What is it?"

A thousand miles to the west a man huddled in a phone booth amidst a cold sleeting rain. On hearing Nevis' voice, Gerald Stevenson, somewhat tarnished union attorney, turned to huddle in a corner of the tiny glass enclosure as if to further cloak his next words. "You sure of this phone, Brad?"

"Of course I'm sure of it," Nevis snapped. "What the hell's going on?"

"Somebody got lucky," Stevenson continued. "They found Kingston and from the reaction down at the District Attorney's office he must be telling them plenty. It's only a matter of time before they dig up his brother-in-law, and I do mean dig him up. They've already placed a twenty-four hour guard at the Dover City landfill. They'll be there Monday morning in full force."

Nevis' face turned red and angry. "Goddamn! Those bastards have got some great timing! And I suppose they know I'm not sitting at home by now."

Stevenson lifted his head long enough to glance quickly around to the outside world, then turned back to his hunched position. "They sure do. Your picture's in all the papers right now under the heading 'Wanted for Questioning'. This time the racketeering angle will just be a lead in to tie you to the rest of it."

"Those bastards! So what have you done so far?"

"What have I done?" Exasperation showed in Stevenson's voice. "I've been trying to get an inside line on this thing without looking too interested. And now I'm calling you. This whole thing just fell out of the sky earlier this afternoon. It's a totally different crowd down there since the last time and they want your ass. This is going to take some time . . . and money. And by the way, I'm not exactly calling you from my office. I'm not sure of anything at this point except I'm sure they can't wait to ask me where you are."

Surprisingly, Nevis appeared a little calmer. "Never mind that. You just get to Johnson fast. Tell him to put everything he's got on these people and don't spare the cash. I want to know how many we can buy or blackmail and then we'll go from there."

"How about Rosetti in Chicago?" Stevenson asked. "He'll be in this sooner or later."

"Hell, he's probably here, or on his way. Things are about to start so we've got to move. You have your home phone checked again and I'll get a coded number to your answering machine later tonight. At midnight here you give me a call from another pay phone. And get somebody to keep your tail clear. I want some good news, Stevenson."

"By the way, they've issued a federal warrant."

"That don't change things here. Nobody's going to be selling autographs at this place. Goodbye."

Nevis exchanged the phone for his drink and took a long swig. Stanley stood motionless waiting to hear what had happened. Ellie stepped to the bar and poured some whiskey in a glass.

"How bad is it?" Ellie asked.

"They found Kingston," Nevis answered.

"Holy shit! Let me go back and take that son-of-a-bitch out once and for all."

"No! I need you here. They'll be plenty of time for that later if it's necessary." Nevis looked down into his near empty glass. "This is probably going to make things harder . . . that is unless I can work it to an advantage." Nevis raised his gaze to some obscure point in space.

"I hope the hell they've got security locked up tight at this place," Ellie said, slowly shaking his head. "I don't like having to trust somebody else's setup."

Stanley remained where he was, looking from one man to the other as if waiting to be directed toward his next move.

Nevis returned his attention to his underlings. "Don't worry about that. These people aren't stupid and in case you haven't noticed, this is strictly hicksville up here. There probably ain't a dozen cops within a fifty mile radius of this Hallingford place."

Bradford Nevis was only nine years old that evening he waited in the alley in back of the tenement where he lived with his mother and older sister. He was waiting for his sister's kitten to come along as he knew it would eventually. The thing had scratched him earlier that afternoon while he held it and Brad was going to get even.

As the kitten approached, purring, Brad slipped on a pair of old work gloves. The animal brushed up against his leg. Nevis buried the lifeless form deep in one of the several garbage cans nearby and went inside to get something to eat.

By the time Nevis reached his mid-teens he had grown into an overweight, alarmingly pudgy individual. The girls at Detroit's Williamson High School were not impressed. Nevis' response to their snickering was usually a tirade of snarling insults. Nevis was far from being popular in any quarter, however, he was not without a following of sorts. Brad found he had a knack for making sure certain people were dissatisfied with their general lot in life. It seemed easy to convince them that their lack of success was not due to any fault of their own, and further, that specific action directed by himself against those supposedly responsible would have positive results. At first, Nevis was surprised to find these so-called disadvantaged types of limited intelligence gravitating to him for advice and council. But quickly, the logic of it all settled firmly in his mind and Bradford Nevis began to formulate some long range plans.

One night when his guard was down, Brad made a feeble attempt to start a conversation with one of the most popular girls in school outside a downtown teen hangout. The girl laughed at him and Nevis, enraged, slugged her in the face, knocking her down. A young man, a year older and two grades ahead of Nevis saw the incident and a minute later Brad had suffered the worst beating he'd ever had.

Two days later Nevis watched with satisfaction as three of his subordinates confronted his attacker as he was heading home after football practice. They broke an arm, an ankle and several ribs as well as making a mess of the boy's handsome face. Bradford Nevis felt real power that day. His future course was obvious.

In the succeeding years Nevis' character had not improved, indeed he had facilitated the deaths of nearly a dozen people who in one way or another had stood in his way. From behind the scenes Nevis presently controlled or heavily influenced the activities of several labor unions headquartered in the upper Midwest. On a parallel course was his deep involvement in organized crime in the same area. Federal authorities were not without extensive knowledge of Bradford Nevis, but though he had been arrested on relatively minor charges on four separate occasions, he had yet to be brought to trial.

Nevis was not a stupid person, else he would not have been walking around loose. He prided himself on figuring all the angles and covering his tracks as he went. He had, of course, known that he was under almost constant surveillance and he also knew that authorities believed he was currently present somewhere within the grounds of his lavish Detroit home. A carefully prepared double had been expertly choreographed to foster this belief.

Naturally, all that was now out the window, however, Bradford Nevis had been in tough jams before. And Bradford Nevis was still around.

Nevis' eyes narrowed once more as he sorted out his immediate course of action. Ellie sipped his whiskey. Stanley moved at last, adjusting his coat and tie. "Well, I guess that's that then," he lamely offered.

Movement at the hallway entrance near the far end of the living room caused the three men to look as one in that direction. Magan Anthony settled her tall frame against the wall. She was wearing an obviously fragile nightgown and nothing else. Magan's primary function of late had been to look absolutely stunning at all times under any condition, a job she carried off with seemingly little or no effort. Gorgeous of face and form under a controlled disarray of long dark hair, Magan glanced briefly at the men, then to the windows and the world outside. "Christ, how long has it been snowing?" she asked.

"Get your things together," Nevis ordered. "You won't be staying here as planned. You'll be coming with us."

"To the party?" Magan brightened. "Great!"

"This is no party. Your job is to look good and be nice to whoever I might decide to point you at," Nevis stated flatly.

Magan suddenly stood erect, and with a single slight shoulder movement, caused the nightgown to slip soundless to the floor. Her calculated intake of breath presented an even more jaw dropping picture to the men before her. She smiled. "In what capacity will I be working may I ask? Maybe I should join your union, Brad."

Ellie shook his head and turned away. "Jesus Christ," he breathed.

Stanley was the closest and again stood motionless, his eyes wide open, his expression awkwardly locked and immobile. Magan took a slow threatening step in his direction.

Ellie turned and laughed nervously. "How's that gun feel now, Stanley? I hope you got the safety on."

"Goddammit!" Nevis roared. "Lets move! I want to be out of here in five minutes."

*   *   *

Gale Mooney sat on the edge of a large overstuffed chair in his den, an old double barrel shotgun laid across his legs. Mooney sprayed a touch of solvent from a can onto a rag and lovingly wiped the firearm a few final times before stretching to place the gun carefully in its cabinet against the near wall alongside several other similar old weapons.

Next to that cabinet was another and yet another, all filled with antique rifles and shotguns. On the wall there were even more along with a few older muskets and a variety of handguns which rested on wooden pegs expertly placed into the knotty pine. Mooney gave a quick but careful glance over their presence as he had thousands of times before.

An old radio on a near table emitted faint garbled sounds. Mooney touched the dial and the station came clear.

*. . . low pressure appears to have stalled over the north shore of Massachusetts and the possibility of a second low forming to the south is now a reality. Folks, it's beginning to look like we could be in for old fashioned winter blockbuster . . .*

Mooney was already dressed in heavy clothing and boots. Frowning, he clicked off the radio, grabbed his heavy coat from the arm of the chair, and stood.

Doris Mooney, Gale's wife, entered the room. Though nearing fifty, Doris would have been judged much younger. Still on the edge of "a very pretty girl" characterization, Doris carried a reasonable ten to fifteen pounds of extra weight. This she viewed with much concern and was forever struggling to recapture her earlier form which, of course, she never would. At the moment Doris appeared in her familiar state of consternation, however, it was not about her weight. "Charlie just called," she said.

"Well, its about time," remarked Gale, putting on his coat. "I was leaving anyway. I don't know what they're doing over there. This thing is going to get away from us if we don't get moving."

Gale Mooney held a particular distinction within the Public Works Department. A year earlier, almost to the day, he had been in the middle of what was clearly the most spectacular accident ever involving a Public Works vehicle. While plowing snow a few miles north of downtown Melonia, along Shoreside Boulevard, Mooney was hit head on by a beer truck traveling south as the other driver suddenly lost control during a heart attack. The huge angular front plow on the city truck is what saved both men as it served to thrust the vehicles to the side away from one another.

The city truck was directed to its left through a guardrail, down over a steep embankment, and onto a foot and a half of lake ice which held like concrete. Miraculously, Gale was thrown clear as the truck rolled over. He landed in soft snow, and although thoroughly pissed off, was basically unhurt. His wingman, who subsequently moved to a southern state, stayed inside the truck, but received only a broken arm and a slight concussion. The other truck was pretty well demolished. Fortunately, the driver survived both accident and heart attack. The beer which was strewn all over the highway was quickly removed by Public Works Department crews before it could pose a hazard to anyone.

Save for an early tour through some of the nastiest fighting of the Korean War, at 54, Mooney had been working for the Public Works Department for most of his adult life. A rugged New Englander, Gale was not known for idle conversation, but rather clipped phrases which came directly to the point. A frequent twinkle in his eyes indicated a man of good humor and further suggested someone looking beyond the moment at hand.

Gale Mooney's main passion in life was his antique firearms. He had begun acquiring some nice pieces while a young man, and in the many years since, his collection was said to have appreciated into the low six figure range. However, Gale enjoyed a discussion of the facts concerning a particular firearm much more than assessing its current dollar value and this was perhaps the one area where he could become quite talkative.

Gale's winter recreation interest was ice fishing which he shared with a few other members of the department, who like he, had "bob houses" out on the lake from the first week of the year through most of the month of March.

In the kitchen Gale collected a large thermos and a paper bag containing a lunch that Doris had prepared for him.

"You be careful, you hear?" Doris admonished. "This is starting out just like that one last year. I don't want to be getting a phone call from the hospital later on."

Gale put a big hand on his wife's shoulder. "Dot, I've told you a dozen times that thing on the boulevard was a freak accident. It's not going to happen again. Dunbar is the one that should be watching out. He's driving even more like a maniac than he ever did. I swear he's looking to go out in a ball of flames."

"Dammit, Gale," Doris warned.

"Sorry . . . sorry. Look, we'll probably be finished by daylight. I'll give you a call anyway. I've got to go. I'm picking Jason up on the way over."

Gale Mooney kissed his wife, opened the door, and switched on the outside light. It was snowing harder and the wind had picked up. Walking to his car, he swept the three to four inches of new snow from the windshield and hood with his free arm. Doris watched through the kitchen window.

*    *    *

The remains of the late afternoon rush hour traffic began to struggle perceptively on the snow covered streets. At a major Melonia intersection an occasional car could be seen spinning it's wheels or sliding slightly as it navigated the deepening ruts. A yellow Public Works dump truck approached the intersection, its rear mounted spreader pitching sheets of sand and salt mix in a wide pattern. As a small car started to slide into its path, the truck downshifted violently almost to a stop to allow the vehicle to pass. One could almost hear the P.W. driver swearing aloud as the gears clashed. With traffic clear, the truck accelerated neatly around the corner and off down the street, the chained rear wheels spinning beneath its near empty load.

*    *    *

The lights were on at the extreme end of the several stalled private garage. Before a long workbench along the back wall a sleek looking snow machine rested on the concrete floor, its forward clip raised vertical to reveal its mechanical innards. Scott Roy, clad in the latest snowmobile cold weather fashion, knelt down over the machine as he accomplished some final adjustments.

Though the machine's engine was running at an exhaust popping fast idle, the sound was almost lost beneath the crash of a current rock tune blaring forth from an elaborate FM radio set up on a shelf above the bench. Proceeding into the darkened portion of the garage one could see a half dozen motorcycles of various types, a red mid-fifties two seater Thunderbird and a late model Oldsmobile sedan. Scott Roy straightened up just as the telephone rang.

In a few quick steps Scott shut down the FM and snapped the phone to his ear. The steady staccato sound of the snow machine's engine now dominated the garage. "Its about time, Charlie. Where you been? . . . Yeah, I know. I'm leaving right away."

Scott replaced the phone receiver, stepped back to the snow machine and lowered and secured its hood. Grasping a rear wrap-around lifting handle, he swung the rear of the machine around so its nose was pointing toward the still closed garage door. Settling himself onto the seat, Scott took the full face helmet from its perch between the handle bars and carefully put it on his head, making sure its fit was just right. Next came the gloves. Scott Roy was not a big man and at the age of thirty his slender frame when completely hidden could well be taken as that of a young teenager.

Scott cranked the throttle momentarily and the machine leaped ahead a foot or two in instant response. He pressed a button on the handle bar and the garage door began to clank upward. Before the door had risen two feet off the floor, Scott twisted the throttle grip wide open. The forward skis rose off the floor as the engine screamed, the spinning steel clad track showering sparks rearward toward the workbench. Suddenly the snow machine lunged forward toward the rising door. It seemed a collision was moments away, but Scott ducked his head behind the tiny windshield and the door cleared both by mere inches. The snow machine disappeared into the night.

Though several Public Works Department employees owned motorcycles which could frequently be found parked at the city garage during nice summer days, no one took these two wheelers quite as seriously as did Scott Roy. Besides a British Triumph and Norton and a full dress Harley, Scott also owned three rare M.V. Agustas. These he had acquired several years before when the value of these exotic Italian bikes was considerably lower than the astronomical prices to which they had more recently risen. The sound of the M.V.'s, even the smaller 250cc café racer, was unlike that of any other motorcycle when they were pushed extremely hard and, of course, that was exactly the way Scott rode them. On occasion he had thoroughly frustrated law enforcement on the open road, but for the most part, seemed to have an uncanny ability of knowing where the police were not. The consensus among local officers was that it was only a matter of time before they were called to scrape Scott Roy off some immovable roadside object. However, this had been going on for some time. Scott was unmarried, and though he got along very well with the ladies on occasion, he appeared unwilling to enter into any long term, time consuming commitment in the near future. Scott's smaller than average size was somehow quickly forgotten after meeting the man. A very complex and changeable person, he could be extremely funny and quick to laugh one minute, very tense and uncommunicative the next. Scott was known to drink more than he had a year or two ago. Reports of a couple fights were not viewed with much surprise. Not one to start trouble,

Scott had very little patience with anyone so inclined. Though giving the benefit of the doubt to friends who might be under the weather, or just in a bad mood, even this charity seemed to be wearing quite thin of late.

Until a couple years ago Scott Roy's love affair with speed was suspended during winter months. The motorcycles, of course, were tucked safely away for the duration, and for whatever reason, Scott's driving habits as applied to his Ford pickup, or any other four wheeled vehicle, had always been quite sane. But then two years ago Scott became involved with snowmobiles, and as if discovering their existence for the first time, his enthusiastic involvement quickly propelled him to the sports state of the art. His current machine was a high powered competition model capable of over 100 M.P.H.

Scott Roy still lived with his parents who incidentally had plenty of money and were gone a great deal of the time. The large home was set on the west shore of a medium sized lake. On the east shore across some railroad tracks and in-town boulevard was situated the city garage. Occasionally, after a fresh snowfall, Scott had taken to riding his snowmachine across the frozen lake to work, usually at wide open throttle. If questioned, nearly all of Scott Roy's friends and co-workers would admit they expected something bad to happen to him soon.

A hundred feet down the winding driveway, the speeding snowmachine suddenly swerved to the right and settled into a sliding hundred and eighty degree turn which pointed it squarely at the frozen lakefront. Down the undulating lawn and out onto the long wooden dock it sped. At the end of the dock the machine became airborne as it stretched into space to fall softly into the new fallen snow. Another slight arcing turn and Scott Roy took aim on a gathering of lights a mile distant on the opposite shore. The pitch of the machine's engine rose perceptively as it rocketed away into the night.

# chapter 4

On Interstate 3 in New Hampshire the Denecy Lincoln headed north amid light traffic. The snow continued. Lorenzo peered out his left rear window at an occasional group of lights seen through the trees along a parallel two lane road. "Tony, how much farther to where we pick up the other vehicle?" he asked.

Tony hesitated only a moment before answering. "About twenty miles, sir. Two more exits and we'll leave the turnpike."

Lorenzo nodded to himself and looked around at his companions. Against the right rear door Frank was beginning to stir from his sleep. At Lorenzo's side, Vincent rubbed his eyes though he was wide awake. Stephen Langella shifted uncomfortably in the front seat still holding the paper packed briefcase on his lap.

Stephen looked across to the chauffeur. "See if you can get a weather report again on the radio, Tony. I'd like to know when this is supposed to stop."

Lorenzo straightened himself and adjusted his tie as he anticipated the end of the long drive. "Remember Stephen? Remember when we pulled into that two bit little town up in the Catskill's? There must have been a dozen black Cadillacs driving around trying to find Carleio's estate. My God, how stupid!"

Langella smiled briefly in the darkness. "Like it was yesterday, Lorenzo."

As Tony slowly turned the radio dial a local station suddenly became crystal clear—*will continue through the night. Several inches of accumulation are probable before tomorrow morning—*

"Damn," said Vincent.

"Not damn, Vincent. Good," Lorenzo replied. "This weather will give the authorities other things to think about. We must just make sure we stay out of trouble. Tony, how is the driving?"

"Very good, Mr. Denecy. Those tires you had me get last week are excellent, sir."

Vincent raised an eyebrow at his grandfather. Lorenzo pretended not to notice, then looked squarely at the younger man. "Details, Vincent. Details. It was good, even necessary, to provide local vehicles for most of those coming, but this time we will go right in with the Lincoln. Out of state cars are plentiful here and besides, such an innocent green. Ha, ha . . . , not so ominous as black, huh? Vincent, we will take you to the other car so you may collect Miss Talli at her hotel and then come to the resort."

Vincent nodded agreement.

Frank Denecy stirred himself awake and was greeted with a wintry scene from his window. "Jesus Christ! Where are we?"

Lorenzo leaned forward to speak to his nephew. "Well, you are finally with us. Those two drinks you had as we were leaving the city put you out cold. You should take better care of yourself. You're lousy company."

Frank didn't respond, but continued his inspection of the landscape. "Christ, I wonder how Carl is getting here. You know, he's probably flying in. Hell, I'll bet he's flying himself."

"Do not worry about Carl Endicott. He will be here," Lorenzo said leaning back in his seat, his tone more pensive.

Vincent looked at his grandfather in genuine surprise. "you mean Carl Philip Endicott? The Endicott Fashion Endicott?"

"The one and the same," replied Lorenzo. "I'm not surprised your father never told you. You were not . . . not family involved then."

"Oh, I'd heard of his connections . . . and the inference, I guess, but I guess I never took it seriously. So . . . who does he work for? What does he . . . ?" Vincent paused to formulate his question.

"Carl Endicott used to work for me . . . for us," Lorenzo stated. "Maybe he still does. I'm not sure. Originally he was Julian's. He was the one that brought Carl out of New York and pointed him at the world. But that was a long time ago. I didn't trust him like Julian did, not that he ever gave me a reason not to." Lorenzo hesitated as he pondered his thoughts. "But then these days I don't really know. Carl was very smart.Carl is very smart. Hell, one reason . . . the main reason I pushed for this meeting was to bring Carl Endicott . . ."

"You? This was your idea?" Frank was incredulous.

"No! Yes, I agreed. It was a consensus!"

Vincent began to mouth another question but thought better of it in the face of the hardening tone in his grandfather's voice.

Lorenzo continued after a silent moment. "This meeting . . . This meeting will hopefully accomplish many things. We must establish a clear direction, a kind of order. We must . . ." Lorenzo hesitated. It was unlike him. The others remained silent as he finally straightened in his seat. "For me, for us," he went on more forcefully, "we must determine just where Carl fits into the scheme of things. I have not spoken to him in two years now. I want to look him in the eyes and I will know. I will know just how big Carl Endicott is. I want to know if we're just along for the ride. Who knows, he may come right out and tell us."

Frank Denecy shook his head as if coming out of a trance. "Christ! And here I was looking forward to an hour or two in the pool! . . . We do have a pool, don't we?" he added in a bit lighter vein.

Lorenzo ignored Frank's attempt at the inane and spoke instead to his grandson with a definite upbeat inflection. "Let us have a drink to begin the evening. Some fresh glasses from the bar, Vincent. We will drink to reality and make believe. It's sometimes difficult to keep them straight these days."

*   *   *

Charlie Hayward had never really wanted to be Street Superintendent. Actually, he'd never given it any thought at all. Though of the honest, hard working, moralistic stock that populates most of middle America, and indeed everywhere else, Charlie's lot in life had historically been determined by outside influences rather than any singular drive or purpose initiated by himself.

Had Charlie's wife Marion known of the possibility of his acquiring the job she would have pushed and prodded him to climb the step up from his long held foreman status. Mrs. Hayward had always dictated the conditions that comprised Charlie's well-being as well as her own. The fact that she made more money as a registered nurse than he did wasn't due to any lack of attention in elevating her husband's lot in life, but rather Charlie's minimal sixth grade education which left him unwilling to fuel his guarded inferiority by possibly biting off more than he could chew.

But several years ago the abrasive personalities of the then Director of Public Works and Street Superintendent had settled all that quite abruptly. After a shouting match heard plainly through the closed door of the Director's office, the feisty Superintendent had emerged red in the face, slammed the door, strode wordlessly past the office staff and out of the building, never to be seen again. Moments later the Director had opened the door, stepped to his secretary's desk and depressed the two-way radio's transmit panel. "Charlie! Drop whatever you're doing and get up here," he had bellowed.

Ten minutes later, after getting not a clue as to what might be afoot from the secretary or the two draftsmen in the outer office, Charlie had wearily entered the Director's domain. After another very few minutes he had stepped from the private office, closing the door quite differently than had his predecessor. "Well, I'll be damned," was all he had to say.

Though a little shaky at first, Charlie quickly showed he had what it took to act as boss, father figure, psychiatrist, and whatever else was required to keep at least most of his work force on the straight and narrow a good deal of the time. Though an outsider might have discerned that discipline was largely non-existent, Charlie somehow knew who to lean on and when. Though some tended to take an occasional liberty with Charlie's good nature, they were in turn kept in check by those who realized when they were well off and didn't want to spoil it. These same few were quick to protect Charlie when criticism might arise resulting from his lack of absolute control of some particular situation. In actuality, everyone knew what had to be done. In large part, the department ran itself.

While normal duties were quite varied, a winter snow storm brought everyone together in an immediate and common goal. At these times Charlie would seat himself at his battered oak desk in the city garage office, pick up the list of names and telephone numbers and start calling. A short time later when everyone had arrived he would scan the faces to see that all were in reasonably good condition and able to work. Such was usually the case. If at a reasonable hour, the atmosphere of this preparatory get-together was somewhat party-like as the men discussed activities from which they were so rudely interrupted or compared storm prognostications. Last minute equipment checks would be made and mechanics would scurry around doing minor repairs on those things that invariably waited until that moment to go to hell.

Whoever arrived first, driver or wingman, would unplug the electric engine heater from their truck and start the engine so it could be warming up. Plows were usually hitched and in place if a storm was known to be approaching, but the driver would decide whether or not to put on tire chains at the last moment depending on snow conditions and what effect they would have on his particular plow run. With cabs warm, windshields clear and wipers slapping rhythmically back and forth, the trucks would then make their way out of their respective parking spaces around the outside perimeter of the garage and head across the street to New England Yard where large stockpiles of winter salt and sand were kept. Here, a payloader would load each truck body with sand for added weight and rear wheel traction and one by one the trucks would go on their way.

With the garage finally empty of men and equipment and the trucks gone, Charlie would retreat to this office to listen in on the radio chatter and to issue any specific orders that would become necessary. In an hour or two when operations had really gotten underway, Charlie would get into his pickup and venture out to see how things were going.

This particular evening started out pretty much as usual. Charlie was behind his desk, the telephone to his ear. Other voices could be heard beyond the office in the anteroom. The sounds of heavy equipment moving about and engines being run echoed forth from the garage beyond.

"When did he leave," Charlie asked of the telephone. "You mean he never came home after work? . . . Yeah, all right . . . Yeah, I know. I'll call there.

Charlie slammed the phone down not in anger, but in frustration from having to make so many calls. Turning to the small blackboard beside him on the wall, he scanned its variously scrawled contents. "Hey, Pat," he yelled.

Patrick Gant leaned around the office door jam to peer at Charlie. The loud conversation of several crew members also in the anteroom diminished for a moment. "Yeah?"

"What the hell is the number of the Country North Lounge? I had it written on the board here, but somebody wiped it off."

"Don't tell me. You can't get ahold of your favorite asshole Powell. Have you called his wingman yet?" Pat moved into the room and slid into the vacant chair by Charlie's desk. He was systematically demolishing the wood end of a long match in his teeth.

"Of course I called him," Charlie replied impatiently. "He ain't home either. I know they're together somewhere getting plastered."

"Well, Country North ain't open yet. They had some trouble last night."

The sound of one of the long wooden benches falling over in the anteroom followed by raucous laughter invaded the office.

"Keep it down out there," Charlie yelled at the open door.

Just then a louder crash of metal hitting the concrete garage floor rose above all else. The same instant a man cried out in pain as others yelled and swore.

"What the hell was that?" Charlie put the phone receiver on the desk as though he might get out of his chair to investigate. Pat didn't move a muscle as he continued to look calmly at his boss.

"I don't want to fucking know, do you?"

Charlie hesitated only a moment, then grabbed for the phone. "What the hell's the Legion number?"

"Nine-seven-four-two," Pat replied.

If Pat Gant's co-workers were polled to name his most worthy attribute, the overwhelming answer would have been his ability to be vulgar. Indeed, in the Melonia Public Works Department, such a title was not without meaning. Though like most everyone else, Pat included swear words into every other sentence no matter what his mood, he exhibited his particular brilliance, some termed it an art form, only on occasion.

When really angered, Pat could unleash a tirade of profanity in such phrases and combinations as never heard before. At such times all other conversation would stop in a moment of silent appreciation. In fact, a few of Pat's originals sometimes enjoyed wide usage for a while. That was until he came up with something better.

But Pat's talent didn't have to wait until he got pissed, for he could, when so moved, paint some of the vilest and sickening word pictures ever heard. On these occasions, usually during lunch, Pat might innocently begin a tale which would quickly degenerate along these lines. More than one worker had been known to puke up his food much to the enjoyment of those able to keep their's down.

At age 29, Pat had been married since a senior at Melonia High. Jackie Gant was one of the few wives to be frequently seen at the city garage looking for her husband, and if he wasn't there, proceed to some job site to find him. Jackie was a pleasant enough person, but she seemed constantly embroiled in some difficult situation that only her husband's advise and wisdom would rectify. The washing machine just sprung a leak, Pat's mother just called from Pittsburgh and was driving up the following day, the cat was sick, etcetera. Furthermore, when Jackie finally found her husband he usually had a cigarette in his mouth and she would sternly remind him that he had quit a year ago.

Pat's co-workers looked forward to these occurrences for they were the only times when he would be on the defensive. After Jackie departed in her orange Mustang the men would slowly embark on what would be about five minutes of good teasing. Curiously, Pat was never seen to be angry with his wife on these occasions and would accept the long moments after she left with relatively good humor. Actually, he would be thinking of things to say the next time he found one of his tormentors eating a jelly donut.

Charlie again grabbed the phone just as the radio base station came to life.

*Seventeen to garage . . .*

Charlie shook his head, dropped the phone and pressed the talk switch on the radio. "What are you doing? The salt trucks were supposed to be in here half an hour ago. Get in here, Hartwell!"

*I'm stuck. It's going to take a loader to get me out,* came the reply.

Charlie shook his head harder this time as he looked across to Pat.

"Christ!" He pressed the mike button again. "Where are you?"

*I'm up by that new motel they're building on the Boulevard almost up to the Center. I was empty and this thing just slid off into the ditch. I'm leaned over pretty far.*

"I'll bet he's been playing with it for twenty minutes," Pat offered. "Truck's probably in right up to the axles. Goddamned fool!"

"Is Oscar here yet?", Charlie asked.

"Yeah, he was out in the garage. That is if he's still alive. Sounded like him screaming before."

"Well if he's still conscious tell him to take the small loader and go get Hartwell out," Charlie ordered.

Pat climbed slowly out of the chair, smiling at the prospect.

"Here, take this," Charlie added as he handed the call list towards Pat. "Call these last four guys from the tool crib. I'll call the Legion."

"Okay," replied Pat, leaving the office.

The radio crackled again. *Seventeen to garage.*

Charlie pressed the mike button, smiling slightly. "Hold on Lester. Oscar's coming to get you. Maybe next time you can manage to keep it on the road."

*Thanks a lot,* came the garbled reply.

*       *       *

The bar at the local American Legion Post still held its share of after work clientele. On Friday night, a large percentage of these would hang around to greet the evening crowd which would start filtering in in a couple hours. Typical in layout, a dozen tables were scattered before the wall to wall bar. At the opposite end of the room a pool table and a ten foot long bowling machine stood waiting for certain more competitive minded customers that were sure to rise from a later, looser crowd to settle their differences on the field of play. In a far corner near one end of the bar, a solitary waitress slipped a couple coins into an aging jukebox.

At a table near center room were seated two men and two women. One of the men leaned back in his chair smiling slightly as he watched the two women seated tightly against either side of the other man. Before them on the table the man held a fresh bottle of beer which seemed to be the center of attention for all three.

"I swear," said Richard Wright, holding the beer tight in his grasp, "you can feel the power in the truck as it comes right up through the shift lever. Sometimes it will shake and jump in your hand."

Richard illustrated the phenomenon by rattling the bottle on the table until the foam of the fresh beer rose to the top and dripped over the side. One of the girls seemed somewhat more intent on the demonstration than the other. Richard shifted most of his attention in her direction.

"Really?" asked the girl.

"I mean it, no kidding," continued Richard, his enthusiasm bolstered by her interest. "Sometimes when you've been driving for hours it can catch you unaware. It can be a hell of a turn-on. Here, I'll show you. Put your hand around the bottle neck above mine."

The girl obeyed.

"Now hold on tight," he ordered.

Roland Powell settled forward slowly and reached for his beer as he watched the other girl. She just sat there watching Richard and the bottle.

"First you bring the lever into first gear and slowly let out the clutch," related Richard as he slid the bottle across the table in an imaginary shift pattern. "You can feel the power coming," he added.

Richard vibrated the bottle in the girl's grasp. The beer dripped down over her fingers. "When the engine's had enough in first, you drop the clutch, go to second and do it again, . . . now to third . . ."

Richard slid the bottle back toward his chest. "In third you've got to really hold on tight," he cautioned. "Sometimes when you let out the clutch the lever will throb back and forth trying to get away."

Roland brought his hand up to rub his face. He wasn't sure how much more of this he could take without bursting out laughing.

"Okay. Fourth gear and you're almost home," Richard proclaimed.

Suddenly, the other girl was rocking slowly back and forth in her chair, moaning softly. Surprised, Richard turned from his intended prey to look at, who up till now, had certainly been the less animated of the two females. All three looked at the girl who appeared to be in something of a trance.

"Linda? Linda, are you all right?" asked the girl with her hand on the bottle.

"Roland Powell or Richard Wright," the voice boomed. The bartender held a telephone receiver in the air, his hand covering the lower part.

The attention of the table's occupants turned to the bartender. The dazed girl seemed to be coming around. Richard and Roland appeared annoyed at the interruption.

"What?" yelled Richard.

"This is for one of you. It's your boss," announced the bartender.

"Jesus Christ, what time is it?" asked Roland.

Richard looked at his watch, the girls now forgotten. "It's after six!"

"I wonder how many places he's called. There must be some snow out there," said Richard.

"Somebody want to take this or not," asked the bartender, waving the phone.

"You talk to him," said Roland.

Richard made a face and nodded. "Yeah, Okay," Richard got out of his chair and made his way to the bar.

"Don't you guys know its been snowing like hell for the past two or three hours?"

"Somebody might have mentioned it to us."

"I am not your keeper and this is not a group home," remarked the bartender.

Richard waved a hand around the room. "Look around. Maybe it ought to be." Taking the phone from the smiling bartender. "Charlie? Am I glad you called. What the hell's the matter with the phone over there?"

Richard Wright had that rare ability of recognizing the humor in almost any situation. Denied the opportunity, Richard could quickly conjure a situation of his own. On occasion he would elevate an ongoing conversation into high gear by directing a continuous stream of dialogue toward his target. Unwilling to pause long enough to allow the other to speak, he would insert their side of the conversation for them until his prey became so frustrated they would scream, "Shut the fuck up, Wright!" and walk away, talking to themselves while Richard laughed uproariously. It had, therefore, become difficult for Richard to lure fellow employees into his trap anymore and the phrase "Shut the fuck up, Wright!" might arrive before he could really get started. However, this didn't seem to slow Richard Wright down a bit for he had an endless repertoire of routines. On occasion he would even play it straight, however, no one was sure when this was taking place so Richard invariably had the upper hand.

But Richard did have some fine qualities. First of all, he had never been heard to say anything bad about someone behind their back. On the contrary, to their face he would compliment them on their work, some special talent, their looks, or their intellect so artfully that nearly always they would be sucked into his grasp and would soon find themselves blushing with embarrassment. As Wright went on he would turn to any onlookers and proclaim something like, "This is one fine man here! And this department is damn lucky to have him. I am proud to work with this man.", etcetera. About this time bystanders would begin to smile as the object of Richard's praise knew he had been had once again. All in attendance would then scream in unison, "Shut the fuck up, Wright!"

But in a serious vein, Richard was fiercely loyal and would defend a fellow employee to the hilt if the occasion so demanded. It was common knowledge that Roland Powell was still driving a city truck because of Richard Wright. Not that Roland could not speak for himself, but he or anyone else could breath much easier when Wright was called to explain what he knew about some misdeed or accident.

Any accident involving property damage, or even the slightest injury, was reviewed before a Safety Board meeting at City Hall twice a month. The City Manager, Assistant Director of Public Works, as well as representatives of other departments would be attendance. The function of the Board to review accidents in order to determine safer and more foolproof procedures was of course viewed by lower echelon employees as being a waste of time. However, one's presence before the board had to be taken seriously from a disciplinary standpoint.

It was here that Richard Wright's eloquence was at its best. Richard played it straight at these meetings, and though he frequently pushed himself close to the edge, he had never quite gone over. Then too, Board members didn't know Richard in his more familiar surroundings, however, other Public Works Department employees summoned and in attendance had, at times, all they could do to keep a straight face. Once, the City Manager had even apologized for calling Roland Powell and Richard Wright away from their work.

At twenty-four years of age, Richard (curiously he was not called Dick) was of medium height and build. The fact that he was quite good looking, coupled with his smooth talking ability, often proved a devastating combination when pointed in the direction of an unsuspecting woman he had taken a shine to. Of course, Richard was not above going overboard here also. He had been married and divorced twice during the past three years as he found he could not kick the lure of a new conquest. On more than once occasion female forms had been observed in the cab of plow truck number twenty-two during night time operations.

If Richard Wright, at least in the short term, seemed to lead somewhat of a charmed existence, Roland Powell's workday often played out quite differently. Indeed, unfortunate things seemed to happen to Roland. This was, of course, the perfect definition of bad luck, many were quick to point out. Curiously, most incidents centered around whatever piece of equipment Roland happened to be operating. As an example, things frequently broke on Roland's truck, or on occasion, Roland's truck would break other things with Roland at the wheel. During snowplowing operations wingman Richard Wright proved invaluable in explaining to superiors that such occurrences were totally unavoidable, but the perception that Roland Powell was somehow jinxed was firmly implanted within the department.

The office secretary greeted his coming with mixed emotions, for though his likable manner might brighten her day, she was usually faced with filling out another accident report. The garage mechanics viewed Powell somewhat more seriously as his presence related directly to their work load. His voice coming over the garage loudspeaker could well mean a following damage report sometimes requiring assistance at the scene. Powell's voice over the speaker evoked even stricter attention from anyone in the end of the building since the previous summer when it was closely followed by a tremendous crash as a street sweeper demolished the large and closed overhead door. A riding lawn mower was totally destroyed and a truck in for a brake job was knocked off its jacks before the sweeper finally came to a stop. Those present had fled in all directions. Powell swore that the throttle had suddenly stuck on the sweeper. As it turned out, he was right.

Roland was a good worker, and his friends said, an excellent driver despite his record. At the same time the computer at City Hall was incapable of assimilating his damage totals, so the magnitude of his true cost to the city had yet to be realized.

An effort to re-nickname Powell "Crash" after the sweeper incident had failed in the face of his incumbent handle of "Duckling" which was used freely with his approval. Shortly after he had started work Roland Powell had leveled a telephone booth with his truck rather than run over a mother duck and her little ones that had darted into the street. On an otherwise newsless day, the local media had christened him a hero. The replacement phone booth even bore a small plaque commemorating the occasion. For better or worse the department was stuck with Roland Powell.

Outside the American Legion Club a single mercury vapor lamp on a high pole illuminated the rear parking lot. The steadily falling snow sparkled in the soft light as it descended to cover all. Roland Powell and Richard

Wright emerged from the back door slipping and sliding as they hurried to Roland's pickup.

"Christ, I thought we were supposed to only get an inch or two of this stuff," Roland observed as he hurriedly swept snow from the windshield of the truck.

Richard was still laughing as he cleared the passenger side. "Did you see that girl? And I was concentrating on the other one! I must be losing it. I'll bet her draws were so slimy she could have slid right off that chair. Damn! And here we are leaving. I don't fucking believe it."

The pair climbed into the pickup which started instantly with a roar. With tires spinning it made a rapid, but controlled exit from the parking lot and proceeded down the street.

# chapter 5

High above south central New Hampshire the executive Lear jet sped northward into the storm. Brian Verrill sat in the pilot's seat hunched slightly forward looking alternately from the expansive instrument panel upward to the blackness outside. Jeff Miles, somewhat less attentive, but appearing markedly more concerned, occupied the copilot's chair.

"He's cutting this a little close, isn't he?" Jeff offered.

"Keep your shirt on," Brian said, not looking up from his instruments. "He knows exactly how far out we are."

The intercom crackled to life with the sound of Carl Endicott's voice. *How far out are we, Brian?*

Brian glanced across to see Jeff slowly shaking his head. "Coming up on forty miles," he answered.

*I guess we've kept them in suspense long enough,* came the response. Jeff, your seat please.

"I guess I'll just go back and have a drink or two or five," remarked Jeff, unbuckling his seatbelt.

"Have one for me," said Brian.

Jeff and Endicott passed each other a few feet behind the cockpit. Now wearing an identical white jumpsuit to the one Brian had on, Carl Endicott looked like a different man than the one that originally entered the plane. Without the two side by side it was difficult to tell exactly why, but clearly, one would not have been mistaken for the other. Carl settled into the co-pilot's seat. "Melonia is closed, I presume," he said.

"They haven't said so, Brian replied. "But they don't profess any emergency standby readiness and I'm sure they're not expecting the scenario we're going to give them."

"How many times have they tried to contact us?" Endicott asked.

"A couple. The last about five minutes ago."

"How's our line?"

"Right on. Concord Air Service has been calling also," Brian continued. "They all sound a little nervous about now."

Endicott smiled slightly. "I really hate to put them through this, but up until now they could have insisted we divert to the coast, probably Portsmouth or Portland, Maine. They still will, but we can bluff our way in from here, what with our communication problems." The smile faded as he reached for the headset and put it on. "I guess its time to let them know we're still airborne before they start contacting a lot of people I'm sure we don't want to talk to."

Brian cast a quick glance at his boss. "I would say." Suddenly, a look of concentration came across his face. "Here's their N.D.B. coming in now . . . we're right on," he concluded, satisfied.

"Good," Endicott said, nodding. "Let's bring her down a little and cut our speed. And move west about a point. We're going to make at least one pass."

Endicott flipped a switch and spoke into the mike. "This is Executive Lear N-741-E calling Melonia. Come in Melonia . . . This is Executive Lear N-741-E calling Melonia. Come in Melonia . . ."

An excited voice from Melonia came on the air. *This is Melonia, N-741-E. Where have you been? We are shut down. Suggest you divert to Portsmouth Air Station.*

"Thank God!" Endicott breathed into the mike. Brian winced in his seat. "We can't do it, Melonia. We've had some electrical problems here. It seems okay for the moment, but it could go out any time. So you're elected. What's the situation down there?"

Melonia was back in a split second. *Repeat, N-741-E. We are shut down! Divert to Portsmouth. We got snow plows on the runway here!*

Brian's face seemed to whiten closer to the shade of his suit, but he said nothing. Endicott continued, calm but firm. "We can't do that, Melonia. I repeat, we have no choice. What are your conditions? Can you contact the plows by radio?"

*Jesus Christ!* came the reply followed by a pause. When Melonia continued the voice was no less animated, but if sounded somewhat resigned. *Conditions are lousy! Ceiling is a few hundred feet . . . maybe. The wind is from the southeast . . . at six to eight miles per hour. Visibility is nil . . . call it variable if you want . . . hell, half a mile if you're lucky. I can't get the plows. It's a private outfit . . . no radios!*

Endicott jumped in to fill the pause after the last Melonia remark. "We're going to make a pass in from the southwest in a few minutes. See if you can locate the plows and let us know how much of a swath they've got cleared." Endicott reached for the controls. "I'll take it now, Brian."

"It's all yours." Brian seemed only too glad to release the controls to his boss. For a moment he tried to settle back more comfortably in the seat, but immediately he was back up in his former tense position straining to see ahead through the windscreen and checking the instruments.

Under Carl's control the Lear settled further into the gloom, the sound of the engines lessening a bit more in pitch.

Again, Melonia was on the air. This time the voice seemed resigned to the attempted landing and eager to relate the necessary information in the least possible time. *Okay, Executive Lear, it's your funeral. Yours and whoever you drop that thing on . . . We've got some hills up to eight hundred feet to the north of the runway. Do keep that in mind. Incidentally, we're at about five twenty U.S.G.S. in case you didn't know it. There's much higher stuff to the southeast. Stay away from there. The plows . . . there's two in tandem . . . have just turned on the east end and they'll be headed back toward you. They'll be to your left of center strip and pushing to the north windrow. They've got sixty or seventy feet of width cleared. You should see some patches of dark pavement.* Melonia stopped for a second to catch its breath. *You reading this, Executive Lear?*

"Loud and clear, Melonia. We should have you in sight any time," Endicott said evenly as his eyes tried to pierce the darkness ahead.

*When you see our lights, get down on the deck. The plows should see yours, and if they've got any sense, they'll pull off the runway. Remember the windrow and stay away from that. If you go around, turn left. I repeat, left, and get back up to a thousand when you do . . . Good luck.*

"There it is," Brian exclaimed, leaning even closer to the windscreen. A vague landscape loomed ahead together with the fast approaching twin lines of runway lights.

On the runway, the two big trucks rumbled along, one behind the other. The collected accumulation of snow was now heavy in their plows as they pushed the growing windrow closer to the line of runway lights.

Suddenly, far ahead down the runway, two lights shown back at the plows. In a matter of seconds they grew to blinding beacons, then disappeared as the Lear thundered overhead. Immediately, the first truck veered to its right, its plows rising as it smashed its way through the windrow and continued over the unplowed pavement to the north line of runway lights. As though choreographed in advance, the second truck duplicated the actions of the first.

The Lear settled into a tight left turn, climbing slightly.

Endicott smiled. "You think they noticed us?"

"I would say they did," Brian answered. "The question is, where will they be when we come around?"

"As long as they're not sitting in the middle of the runway, I don't really care."

The Lear continued in its turn, flashing through the night a few hundred feet above the northern hilltops.

"By the way, how do I look?" Endicott asked.

"Different," Brian observed. "Different enough. A disguise that doesn't look like a disguise. I don't know how you do it."

"I've been doing it for a long time. Maybe too long," Endicott mused. " . . . After we land I want to find the man we've been talking to. That shouldn't be hard. We want to thank him very much for his cooperation as we give him . . . say a five hundred dollar tip for his professional courtesy and another couple hundred to pass out to the plow truck drivers. We also mention that we would appreciate his not making much of our landing should anyone inquire as our boss would not be pleased if he knew we were taking chances with the corporate aircraft. And oh, we'll be having our equipment checked out before we leave the first of the week."

"Sounds good," said Brian. "It will sound a lot better when we're on the ground."

"One more thing," Endicott continued without acknowledging Brian's remark. "We ask him if he could recommend a good hotel about thirty miles north in the Plymouth area as our reservations got fouled up in Waterville where we're covering the World Cup ski competition this weekend. This is one time we'll be putting our prepared cover to good use even if it's only here."

Endicott glanced quickly to his left, making sure his companion had understood everything he'd said. Brian nodded to his boss.

Endicott started to bring the plane slowly out of its turn. "When we get our cargo and equipment into the van and on the road the first thing I want to do is check all the local police and emergency channels to see what kind of a disturbance we've caused, if any."

As the Lear straightened into its short approach, the two plow truck drivers were standing to the rear of the first truck to see what manner of aircraft dared challenge nature's worst. Again, the glaring lights as the plane lowered itself gingerly onto the far end of the runway. Straight and true it came until just before where the plow trucks were parked, it turned and taxied through the snow to the small terminal building.

*       *       *

Dwane Huckins brought his pickup to a sliding stop at the snow covered intersection and reached down to flip a switch on the expansive array of radio equipment located beneath the truck's dash.

"Can you believe that? The bastard made it! Slid that thing in just as nice as you please. I swear some of those guys are getting really crazy. That was a few million dollars worth of aircraft that just set down." Dwane shook his head, changed gears and the truck accelerated slowly away over the snow.

In the passenger seat, Bob Garnett waited for a moment as though deciding if indeed Dwane's comments required an answer. "Hey, the airport's going big time. You know what its like in the summer over there. There's money laying all over the place," Bob finally offered. "It must be nice," he added.

"I'll tell you, one of these days someone's going to make a mistake. They're long overdue. It's not going to be pretty." Dwane scowled as if visualizing the terrible consequences of his prediction.

A lot went on in Dwane Huckins' head that no one knew about. And that was probably just as well. Dwane was friendly enough, but periods of silence and obvious tension were observed with a limited respect by the rest of the Public Works Department work force. Having been with the department for eight years, he had previously spent a year on the Melonia Police force. However, his severe treatment of a rape suspect had led to a reluctant request for his resignation.

Huckins had served in Vietnam in some sort of Army Intelligence role and it had been said he was one of the last Americans to leave the country during those dramatic final moments at Saigon. During the years since he had very little to say on the subject.

Originally from the west coast, it was not known why he had chosen to settle in the far away and foreign northeast. A couple years ago he had spent a month's vacation in California and when he returned he was married. Wife, Jean, was quite young and very flashy. After that, Dwane didn't spend as much time drinking with the guys after hours as he had. Not that it had ever been that much, but he seemed a little more easy going at work.

If Dwane Huckins had a hobby it was certainly his continuing interest, indeed obsession with criminology and related police sciences. The local department had hated to let him go and had done so only in the face of an impending lawsuit. Few knew that Police Chief Justin Mars had recently asked Huckins to return to the force, but apparently Dwane had other plans.

Dwane was not one to insist that others should share his interest in what was intellectually termed a dark science, however, there was one constant and obvious reminder that all could see. Dwane Huckins insisted on being able to receive radio transmissions from any government agency so equipped and to that end his personal pickup truck bristled with antennas and various radio gear. Had such an idiosyncrasy belonged to anyone else, that person would have been a perfect target for teasing and ridicule. But not so with Dwane. At times many of the guys were welcome recipients of some informational tidbit that certainly the general public was not privy to.

Most of the public works vehicle two-way radios included the Melonia city police band as well as their own. This was partially due to a screw-up when they were ordered. However, during winter months when long hours were likely to be spent in the same vehicle, Dwane's plow truck received a system roughly equivalent to that in his own truck by which he could receive signals from the State Police, the Fire Department, County Sheriff's office, Department of Safety and the Melonia Airport, as well as a couple others that only Dwane knew the origin of. Dwane Huckins simply wanted to know what was going on around him.

Bob Garnett's true talent was his ability to alter his character to fit his surroundings and to better adjust himself to those with whom he had to associate. This is not to say that Bob didn't have a mind of his own, or could be used or kicked around. It simply meant that Bob Garnett wasted very little time in needless personal conflict with others.

Of course few, if any, would have described Bob in those terms. Instead, they might have declared Bob a likeable sort who could get along with almost anybody. However, anyone who knew him reasonably well would have been eager to expand on another facet of Garnett's abilities. For Bob was recognized as a supreme arbitrator. But Bob was not concerned with complex issues argued between civilized men who knew in advance that an agreement would inevitably be reached after long and difficult and probably very boring negotiations. No. Bob Garnett liked the action of a more immediate challenge.

The scene was usually some neighborhood bar in which the locals had been busy getting shitfaced for the past couple hours. Sooner or later, a heated argument between two of the more stupefied individuals would become particularly abusive. At some point, they would rise from their chairs, upsetting drinks, ashtrays and anything on the table. The screaming and name calling would then reach its all too familiar levels.

"Why you cocksucker!" one would exclaim, trying not to drool. "Your wife's a whore . . . always has been! And those fuckin' kids . . . couple of little faggots if I ever saw any!"

The other would naturally reply in kind. "Why you low life pigfucker! You'd fuck your own mother . . . probably have! Come outside and I'll . . . Fuck outside! I think I'll rip your fuckin' bag off right here . . ."

Each lurches forward to engage the other. Suddenly, Bob Garnett is between them. "Hold it fellas," he says and raises his hands as if to freeze their initial blows.

Two or three minutes later, the would-be combatants are proclaiming life long friendship and are buying each other a beer. Both buy Bob a beer. Bob returns to his own seat and the bartender buys him a beer. A couple amazed bystanders do the same. Bob drinks for free as long as he cares to hang around. It is truly an astounding phenomenon.

Fortunately, Bob seldom got the chance to exercise his strange tranquilizing ability, for it would surely have lost its edge after frequent performances. Once, a couple of Bob's fellow workers decided to put him to the test and staged a particularly nasty confrontation at a local club. As always, Bob rose to the occasion, but after a few moments, must have sensed he was being had. Another minute and he had nearly succeeded in pitting the two against each other for real and finally shouted at one. "I wouldn't take that shit from him if I were you. Kill the son-of-a-bitch!" Bob had returned to his seat while his two friends stood there feeling stupid. Many people in the bar thought the scene quite amusing. The bartender bought Bob a beer.

Bob Garnett's winter duties included acting as wingman on the plow truck driven by Dwane Huckins. To say that his easy going nature might have come in handy while working with Dwane may have been unfair to the latter, however, it was true the two were good friends.

Bob had structured a pretty stable existence around and outside of his occasional barroom activities. Having been married for nine years, he and wife, Lee, had two boys, six and eight years of age. The couple were about the only people that Dwane and his wife saw socially and the foursome could occasionally be seen dining at one of the area restaurants.

Bob had once worked as a radio and T.V. repairman and still did on a once in a while basis. However, recently his chief interest along these lines had been the installation of the radio system into a brand new Ford Louisville plow truck that would be he and Dwane's. The truck was to see its first service during the present storm.

Dwane expertly altered the course of his pickup toward the side of the road to avoid an approaching car that strayed across the yellow line as it came around the corner. The traveling was getting quite bad in the deepening snow. With a smooth downshift and light pressure on the accelerator, Dwane brought the pickup back on course with hardly a slip or slide. Neither man spoke of the minor, non-incident which had just occurred, but plainly, Bob was becoming a little edgy.

"Christ, will you look at this stuff come down. I'll bet Charlie called us last. He always does."

Dwane gave a quick laugh. "That's because we're the best," he said.

*   *   *

A few cars were gathered around the entrance of the convenience store, a couple with their engines running, lights on and wipers flapping back and forth. The four or five inches of new snow on the ground was deeply rutted from recent traffic. A couple outside lights illuminated the immediate area and the street several yards away where a few cars ventured slowly past.

The door to the store opened, clanking a small cowbell suspended overhead on a spring. A tall, barrel chested man in his late fifties ventured out on the landing where he hesitated momentarily. In one arm he carried a large paper bag of purchases. Under the other he secured a couple thick newspapers. With a careful glance at the snow covered steps, he proceeded down, appearing mindful of where he placed his lightly rubbered black wingtips.

One could hear the snow machine's engine before it was apparent where it was coming from. Suddenly, it cut across the street and slid to a stop a few feet from the steps and the man who had just carefully finished negotiating the last one. Startled, the man turned, lost his footing and slid to the ground. The snow machine rider got off his mount and moved to assist the man who was quickly gathering up the last of his purchases out of the snow and stuffing them back into the bag.

"Stupid fucking kid!" the man snarled as he quickly stood and planted a right hand solidly on the chest of the snow machine rider, shoving him to the ground.

Instantly, the rider was on his feet, and tearing the full face helmet from his head, thrust it aside into the snow. Scott Roy raised both fists and again approached the older bigger man. "I was just trying to give you a hand, but if that's the way you want it, I'd rather kick your ass," he snarled.

Stanley Fagner mouthed another obscenity, dropped his parcels and assumed a fighter's stance which hadn't been in vogue since the forties.

On the opposite side of a white Cadillac parked a short distance away the driver's door opened and John Elvio stood to look across the roof of the car. "That's enough," he ordered. "just pick up the stuff and get over here!"

Stanley took no notice of the command, but stepped to circle the younger man. One could picture countless confrontations in the ring beginning to play back in the man's head. Scott Roy stood his ground, becoming more fascinated than angry.

The rear window of the Cadillac rolled down and Bradford Nevis loudly enforced Ellie's order. "Stanley! Get in the car!" Nevis looked from Stanley to Scott who met his gaze. Stanley shifted his attention back and forth from his boss to Scott as if still not convinced exactly what he should do.

"In the car! Now!," Nevis exclaimed angrily.

At once, Stanley obediently reached for his bag and papers, stepped to the car, opened the front door and got in. After the previous hesitation, the moves had been sudden, almost programmed, in their execution. Scott Roy slowly lowered his fists and looked again to where the final command had emanated. The rear window rolled up cutting off eye contact between the two men.

The Cadillac moved out onto the highway and away. Scott retrieved his helmet from the snow and gave the car a parting glance as he quickly sprang up the steps to the store.

*     *     *

The asphalt expanse surrounding the city garage was ablaze with activity. Most of the plow trucks parked around the buildings perimeter were not running, the mantle of new snow being swept from cabs and windshields by forearms, push brooms, or anything else that was handy. The last employee vehicles filtered in, heading directly to the rear of the lot to be parked alongside those that had already arrived. Also to the rear of the building, a few trucks were gathered at the gas pumps. Those few drivers without full tanks now realized that the intensifying storm would require more than a single circuit of their routes. Under such circumstances it was well to put off a second fill-up as long as possible. During a premature trip back to the garage, heavy snow could reach unmanageable depths back on one's run.

The man currently pumping gas into his Louisville Ford was not in a good mood. It was becoming increasingly obvious that the crew would be getting a late start on a storm that now promised something more than the average snowfall. Bill Board's route included some steep hills and several inches of depth on that first go-around could cause all kinds of problems. For that reason, Bill nearly always managed to have his dump body already filled with sand and thus avoid waiting in line for a payloader at New England Yard across the street. Tonight was no different, however, he was angry at himself for forgetting to fill up with gas earlier in the afternoon.

From the line of personal vehicles, a somewhat younger man approached the truck, his progress slowed only slightly by a case of beer under each arm. James Anasty's given name, at least at the city garage, had long since given way to the handle of "Custer", the idea of which he freely enjoyed and cultivated. Custer stopped in front of Bill Board and carefully lowered his cargo to the ground.

"Click that pump off long enough to pass this beer up to me before someone comes out here," said Custer, quickly looking around.

Bill Board left the gas nozzle sticking in the saddle tank and himself cast a look toward the back door of the garage. As Custer climbed up into the dump body, Bill reached for the first case. "Who the hell designated us as a carrier tonight?" he asked.

"Nobody. I'm sure Hartwell and Scott will have some on board. And probably Richard. Christ! Look at it come down, will ya?" Custer placed the beer in the front passenger side of the body on top of the sand, but out of view of anyone on the ground.

"Don't forget Dunbar. He's always got something tucked away," Bill added.

"Fuck The Fly!" exclaimed Custer, climbing down to the ground. "Drinks nothing but scotch. Blaaaaa!"

"So you think we're going to drink all that? Are you nuts?"

"Look," Custer explained. "The stores are going to be closing early which means pretty damn quick. Somebody's going to want a beer or two later on and at three in the morning the price goes up."

Bill Board shook his head at Custer and went back to his gas nozzle.

At age twenty-six, Custer was totally consumed by the heavy metal music scene and its culture. While most fellow employees were loosely committed to a diet of pop rock or country western, a blatant attack by Custer's favorite sounds produced screams of pain and anger. Those who had visited his apartment spoke of another world where amplifiers, speakers and an array of electronic audio gear accompanied by a complex system of colored strobe lights was capable of literally raping one's senses. Custer also owned an assortment of strange looking guitars. No one had determined just how good he really was, but the sounds he made could drop flying insects anywhere in the room.

Custer spent most weekends in and around some of the wilder, big city type night spots to the south and frequently attended rock concerts in Boston and New York. His goal was to someday establish a northern annex emulating the best of these establishments. It had been wondered why indeed Custer chose to work for the Melonia Public Works Department, but somehow he seemed content, at least for the moment. During winter maintenance months Custer was teamed with Bill Board in plow truck number fifteen. They presented an odd couple if ever there was one.

In their truck Custer had installed not simply an AM-FM radio, for almost every truck had one of these, but a sophisticated, high powered sound system. One might have imagined this would drive B.B. nuts and indeed he was having a problem along somewhat predicable lines.

Custer was quite a striking looking individual and encountered little resistance from the ladies. Though his five foot, ten inch lean frame and finely chiseled features were handsome, it was his hair that would jerk one's head around for the first time. Shoulder length, honey blond, and naturally wavy, Custer always looked like he had just stepped out of a Lady Clairol commercial, though he swore he gave it no special care.

Hence, the "Custer" moniker was almost automatic. Occasionally, he wore an old Cavalry hat to further the image.

Bill Board, on the other hand, would not be working for the city very long. He would tell you that in no uncertain terms. Of course, he would have said the same thing five or six years ago. William was destined for bigger and better things. Though some applauded his desire to improve himself, most agreed it was a lost cause. Bill Board had taken innumerable courses at the local State Vocation School over the years. From computer programming to animal husbandry, Board had been exposed to it all. He should have been a thoroughly educated individual by now, and indeed had collected a wide assortment of mostly useless information. But Bill claimed not to have found his special niche in life, that which would lead him towards a respected well-paying career in the community. Through it all Bill had sought to improve his manner of speech and vocabulary, however, this too had somehow fallen short of the mark.

Although frequently appearing angry to those who didn't know him, only rarely did Bill Board lose his temper. This state of mind was not freely sought by fellow employees because Bill was a large, well put together man. However, this was not the only reason that Board was not teased or made fun of from time to time though he might have seemed a prime target. Bill was fairly good looking in a large cuddly animal sort of way, and as a result, somewhat of a ladies man. Though his dates seemed to change with the course he was currently taking, some of Bill Board's companions had been fleetingly gorgeous. The guys at the garage had been impressed from time to time.

At the beginning of the winter Custer had sought to widen his driver's outlook on the hard rock music scene, so as to pave the way for the installation of his sound system. Although not taking very well to some of his wingman's favorite selections, Custer still had the upper hand, having convinced Bill that the sexiest women were to be found to the south, but only a heavy metal aficionado could hope to make it to first base.

Custer turned for the garage, then stopped and looked back at Bill Board. "Hey, you try those new outside speakers yet? I've got a couple tapes that will wake up everybody within a mile of this truck."

"No, I haven't. And see if you can resist turning that thing on until we get the hell out of town. And by the way, I don't want to hear no more of that acid rock shit you had last storm. That stuff has no melodic quality at all."

Custer laughed out loud. "Melodic quality, huh? Ah, the music a man loves can carve chunks from his soul." Laughing again, he continued toward the garage.

"Well, I'll carve a chunk or two from your ass if you try playing that crap," Bill warned at Custer's departing backside.

# chapter 6

At the other end of the garage Scott Roy brought his snow machine off the street at high speed and barreled it up atop a high snowbank at the end of the parking lot across from the main garage equipment door. Grabbing a paper bag he had pinned between his legs on the seat, Scott half stepped, half slid down the steep bank and walked toward his plow truck parked at the corner of the building. At that moment a payloader pulled into the driveway and headed for the big main door which was clanking slowly upward to accept it. Sliding to a stop, the payloader narrowly missed hitting Scott Roy.

Scott stood his ground and yelled angrily up at the cab of the machine. "Go ahead and hit me and you'll be wearing that Goddamned thing!"

Dennis Atherton pulled the side window of the cab open and leaned his head out. "What the hell's the matter with you? The night ain't even started yet."

Scott grimaced to himself and finally waved his free hand in a northerly direction. "Ah shit, I damn near got into a fight up at the variety store, can you believe it? Fucking flatlanders think they own this place."

"Well, take it easy, for Christ's sake. I almost had your ass just then. Me? I got to fix this son-of-a-whore. Just split a hydraulic hose and the other loader is up at the Center."

Scott waved his bag of beer at Dennis as a sign of apology and continued toward his truck. The loader stormed into the garage.

Scott looked at the snow covered truck with disgust. Unlocking the driver's door, he deposited the beer on the floor, climbed into the seat and inserted the key into the ignition. With a couple groans of the starter the engine started obediently and settled into a smooth throaty idle. Swinging out on the step again, he grabbed a long handled brush from the seat and started wiping snow from the windshield and hood.

Dwane Huckins' pickup pulled up behind the next truck in line. Bob Garnett got out and stepped toward the larger vehicle. Dwane continued on toward the rear parking area.

Scott stopped work long enough to look over at Bob. "Hey, you didn't see Lester on your way in did you? You go right by his house. I haven't been inside yet, but it doesn't look like he's here or he would have had this thing running."

"I ain't seen him, but I can tell you where he is courtesy of Dwane's radio. He put a salt truck off the road up at the center. Oscar went up to pull him out," Bob answered, sweeping snow from the driver's door of the new Louisville Ford.

Scott shook his head and stepped down to the pavement, as though with that news, he was in no big rush. "That's right. Goddammit! I forgot he had salt truck duty this week. Well, that's just great. I can see myself sitting around here for the next hour, or maybe Charlie will stick me with another wingman."

"Hell, he ought to be back pretty quick. Oscar will yank him out of there if he has to do it a piece at a time," Bob offered.

In the garage office Charlie Hayward stood behind his desk. The phone to his ear. A couple other men stood waiting nearby. "Yeah, there's a pickup scraping hospital hill now and a couple more on the other hills in the city. The big trucks will be out as soon as they're loaded. What's the latest on the storm? . . . Wonderful!" Charlie scowled, hung up the phone and pressed the radio mike.

*       *       *

Oscar Scovill bounced along in the payloader at a reasonable payloader speed of fifteen miles an hour. A small wizened man looking much older than he really was, Oscar had both hands on the big steering wheel as he concentrated on keeping the unwieldy machine pointing straight ahead.

*Garage to sixteen. Oscar?* came Charlie's voice over the radio.

Oscar reached for the radio mike, and with it in his hand, reached back to grasp the wheel as well. With a free finger he pressed the button. "Sixteen," rasped Oscar Scovill.

Oscar Scovill complained about nearly everything and started each job under protest. His bitching and moaning would commence when the man was prodded into conversation and frequently when he was not. According to

Oscar, things were so screwed up that it was a wonder that the department, the city, country, or the whole fucking world for that matter, managed to make it from one day to the next. The forecasting of doom was Scovill's favorite pastime.

This was old stuff to the rest of the men at the city garage. It was expected and even courted at times. Remarks such as, "Oscar, I've been really depressed today. How about cheering me up," or "Boy, I feel so damn good I'm starting to get paranoid. Where the hell is Oscar?" were frequently heard.

But Oscar Scovill had a right to his morbid depths. Fifty-seven years ago when God kicked him downstairs, Mother Nature must have been having her period. Oscar was born on February twenty-ninth, so for three years running he would be reminded occasionally that "his day" would be done up in grand style. When "his day" finally arrived everyone would act like they had completely forgotten and the subject would never be mentioned.

Certainly, Oscar seemed to have his share of bad luck. Last July third he had headed for Maine on his annual three week vacation. It wasn't until he reached his summer camp the following day that he opened his vacation pay envelope to find that the City Hall computer had printed him a check for nine dollars and eighty-one cents.

And the shithouse incident of the previous fall belonged somewhere in the Twilight Zone. About eleven o'clock in the morning on the day in question Oscar was in the can taking a crap. Suddenly, screams of pain and anguish were heard from the garage restroom. Everyone within earshot went to investigate. Somehow, while performing this simple body function, Oscar Scovill had broken his ankle. The most touching, sympathetic comment heard was, "Get away from me! You're fucking cursed!"

But somehow, Oscar still managed a perverted sense of humor and was actually quite well liked. He would, of course, laugh at someone else's misfortune. If one felt the need to secure Oscar's smile on demand one had to skillfully embark on a discourse that would top his current prediction of doom, or at least give him ideas he could use later. If the attempt was successful, Oscar would show an even line of brown teeth and maybe even chuckle.

Oscar Scovill's duties with the department were somewhat basic, but quite diversified and ranged from garage work such as replacing broken springs or axles on the big trucks to lighter mechanical tasks of a repetitive nature. Although heavy equipment was not his forte, occasionally Oscar was permitted some small job with one of the city payloaders, an assignment he dearly loved. However, Oscar's winter storm duties typically involved operating one of the city's four small Bombardier sidewalk plows. These narrow one man tank-like vehicles carried a single vee plow. They operated singularly and their work was long and lonely.

There was a constant battle between the sidewalk plows and the big city street plows which stemmed from plowing snow in each others territory after such an area had been cleared. City plows had been known to harass, or even terrorize these smaller vehicles at times for such infractions and the Bombardiers had to use all of their superior maneuverability and forty mile per hour speed to escape.

Oscar Scovill reached quickly with his microphone burdened hand to turn up the radio volume just as Charlie's reply came back over the air.

*Listen, if you can't get that salt truck out, just leave it there for now if it's off the road and pick up Lester. I need that loader back here.*

Oscar brought the mike close to his lips. "The truck's out. We're headed back," he reported with a brown smile.

Very close on the tail of the bouncing payloader, Lester Hartwell was getting madder by the second. "Goddamn son-of-a-bitch! You fucking son-of-a-bitch!"

Oh, how Lester dearly wanted to ram the ass end of the payloader and move it out of his way so he could get back to the garage where he knew Scott was waiting to get started on the night's work. With another expletive, Lester threw the useless radio mike against the dash where it clattered to the floor.

Oscar, that weasely little pigfucker, had done it on purpose. After scaring the shit out of Lester by nearly tipping over the salt truck as he unceremoniously yanked it out of the ditch, Oscar had taken the lead on the five mile trip back to the garage ahead of the much faster truck.

Now, Lester was forced to creep along behind the payloader when he could have been back there already. Lester seriously contemplated giving the loader a nudge, but with his luck he knew Oscar would probably lose control and wreck the damn thing. If Oscar survived, then he'd really be in trouble.

Oscar knew he was there, wanting to get by, but he refused to pull over. Lester had yelled several times at him over the radio, then finally to the garage before realizing he apparently couldn't transmit anymore. That slimy little bastard! Lester Hartwell was going to do something bad to Oscar Scovill in the near future.

The Melonia Department of Public Works was indeed a collection of very talented people, and Lester too, possessed his own special gift. Lester Hartwell could let the loudest, juiciest sounding, nose curling farts imaginable. And what's more, he could produce them at will.

Admittedly, no one can endure a steady diet of farts, not even Lester, so the popularity of this phenomenon ebbed and flowed with either the rising tide of the saturation point on one hand to someone saying "you know, I haven't heard a good fart in days," on the other.

Lester's favorite ploy was to start the sequence by taking the microphone from the truck radio while riding along and inserting it under his ass. At this point a tremendous fart was born. Other passengers that might be in the vehicle at the time frantically rolled down all windows no matter what the outside temperature and started to moan. If this was during normal working hours the Public Works secretary at the City Hall office would utter "Oh, my God," as the fart dribbled in over the radio base station behind her desk.

This, the opening fart, was a signal for others to join in, and though none could approach Lester's magnificence, soon one could hear a varied collection of "phheppps, phropps, pops, and staccato-like snaps as a veritable symphony of farts went booming out over the air waves.

At this point, Public Works Director, Walton Conover, whether in his car or in his office, which was some distance from the base station, would usually wait thirty seconds or so and then reach for the microphone and slowly drawl, "Alright, you guys, I guess we've had about enough of that." The farts would sputter to a stop until the next time, which might be an hour or a week hence. Such Famous Fart Festivals were eagerly awaited by that segment of the populace constantly tuned in to police, fire, and most of all, the Melonia Public Works Department frequency.

Not all of Lester Hartwell's demonstrations were for public broadcast. Indeed, some of those privately held brought the most startling results. Lester could clear a small to medium sized room in seconds. Victims claimed that any food so exposed would spoil immediately and that three or more applications in the same locale would start peeling paint from the walls.

Anyone trapped in close, non-ventilated confinement with Lester for the full duration of "A Fart" frequently suffered a strange psychosis, as yet unidentified. There was one case on record where an individual received workmen's compensation for nearly a week.

Farts, however, were only an idle pastime with Lester and there was, after all, much more to the man than that. Lester Hartwell, at fortythree, was a rather large individual and seemed to be adding ten to fifteen pounds to his frame every year. Possibly, this was due to Lester's fleeting associations with any laborious physical activity. The only real exception was Hartwell's active participation in the eagerly awaited fall deer hunting season, an interest held equally by fellow workers Dean Smith, Donald Masse, and at times, a couple others. During this period many hard miles would be trekked through the woods. "Hardens you up for the coming winter," Lester would proclaim in a wise and thoughtful tone. In the last couple years Dean Smith had gotten Lester to widen his hunting schedule to include ducks whose season immediately preceded that of deer.

Lester was an excellent driver and equipment operator in his own right, but a limited number of these positions during the winter forced him to serve principally as a wingman which he really didn't mind for he and Scott got along quite well.

Lester was not presently married and his current interest revolved around his brand new, elaborately outfitted four wheel drive Dodge pickup truck. Although equipped with oversized tires and plow, Lester would not think of making extra money with this truck plowing driveways. The new Dodge was for Lester Hartwell's private use only.

Lester had just heard the brief conversation between Charlie and Oscar. There was nothing wrong with the receiver. Lester got even madder when he thought of Oscar's smug tone as if he had heroically rescued Lester and his salt truck. And here Lester couldn't even say a word in his defense.

*   *   *

"Well, at least something's going right," Charlie said and released the mike switch. Looking at the older of the two men in the room,

"Dean, go tell Dennis not to sweat the loader. I'll send Oscar to the yard as soon as he's back. And find Simpson and tell him to come in here." Dean Smith left the room without a word just as Dennis Atherton appeared in the doorway. The large wrench he was holding and most of his right hand and wrist were dripping with hydraulic fluid.

"Christ Charlie," he said, almost pleading, "don't let Oscar down in the yard to load the rest of the trucks. He'll probably kill somebody. We'll have the Michigan fixed in a few minutes."

It was hard to imagine a time when there was no Dennis Atherton at the city garage although only twelve years ago such had been the case. An imposing figure, Dennis was a shade over six feet and weighed a good two hundred and eighty pounds including fifty pounds of gut.

Usually good natured despite appearances, Dennis was quick with a smile, but a reserved twinkle in one eye seemed to say, you'd better be my friend.

Atherton's demeanor was deceiving for he got angry a lot, swearing a blue streak to himself, at a fellow worker, or at some tiny screw that refused to do its job. His ultimate profanity was "son-of-a-whore" after which he usually seemed to calm down and the smile returned.

Dennis was a good mechanic, but an even better diagnostician and often declared what was ailing a sickly engine before it clunked to a stop. The man's further worth was evident when he was called upon to operate heavy equipment such as a grader, backhoe, or payloader. Atherton's fluid precision at these controls was second to none.

Dennis' most endearing quality was frequently exhibited, but wholly involuntary. It had been found that the man would react dramatically to sudden loud noises or unexpected movements. A feigned punch to his gut would produce a deep grunt as he grabbed for his stomach. Slamming a heavy metallic object into a truck body or tailgate behind his back would send Dennis high into the air, sometimes pulling a muscle and yelling in pain. No matter how many times this happened, onlookers never tired of the amusing spectacle. "You fucking sons-a-whores," Atherton would scream and then smile at their joke.

Occasionally Dennis would return such pranks in kind. Over the period of one morning several months ago these activities had steadily escalated until a quarter stick of dynamite blew the door off the sign shop.

As Dennis finished asking Charlie not to send Oscar to the yard with the loader, a hand appeared around the office door casing holding an inflated potato chip bag. A second hand emerged and punched the bag which exploded in a loud pop. Atherton's body jerked with the predictable reflex action and the heavy wrench struck the office wall with a thud. Drops of hydraulic fluid sprayed about the room.

"Fuckin' sons-a-whorse!" Dennis said.

Laughter was heard from the anteroom. The younger man left of Charlie nervously stepped to a more secure position behind the desk.

Dennis quickly moved to the office door and confronted the half dozen men in the anteroom. "Alright, which one of you bastards did that," he asked, angrily.

A couple of the men eyed Dennis with poorly feigned surprise as they sat sipping coffee from Styrofoam cups. The remainder closely inspected the couple dozen words on a poster taped to the wall. "Annual Dwarf Throwing Contest, February 18th," the notice proclaimed. "Dwarfs supplied by American Small People Corp. Sponsored by the Melonia Rod and Gun

Club. Proceeds to go to the Melonia Mental Health Clinic. Ambulance in attendance."

"You sons-a-whores," Dennis repeated, a slight grin appearing.

Charlie appeared at the doorway behind his mechanic. "You guys got nothing to do?" he asked. "Trucks cleaned off and gassed up? Some of you ought to be thinking about chains. I don't want anybody back here in half an hour putting them on, and if you get stuck you'll probably be sitting there awhile. We're going to be behind on this one. The old man called it in late and that's when this was supposed to be a few inches. Now they're talking a foot or two!"

There was a few groans mixed with a couple cheers from the room. The men wandered out, either to the garage proper or in the direction of the toilet. Others entered from outside with new snow glistening from heads and shoulders. The coffee and candy machines became centers of interest. There was a general milling around of personnel.

Dennis Atherton headed for the interior garage door, but stopped momentarily as Custer inserted a key into his locker against the far wall. With his back turned, the long blond hair, short jacket and shapely backside, Custer could easily have been mistaken for a female.

"Hey, nice ass," Dennis teased.

While rummaging in his locker with one hand, Custer gave Dennis the finger with the other and wiggled his ass. Dennis laughed and continued into the garage.

Dean Smith warily approached the grimy and dented coffee machine and gave it a hard kick. "You gonna give me some coffee this time? I ain't in no mood to get fucked by some machine," he warned.

Dean deposited his money. The machine clunked several times and successfully poured coffee into a cup. As Dean reached to extract his purchase from the machine, the cup caught on the small plastic door and some of the hot liquid spilled on his hand. The cup slipped from his grasp and fell to the floor, splattering its contents.

"You fucking son-of-a-bitch!" Dean exclaimed, then commenced to kick the machine several more times.

Simpson Dunbar walked into the garage office. At sixty-one, he had been working for the department for thirty plus years. Six feet tall and one hundred and thirty-five pounds, Dunbar's thin body possessed more strength than it appeared. His stiff, straight black hair was seldom restrained, and together with a general gaunt appearance, was responsible for his somewhat wild look.

Sometimes referred to as "The Fly", usually behind his back, Simpson had a habit of rubbing high on his forehead with the backs of both hands and wrists rapidly back and forth with fingers outstretched. No one knew why he did this and he had never said.

Simpson Dunbar drove his city dump truck fast both summer and winter. He appeared rough on his machinery, but nothing ever went wrong with his truck. Dunbar did most of his own maintenance. For some unknown reason he was offered the use of a new truck when it was purchased, however, a month ago when two new Ford Louisville's arrived he had chosen to stay with his diesel powered GMC. His wingmen swore they had plowed snow at over fifty miles per hour. No one believed them, but nobody offered to take their place either.

Dunbar never missed a day of work and only last year was forced to take some vacation time which he usually lost due to its growing to such proportions. He appeared to scheme to get more overtime, particularly during the winter which sometimes produced gripes from fellow workers.

Dunbar talked in a snappy, wisecracky manner, smiling freely at the end of some paragraphs, swearing at others. The Fly had had any woman he ever wanted, but no one knew any of them. He would, however, relate these torrid tales at the least provocation. He had been married for many years. Few had ever seen his wife.

Simpson Dunbar lived at 57 Larson Place, only a half mile from the city garage.

"Simpson, I don't know if you've met Dustin Eaves here," Charlie said, indicating the young man beside him with a wary look on his face. "Dustin came over from Parks and Rec last week. He's going to wing for you tonight." Charlie turned to Eaves, "Dustin, this here's Simpson Dunbar, our senior man in the department."

Dustin Eaves cautiously moved to offer a hand to Dunbar, but Dunbar had not taken his eyes from Charlie. He was obviously not pleased.

"What do you mean, senior man?" Simpson snarled.

Charlie shook his head in mounting frustration. "I mean you've been here the longest so you've got the most experience, okay? And with Henry in the hospital, you need a wingman."

Simpson shifted his gaze to Eaves, but didn't change his expression. "For Christ's sake, Charlie! On a night like this? For the first time? God!"

"Simp, you do seem to go through wingmen," Charlie answered, then noticed Eaves' mouth opening slowly and the remains of his color departing his face. "Er . . . don't take that like it sounds, Dustin. It's kind of a private joke . . . we, we've had some turnover lately . . ." Charlie looked back at Dunbar and tried to gather his authority. "I wouldn't send him out with just anyone, Simpson."

Dunbar looked back at the younger man. "You ever had any experience with these plows?"

"No," Eaves answered softly.

"You ever sat in one?"

"No," Eaves answered, even more so.

Simpson rolled his eyes toward the ceiling, then locked Eaves with an icy stare. "Well, come on. You can help me finish putting on the chains, then you'll get a crash course on the plows right here in the garage. I might as well tell you right now, I used to be a nice guy, but the older I get the more I realize how much fun it is to be a mean bastard. Let's go!"

Simpson gave Charlie one last dirty look and strode from the office. Eaves started to follow like a lamb going to slaughter, but turned and gave Charlie a final, almost tearful glance.

"A pussycat, really," said Charlie, managing a weak smile.

Dustin Eaves had only worked for the Parks and Recreation Department for a few months when he had been transferred to the Public Works Department. Curious, because ordinarily he would have been laid off in the late fall along with a few others for lack of winter work. However, Walt Conover had mentioned something to Charlie about Eaves' parents being friends of the city manager, or mayor, or the like, and let it go at that.

Eaves had not yet begun to penetrate the overall clique of P.W. work force, therefore, he was simply called Eaves for the time being. Of medium size and slender build, Dustin looked to be a clean cut youth. However, he appeared very unsure of himself and further radiated an aurora of vulnerability. One could sense others beginning to zero in on a potentially new target for assorted practical jokes.

Tonight would be Eaves' first snow storm with the department. It was important that he asserted himself or he could be lost in a sea of vicious ridicule just for the hell of it. There upon he might rebound in kind and in good humor, or he would leave.

# chapter 7

The garage proper was a center of last minute activity comprised mostly of those small maddening tasks that one doesn't realize need doing until they jump up and bite you in the face. The center of attention, parked well up into the mechanics work area, was the leaking payloader, its repaired hydraulics nearing operational status once again. Behind the loader, two plow trucks were being fitted with heavy tire chains about their dual wheeled rear axles. This process, no matter how many times it had been performed in the past, was always cumbersome, sometimes injury provoking, and required a continuous accompaniment of foul language.

To the street side of the building rested two of the city's large salt and sand trucks, their job now finished for the evening. Silently they stood except for the dripping of melted snow and the sizable globs of slush that intermittently fell to the floor with audible phlops whose echo could be plainly heard amongst louder, more functional garage clatter.

In the far corner, past two parked backhoes, the Sno-Go, a specially equipped truck housing a huge diesel engine to the rear of the cab which powered a six foot high by eight foot wide snow blower affixed to its front, idled obediently its exhaust piped through a wall fitting to the outside air. Tomorrow would be its first outing of the winter. Another foot or more of new snow added to what had been previously plowed would clearly require snow removal downtown and along the main drags. Well into next week the Sno-Go would feed a fleet of a dozen ten wheelers in this off hours operation as the trucks made countless trips to various snow dump sites along the river which ran through Melonia.

Ahead of the payloader, over which Dennis Atherton, and another mechanic, Donald Masse, still slaved, drivers and wingmen gathered around the screened tool crib or wandered to and from the anteroom awaiting the final word to go. Some appeared clearly anxious to get on the road. Others seemed more than content with the delay.

Roland Powell watched Richard Wright carefully set what was left of his third cup of coffee amidst the parts and tools scattered over the iron workbench outside the tool crib door. Satisfied with its temporary security, Richard selected a semi-clean rag and commenced to wipe the first portion of the coffee from the front of his shirt.

"You know, I'll bet you ain't had nothin' to eat all day," Roland observed. "Just how shitfaced are you anyway? I swear if you go falling asleep on me tonight I'm going to bounce you off something solid."

Richard finished his wiping and tossed the rag back on the bench. "Hey, let me tell you something. You don't realize it, but I live on the ragged edge of some really heavy depression here. However, over the years I've learned to jiggle my psyche around just enough to keep from falling into the deep dark hole of final and catastrophic doom. But I can tell you its damn tough walking that fine line and that in itself is depressing. So you know what I do? I drink, that's what I do. It's the fucking cornerstone of my mental health."

"And you wonder why I'm starting to show some wear and tear? After listening to fucking drivel like that? First thing we're going to do is stop and get some coffee in something that you can't slop all over the place. Like a baby bottle maybe."

"You seem to forget, we got no coffee stops on our run. Which is why we're forced to drink beer. Luckily, you drive the truck off into the woods a lot, so I can piss almost any place. You just worry about yourself and try to leave a few guardrails standing this time."

Dean Smith approached the pair, put a hand on each of their shoulders and leaned close as if to impart some secret gem of knowledge far too juicy for general consumption. "Hey, Wayne just went into the shithouse. Maybe he's on the can."

The three men looked at each other while they considered this significant development. Without a word Richard reached into his jacket pocket and produced a sizable red firecracker. Roland grabbed a spray can of Gum-Out from the bench and the group headed for the anteroom. Trailing, Dean looked back to catch the eye of Dennis Atherton who momentarily looked up from his work.

Roland and Richard stopped briefly at the bathroom doorway, the actual door to which had been missing well past anyone's ability to remember. The trailing onlookers, now numbering half a dozen, gathered close behind. Past the grimy shower that no one ever dared use, a long several fauceted sink dominated the remainder of the wall. On the opposite wall a long urinal did the same. Alone and vulnerable in the center of the room's end stood the single plywood enclosed toilet. Beneath the stall door two feet could be seen with pants down around their ankles.

With over stated stealth, Richard approached one side of the stall, firecracker in one hand, cigarette lighter in the other. Roland sneaked to the other side of the enclosure armed with his can of Gum-Out. Behind them, the doorway became crowded with eager faces.

Richard lit the firecracker and held it at arm's length. Roland reached over the side of the stall and sprayed the Gum-Out toward the rear of the enclosure. Richard dumped the firecracker in that direction. Both men flattened themselves against their respective walls.

From the box came a troubled voice. "Hey . . . what . . . oooh . . ."

Wham! The explosion rattled the stall, its flash erupting upward and outward into the void. The plywood door twisted awkwardly on its remaining upper hinge as Wayne Harrington was thrust through the opening to sprawl face down on the concrete floor, his white ass now the brightest thing in the room.

The laughter started and quickly rose in crescendo out in the hall. Richard and Roland awkwardly stepped over and around Wayne as he started to move and groan. Valiantly, they tried to keep from laughing until they got out of the room.

*　　*　　*

The rear of the truck was jacked free of the floor. Over one pair of wheels bright new tire chains, their cross links shiny and unblemished, were tightly fastened and ready for the night's task. On the other side the chains were still slack. Under the axle Simpson Dunbar, his back planted firmly on a wheeled garage creeper slid back and forth tugging at the chains, trying to get them to fit. On the outside of the wheel Dustin Eaves knelt on the floor vainly pulling on the chains in an effort to help. Dunbar's profane directives at Eaves and the chains didn't seem to help.

A few feet away, Jason Peck, the only black man in the Public Works Department and indeed one of the few blacks in Melonia, stood next to Pat Gant as the pair watched the chain installation process from a seemingly safe distance. The explosion in the bathroom had been less resounding at this end of the garage, but could be hardly overlooked.

"What the hell was that?" Jason asked.

Pat pretended not to have noticed. "What? Oh that? Sounded like the old cherry bomb, Gum-Out routine. Somebody probably got blown out of the shithouse. I'll bet it was a good one."

Jason scanned what he could see of the garage interior. "I'll bet it was Wayne. He said something about taking a crap before we went out."

"Wayne?" Pat laughed. "What'd you think of his face? Lester opened a door into it this morning. He won't be worth a shit the rest of the night."

Simpson Dunbar slid out from under his truck far enough to look at Pat and Jason. "For Christ's sake! Will one of you get your ass over here and give me a hand with these chains?"

Pat was nearest to the truck and reluctantly took the few steps to the scene of the struggle. Jason followed. Dustin Eaves rose to his feet, his feeling of helplessness plain on his face. Pat knelt by the outside wheel and grabbed the chains at ten and two o'clock.

"That's it," yelled Dunbar. "Take up some slack while I try to snap this clip. Some son-of-a-bitch has been fuckin' with my chains again."

Frank Hobbs, chief mechanic, walked up to inspect the operation. Dean Smith was on his heels, just waiting for him to come to a stop.

"Frank. What the hell did you do to the hydraulics on number nineteen? I pulled the lever and the front plow jumped right up in my face. Scared me half to death."

"Good," Frank replied, not taking his eyes from the chain operation. "Maybe you can see your way clear to lifting it over the railroad tracks on North Main next time instead of ripping off the cutting edge."

"Yeah, maybe." Dean seemed taken only sightly aback by the remark as he turned and left.

Frank addressed the chain applicators in general. "How long does it take you guys to put on chains these days? You're going to have to move this thing pretty quick. The loader's almost ready and B.B.'s finally got his lights working."

Dunbar gave a mighty tug on the chains from his prone position and grunted his answer as loud as his remaining breath would allow. "Well, don't just stand there and piss all over yourself in anticipation, Frank. We'll be done in a second."

Frank smiled. Dunbar continued.

"And then I've got to show Eaves here how to operate the plows. Ain't that great?"

Frank turned to look at the younger man for the first time. "Eaves? What's your first name again?"

"Dustin," answered Eaves.

"Well, Dustin," Frank spoke in a matter of fact manner, "don't pay much attention to Dunbar's ravings. He's quite old as you can see and most all of us think he's going to die soon."

Eaves smiled weakly and appeared on the verge of saying something, but Frank suddenly looked down at Dunbar and continued in a hardened tone.

"And Simpson, don't you go scaring the hell out of Dustin here with your tales of horror like going through the windshield or having the wing bounce up in his face. I'm not putting anymore glass in your truck this winter!"

Frank Hobbs turned and walked away. Dustin Eaves regained his bleached expression of concern. Jason Peck looked away so as to keep his smile to himself.

Finally, Pat and Simpson stood from their completed task. Almost immediately, Simpson raised the backs of both wrists and alternately used each to scratch his forehead. Pat took this cue to step forward and gesture toward Jason and Dustin Eaves.

"Ladies and gentlemen, I give you, The Fly."

Jason laughed and even Simpson flashed a hint of a self conscious smile until he glanced to catch Eaves with a snicker about ready to dribble from his lips.

Simpson Dunbar fixed his new wingman with a cold stare. "You! Eaves! Get in that truck!"

$$*  \quad  *  \quad  *$$

Scott Roy walked into the empty garage office, plunked himself in Charlie's chair behind the desk and reached for the radio mike. "Garage to seventeen." Scott idly pressed the mike to his chin and glanced at the evening Boston paper eschew on the desk. Still waiting for a reply on the radio, he turned the first couple pages. "Garage to seventeen," he repeated.

At page three Scott looked away momentarily, then jerked his gaze back to the paper and sat up straight in the chair.

Dwane Huckins strode into the office. "You trying to get Lester?"

Scott answered, not taking his eyes from the paper. "Yeah."

"Well, they just drove in. Lester's grabbing a coffee and Mr. Gloom and Doom took the loader down to the yard. Presumably to load our trucks. What a Goddamned treat this is going to be."

Scott stood behind the desk and turned the paper around so Dwane could see it. He punched the photo of a man repeatedly with his forefinger. "I saw this guy tonight! Here in town. I'm not kidding you. It's him!"

Not changing his stance, Dwane turned his body toward the paper as though figuring he'd take a second or two and comply with Scott' request. A second or two passed and Dwane grabbed the paper. "Christ! You know who this guy is? Are your sure?"

"Hell yes, I'm sure. And I see who he is. I can read for Christ's sake."

Dwane continued staring at the paper. "Bradford Nevis? Here in Melonia? Hell, this union of his is just a front for organized crime."

"Hey, I'm sure you know his whole damn background."

"So, they're on him again, are they? Are you positive it was him?" Dwane asked again, finally looking up.

Scott appeared somewhat exasperated. "Once more. I looked at him. He looked at me. Distance about ten feet. Good light. It was him."

"No shit! Where? How long ago?"

"Hell, about twenty minutes ago. I stopped at the variety store to pick up a six pack for tonight. When I pulled in this guy coming down the steps sees me, thinks I'm going to run into him, I guess, and falls on his ass. Well, I start to help the guy and I'll be Goddamned if he don't get up and shove me. I couldn't fucking believe it. Anyway, we're about to get into it and the driver of this white Caddy steps out and tells this guy to get in the car. Well, he don't pay any attention. Just then this Nevis character rolls down the rear window and yells at him. Stanley, he calls him. Stanley, he says, get in this car. And Stanley, he gets in the car."

"Stanley?" Dwane questioned.

"Yeah, Stanley. His name's right here in the paper."

"Stanley Fagner," said Dwane, now somewhere in thought.

"Yeah, that's him."

"Well, where did they go?" asked Dwane, looking at Scott. "What about the car? Did you see the license?"

"Hell, they left. Headed north. The car? I told you. A white Cadillac. New or close to it. Massachusetts plate, but I didn't pay any attention to the number. I was still pretty pissed off and I wanted to get back here."

"Goddamn! Nevis!" Dwane tossed the paper back on the desk. "What the hell is he doing? He slips surveillance in Detroit to come here?"

"So why don't you give Mars a call? It ain't like you don't know him and I'll bet he's there right now what with this storm."

Dwane looked at the phone. "I'd like to, but what the hell have we got? Mars would really think I've gone off my rocker." Dwane shook his head. "By now they could be on the turnpike in either direction. They could have taken 16 east or stayed on 5 north. They . . ."

"They could be holed up a mile from here," Scott interjected. "Hey, it's your call. Don't matter to me . . . unless maybe if I run into that Stanley asshole again."

Charlie Hayward stomped into the office, shaking new snow from his boots. "Okay, lets go. Get your trucks down to the yard. Oscar's down there with one loader and Dennis is going down with the other. We'll use 'em both. The police have called twice in the past ten minutes wanting to know where the hell we are. So get loaded and get on your runs!"

Simpson Dunbar eased off the throttle and the big truck's engine slowed to a rumbling idle. Dustin Eaves, on the passenger side, sat back in his seat in an attempt to relax for a moment, though his gaze was still firmly affixed to the five one foot long levers mounted before him.

Simpson took a quick deep breath and continued his lesson. "All right, let's go over it again. Forget the first and third levers closest to me. You won't need the first one, that's the dump body. The other is for the wing jack and we won't be using that for a while, so leave it alone. Now, the fourth lever from you is for the front plow. Back toward you to pick it up. Forward all the way to let it down. The controls are just the opposite on some of the other trucks, but you don't care about that now. And sometimes we'll have to hang the front plow just barely off the ground so's not to rip the shit out of some dirt road that ain't frozen yet . . . But don't worry about that now either. Alright, pick it up . . . I said pick it up . . . Pick up the fucking front plow! Jesus Christ!"

Eaves finally grabbed the lever with a lightening fast movement and yanked hard on it. Simpson provided more engine R.P.M.'s and the massive front plow rose into the air where it rocked back and forth a couple feet above the garage floor.

"Good," said Simpson, continuing with his rapid fire dialogue. "Now remember what I told you about those two levers on your right. They operate the wing and you have to use them in a certain way. The first lever raises and lowers the back of the wing. The next lever operates the front. Always raise the front first. Always lower the back first. Remember that! If you do the opposite and we're traveling at say forty miles an hour you could catch the wing against something or in a hole and rip it clean off the truck. We could run over the damn thing and roll this pig fucker right over. We'd probably both be killed. Now, pick it up . . . I said pick it up!"

Eaves raised the front of the wing with his left hand, his right poised and ready over the lever next to the door.

"Okay. Alright. That's good with the front," said Simpson approvingly. "Never more than that. Now, up with the rear."

Eaves pulled the right hand lever. The back of the wing rose swiftly.

"Good. Easy . . . Not too much!"

Eaves stared out his side window at the wing, seemingly transfixed as its rear scribed a circling arc while it came closer and closer.

"That's enough! Let go the lever! Don't you dare break my fucking mirror!"

The wing stopped inches from the door and Eaves shrank back from the sight of it. He was breathing heavily. Simpson rolled his eyes and took a second to scratch his forehead in his customary manner.

"Good!" he said. Now put 'em down. Everything." Eaves operated the levers correctly in reverse and the plows clattered to the concrete floor.

Frank Hobbs stepped up on the driver's side running board and peered into the truck. "You're going to have to finish this outside. I'm not routing everything out the side doors and Dennis is about ready to drive the loader through the side of the building." Frank looked across at Eaves who was still clutching the levers even though the plows were now resting on the concrete. "How we doing, Dustin?"

Eaves nodded his head and managed to make a sound in his throat.

Frank looked back at Simpson. "You ought to be ashamed," he said.

Simpson grinned silently at Frank, then turned back to Eaves. "He'll be just fine. Just fine once he gets the hang of it."

Frank acknowledged Simpson's assurance with a final skeptical glance, stepped down off the truck and walked away. Simpson raced the truck's engine to build hydraulic pressure.

"Alright, raise 'em! Everything," Simpson ordered. "But not quite so close with the back of the wing."

The front plow rose into the air and Eaves grabbed for the wing levers.

"Eaves?" Simpson asked.

"Yes?" Eaves answered, surprised at his name in the form of a question.

"Do you drink, Eaves? I mean liquor, booze, beer, whatever?"

Eaves hesitated, unsure what his reply should be. "Well . . . yes. I guess. Some. Sometimes . . ."

"Well I do, Eaves," Simpson announced. "And if you know what's good for you, you will too. Now finish with the Goddamned wing!"

Simpson grabbed the microphone from the radio and put it to his mouth. His voice could be heard echoing through the garage loudspeakers. "Open the damn door or I'll take it with me."

Simpson tossed the mike to clatter on the steel truck dash just as rock music started to emanate from the loudspeaker inside the garage. Simpson watched the big door slowly raise in his rear view mirror. "Damn that fucking Custer. Someday I'm going to smash that radio of his."

Simpson carefully released the clutch and the truck gathered speed in reverse. Barely clearing underneath the still rising door, Eaves just managed to snatch the wing far enough in to miss the door jam as they passed by it. Simpson had of course been keeping track of the situation through Eaves' door mirror and smiled at his wingman's momentary frantic concern. Then the rock music returned.

Outside, the snow settled heavily through the assorted glares of many lights. After Simpson's number forty-one cleared the building another followed, and after it, the payloader darted out and expertly maneuvered to get into the street ahead of the trucks. Around the garage the remaining trucks started to move, some spinning their rear wheels in the snow as their unweighted bodies afforded little traction. Struggling into the street the haphazard parade accelerated the short distance to the New England Yard entrance.

Down the long curving driveway the remaining trucks came, their yellow flashers ablaze. Past the utility sheds and storage buildings, the trucks gathered in two rows in the large courtyard beside the huge pile of winter sand perhaps thirty feet high. At its base two payloaders dove into its soft body, each time removing a tiny fraction of its total mass. With front buckets full and rising, the loaders approached the first truck waiting in their respective lines to deposit their measures of sand.

Gale Mooney opened his door and stood on the sill to look over his cab and catch the eye of the loader operator. He waved three fingers in the air and got back in the truck. "Well Jason," he said, looking over at his young wingman, "this will be your biggest storm so far. What do you think of it?"

Jason Peck, age twenty, arrived in Melonia last summer along with his mother and three younger sisters. Laura Peck had been determined to remove she and her four children from the decaying social fabric surrounding their Bronx, New York apartment. Jason had already been arrested on more than one occasion for his activities with a local street gang and Mrs. Peck could see an even darker future for her daughters, the oldest then seventeen. Desperately, she had arranged for a new beginning with the help of a distant cousin living in Melonia. No one in her immediate family had ever been farther north than New Haven, Connecticut. Laura viewed New Hampshire as a clean, cold, back to nature chance for a new life.

Jason had not wanted to leave the old neighborhood and had done so only in the face of his mother's iron will and the families' close ties with one another. Even then, he promised to stay for only a six month trial period. Upon securing a job with the Public Works Department, Jason was accepted with the reserved friendliness afforded most new employees, but with an added curiosity, and perhaps an emphasized courtesy, because he was black. Racial prejudice on a gut level was somewhat foreign to whites who encountered almost no blacks and an opportunity to prove that they were above such character flaws as shown on the nightly news and prime time dramas was sometimes overstated.

However, it soon became evident that Jason Peck regarded most of his co-workers as hicks and bumpkins, and while they were ready to accept this New York ex-street gang member, who was seen to still carry a switchblade, his attitude was becoming tiresome. Peck had difficulty taking a joke directed anywhere in his vicinity, so this further eliminated much of the accepted break-the-ice conversation. His work, which had been acceptable and even enthusiastic at times, was becoming much less so by late fall.

Charlie Hayward knew that some corrective measures would have to be taken, but had kept putting off anything drastic, hoping that things would work themselves out. When it came time to post winter work schedules, Charlie had thought about teaming Peck as Gale Mooney's wingman. Before he could, Mooney suggested the pairing himself.

During the last couple months Jason seemed to have become somewhat more at ease in his surroundings, and had even started an occasional conversation with fellow employees. A couple of the guys had been heard to shorten his first name to "Jay", a sure sign of easing tensions.

It was, of course, because of Gale Mooney. Although no one knew that it was he who suggested Peck as his wingman except Charlie Hayward, it was evident to anyone who cared to look that the older man had a thoughtful, steadying influence on the younger black who was clearly out of his element. Jason's first reaction to Mooney's firearm collection had been one of disbelief. To the young New Yorker, a gun was illegal and its use probably more of the same, so anyone who owned that many guns without being arrested was someone out of the ordinary.

After taking Jason out to his bobhouse on the frozen lake on the back of his snow machine a couple of times, Mooney had mentioned that Jason was getting a machine of his own. A further surprise to Peck was finding that auto insurance rates were a fraction of what they were in New York. It was not hard to believe that Jason Peck didn't think Melonia quite as boring as he had once thought and his six month imposed time limit passed without a word.

The second bucketful of sand rocked the truck. "Man, lets do it," said Jason.

"I hope you're that enthusiastic about noon tomorrow," replied Gale.

"Say, what's this I hear about you putting this thing in the lake last year?" Jason asked.

"Who told you that?"

"One of the guys. I forget who."

"Yeah, well its no secret I guess." Gale appeared a little uneasy as he placed his right hand on the shift lever for no apparent reason. "Except it wasn't this truck and we didn't go in the lake. The ice was good and thick about that time which was lucky because right along there you go twenty feet from shore and the water's twenty feet deep."

"They said you crawled back up to the road and gave the other driver that C.P.R. stuff until the ambulance got there. Saved his life, probably."

"They did, huh? Well, I'm not looking forward to doing it again just to liven up the evening."

Jason smiled, maybe a bit at Gale's discomfort. "Naw, but it's nice to know that . . ."

"Pull that wing up a little, will ya?" Gale interrupted.

The third and final bucket of sand stirred the loaded truck only slightly. Gale put the truck in gear and got under way.

In the other line, truck twenty-two of Roland Powell and Richard Wright, was also being loaded.

"Hey, guess what," asked Richard.

"What?" answered Roland, resigned to the obvious reply.

"Tomorrow is garbage day on our run."

Roland started to smile. "You know, I do believe you're correct."

"So, tonight we get that slimebag over on Lexington!" Richard vowed. "You know, that asshole that calls the office, says we plow the street all wrong. Said we clipped his car when we didn't. Swears at us . . ."

"I know. I know. We've never seen his garbage cans that I can remember. Just hasn't been the right night, I guess. I wonder how many he's got."

"You mean how many he had," Richard corrected, clenching both fists in front of his face. "Slimebag, you are mine!"

The horn sounded on the loader as the last bucket of sand descended into the dump body. Truck twenty-two moved away, Richard continuing to mutter additional threats.

In truck thirty-nine Bob Garnett reached down to adjust a couple controls on the new radio installation. "Well everything seems to be working. I don't know why, but it is. I hope they don't give us the next new truck that comes in."

"Maybe we'll hear something about Mister Bradford Nevis. It's hard to believe . . ."

Slam! Oscar Scovill dropped the payloader bucket directly onto the truck body while depositing the first measure of sand into the truck.

"Goddammit!" Dwane grabbed the radio mike. "Leave the damn sideboards, will ya?"

Bob appeared not to notice. "Hey, even if it was him, he's probably miles away by now."

"I don't think so," Dwane mused. "It doesn't make sense that anybody would be traveling any distance on a night like this. And Nevis isn't stupid. No, I'll bet he's somewhere in the area. If I knew why maybe I'd know where."

"Then call Mars, for Christ's sake! You've got the police radio right here."

Dwane nodded slowly. "Yeah, I probably ought to. Maybe I will. In the meantime we'll see how good this truck is cause I'm going to be pushing it. That way if we want to take some time somewhere we can do it without being any further behind than we already are."

"Why would we be doing that?" Bob asked suspiciously.

"How do I know? Say, we ran across that white Cadillac somewhere. If we could identify Nevis in the car we'd run the son-of-abitch off the road!"

"What the hell's this "we" shit? And even if we were that stupid, we'd be up to our ass in trouble."

"What do you mean, trouble?" Dwane asked. "You'd be a fucking hero."

"Yeah, sure. Or dead," said Bob.

"Really," Dwane shook his head in disgust. "So just as a precaution I'll just swing around back of the garage and get my forty-five out of the truck."

"Jesus H. Christ! Look . . . you . . . we got no cause to apprehend anybody."

"Then don't worry about it. Like I said, just a precaution."

The last bucket of sand rocked the truck slightly. Dwane put the truck in gear.

"So, call Mars," Bob repeated.

"Yeah, I will."

"When?"

"Later."

"Damn!"

Truck thirty-nine gathered speed and headed for the gate.

# chapter 8

As the snow continued to settle steadily, what evening traffic there was crept about the city's now whitened streets cautiously treading its way to final destinations. The muffled sound of rubber on the hard packed surface was punctuated occasionally by the more distinct "whish" of tires slicing through salt melted areas of slush. Louder still was the clank of heavy metal on asphalt as the city plows finally sank their teeth into the building storm.

To an experienced eye, the city's approach to the night's work might have correctly seemed somewhat more inspired than usual in its initial stage. Plow drivers willingly assumed personal responsibility for the condition of their runs and with rapidly increasing snow depths, completion of their first circuit was vitally important. With plowing speeds a little more than usual snow could be seen cascading farther from the road as it streamed forth from front plow and wing. Cosmetic clean-up, and certainly sidewalk clearing, would be of secondary consideration this evening. Customary slow downs in approaching homeowners seen clearing snow by hand or machine near the mouth of their driveways would be held to a minimum, or entirely disregarded. Most seasoned citizens so involved would be instantly receptive to the city's late start and the resulting higher truck speeds and engine revs. Naive souls expecting a city plow to bow to their presence would be in for a surprise.

At the city garage office Charlie Hayward sat down behind his desk and punched the radio microphone. "All right, listen up you guys. We've got six inches on the ground now and we're going to get a lot more. So just open up your runs for now and make 'em passable. Main drags first. We'll push back and clean up later. So, take it easy and take it safe." Charlie settled back in the chair.

The radio came alive immediately. *You saying we're going to get a foot and a half of partly cloudy? It time for coffee yet?* The voice was replaced with the heavy beat of a rock tune.

Charlie reached forward to slam his fist on the radio mike button. "Can that radio, Custer."

*It's not me, dammit!* came the reply.

The music continued for another couple seconds and then stopped. Charlie Hayward sat back again and shook his head.

On the outlying country roads conditions were combining to present a situation wholly unappreciated by Public Works Department crews. With almost non-existent windrows from previous storms, and little or no traffic, plowing that first path through winter's wilderness could be difficult indeed.

Among those least concerned at the prospect was Simpson Dunbar. At thirty miles per hour the sound of the engine and that of the plows was almost deafening in the truck's cab. The view out through the windshield displayed a landscape of windswept whiteness in this area where open fields bordered the highway. Only the faint tracks of a couple vehicles that had passed some time ago indicated where the road was supposed to be, or indeed that there was a road at all. The only solid objects to be actually seen was the occasional telephone pole as it flashed by close on the wing side of the truck.

The hands of Dustin Eaves were white as death as they clutched two of the plow levers ahead of him next to the dash. Dustin stared blankly ahead into the approaching gloom.

On the other hand, Simpson seemed without a care. A cigarette dangled from his lips, his left arm rested on the open window frame. His countenance suggested a man on the open sea not expecting anything important to happen in the immediate future.

"H . . . h . . . how d . . . do you know where the road is?" Eaves managed to get heard above the din.

Simpson glanced over, seemingly surprised to hear so many words all at once from his rookie wingman. "I can feel it," Simpson replied in a voice of appropriate volume. "Don't worry, I know where it is . . . You know, you don't have to hang onto them levers all the time. They're not going anywhere."

Eaves slowly released his grip of the levers and brought his hands cautiously into his lap. Just then a series of loud thuds came from the right side of the truck, and with a loud wham, the wing suddenly rose into the air dangerously close to Eaves' window before it fell harmlessly back to earth. Eaves emitted a choked sound from his throat and grabbed the levers again.

Simpson laughed. "Don't worry about it. That's only some loose pavement along the shoulder. Relax! Here . . ."

Simpson produced a pint bottle from under his coat on the seat and thrust it at Eaves. "Here, you like scotch? Take a good slug of this."

Eaves just stared at the bottle.

"Christ, take it! In your case its strictly medicinal. And don't spill any!"

Eaves took the bottle as ordered, carefully unscrewed the cap, and took a couple good swallows. No sooner had he gotten the cap back on than he started to cough violently.

Simpson grabbed the bottle. "How's that? Better? Ha, haaaa . . . , old Doctor Dunbar here. Another dose in fifteen minutes. Hell, you'll be fine in no time." Simpson stuck the bottle back under his coat. "Pints are always better than fifths, you know," he added. "They don't roll around in the truck as much."

Truck twenty-two pulled out of Willow Avenue and onto Landaw Street. A stop sign momentarily seen behind the right side of the truck on the corner suddenly disappeared.

"That was a stop sign back there for your information, Richard Wright announced. "Now it's just another piece of garbage."

Roland Powell reached forward out his open window, grabbed the windshield wiper at its farthest travel to the left, lifted it, and let it snap back onto the glass. "I can't see shit out of this windshield. These fucking wipers aren't worth a fuck!"

There was a slight thud to the right of the truck.

"Christ, I think you got that mailbox," remarked Richard, twisting his head quickly to the right against the closed window.

"I didn't see it! Why the hell didn't you pick up the Goddamned wing?"

"And leave a pile of snow behind? I think the way it works is we're supposed to just miss these things and plow the road at the same time."

"You drunk cocksucker!" Roland roared. You better wake the fuck up and soon!"

"The trouble is we're going too slow! I can't gauge distances at fifteen fucking miles an hour. Hey . . . watch out for this pole!"

"Fucking Goddamn!"

"Christ! Will you get this piece of shit moving? I have to get into a certain rhythm so I can get my timing down." Richard rocked back and forth in his seat. "Come on, let's go! Jesus, I hope you don't fuck like you drive."

Truck twenty-two gathered speed on Landaw Street. The streaming snow from the wing crossed the sidewalk and started its assault on the assorted picket fences and shrubbery beyond.

*       *       *

At Melonia Police Headquarters a cruiser pulled into the driveway and proceeded carefully through the snow to park up against the two story brick building. Presently, an officer got out of the car, took a shortcut across the landscaped area to the front of the building and entered through the main door.

Stamping snow from his feet in the anteroom, Sergeant Greg Budner glanced to his right at the female dispatcher behind the glass partition. She looked up and smiled with a certain smugness which clearly illustrated the fact that she would be spending the immediate future inside where it was warm and dry whereas Budner would of course have to face the storm again soon. Greg Budner shook his head at her and reached for the hallway door.

In an interior office of several desks and assorted file cabinets Police Chief Justin Mars stood before a window looking out over the floodlit rear parking lot to the river beyond. Individual areas of swirling, winddriven snow played tag with one another across the open area. Irregular, but neat, straight sided pieces of ice covered with snow appeared as strewn puzzle pieces on the cold black expanse of open river. Slowly, the current carried the varying patterns from left to right.

Mars turned back to the room and briefly eyed the lone officer in attendance a couple desks away as he separated a large stack of paperwork into three separate piles. Sergeant Budner stepped through the half open door and began removing his coat.

"How's the driving?" Mars asked of his sergeant.

"Not that great," answered Budner. "It's really coming down now."

"Well, at least the plows are finally out."

"Yeah, and it looks like they're trying to make up for the late start. Some of those guys are moving right along. I hope nobody gets in their way."

Mars opened his mouth to say something, but didn't. Instead he simply nodded agreement.

Five years ago, upon taking over as chief, Justin Mars stated flatly that he would bring Melonia's force of twenty-eight officers up to date in terms of equipment and training. Some of the older officers viewed such action as unwanted and unnecessary, particularly as being orchestrated by an outsider. Over the next three months four had chosen to retire.

A couple years later Mars wangled a new headquarters building to compliment his "new look". While complaining about the expenditure, a few citizens further chided the department for its big city airs, citing its complex radio call system and new headquarters security apparatus. However, most people couldn't have cared less.

Forty-six years of age, Mars was about five foot ten and blonde. His muscular frame indicated regular workouts certainly at home. Shortly after being selected as chief, Mars had shed his uniform in favor of a varied plain clothes wardrobe, however, until recently Justin Mars had been seldom seen out and about. It was said he could be found in his plush office deep in the recesses of his concrete and brick headquarters building available by appointment only, and then requiring a guide through the security system.

But of late, the chief had been much more visible. And very friendly. A high State Police position or other political appointment was rumored. The uniform had even reappeared.

Mrs. Mars had faded from view some time ago. The divorce rate in the department was extremely high. Curiously, all female employees, whether uniform or clerical staff, were extremely good looking. More rumors.

Through it all the Melonia Police Department enjoyed a good reputation gained simply by the professional, yet courteous service it provided. Outside of town, particularly among those inside the state capital to the south, the Melonia force was held in even higher regard.

The telephone on the desk where Mars stood buzzed for attention. The chief picked it up. "Yeah? . . . Fine, put him on." Mars raised an eyebrow at Budner who walked closer and leaned on the desk.

"Well hello there, John," Mars continued. "You ought to be tucked away safe and sound at the Elks Club on a night like this." Initially smiling at his own remark, slowly the expression became more serious.

Having been included in whatever was being said by Mars' initial glance, Sergeant Budner patiently watched his boss.

"Yeah, I remember him," said Mars into the phone. "Hell, he's got to be well into his eighties by now. This must be the first time anyone's seen him around in years. Any idea why he was headed your way?"

Mars looked back at his sergeant as the caller continued. Finally the Chief smiled again. "So, I guess you've got a couple things to do tonight except watch it snow . . . Well, I suppose even though he was headed for Concord he could be anywhere. We'll keep our eyes open . . . Say, you going to get up here for some salmon fishing this spring? . . . Yeah, I know. Okay, then. It's been nice talking to you John. Thanks for calling."

Mars replaced the phone. "Nino Valachi," he announced to Budner. "That name mean anything to you?"

Greg Budner thought for a long second. Yeah . . . Mafia, old time Mafia. Isn't he dead?"

"Apparently not because he was positively identified by a couple retired Boston cops working security at Logan Airport. Seems Valachi and two "associates" disappeared in the crowd. I guess these guys are sorry they didn't follow him now, but at the time they didn't have any reason to and besides, he's nothing to them at this point. Anyway, one of them called it in and obviously there was enough interest to do some checking. Valachi and company came in from Miami on one of the last flights before Logan closed down. They had a charter set up to fly into Concord which of course never left the ground. Supposedly, the old man was none too happy about it and one would assume he found other transportation."

"Really. Well ain't that something? Who was that on the phone?"

"John Griffin, State Police in Concord," Mars answered.

"Oh . . . oh, yeah," Budner nodded.

"Says he's calling most of the towns in the central part of the state just to let them know. Hell, I'm sure there aren't many that even know what Valachi looks like, or did. We've got a picture on file. Better dig it out. The Feds are checking the Miami end of it. Apparently, there's still some regard for the old man."

Mars paused in thought for a moment. Budner turned to go, but stopped when Mars continued, possibly more to himself. "Why the hell would he come here . . . this time of year? . . . Boy, if this had been fifteen years ago, even ten, when Valachi went somewhere, something was going on . . ."

\*    \*    \*

Dwane Huckins stopped the truck opposite a late model black Buick that had slid off the road into the shallow gutter. Though on the other side of the highway, the car appeared to have been traveling in the same direction as the city plow. There was no evidence of a spin. The car didn't look that badly stuck. A man had gotten out of the driver's door and looked questioningly across at the city plow.

"We can't leave him there," related Bob Garnett. "He's going to be right in our way. Let's see if we can push him out."

Dwane continued to look across the road. "Wait here a minute. I want to take a closer look." Dwane started to open his door.

"At what, for Christ's sake. That ain't no white Cadillac."

Dwane stepped down to the road as the driver of the other car, a tall, well dressed man wearing a black top coat, started across to meet him. The pair walked back to the Buick. Dwane walked around the car, then stuck his head in the driver's side window. The man kept talking and gesturing at the plow truck. Dwane stood, nodded, walked back to the truck and got in.

"What's going on?" Bob wanted to know.

"Up with the plows. We're going to push them out."

"So, let's get out and do it."

"We can't. They're on glare ice."

"Well, we got plenty of sand."

"I don't want to take the time. Will you pick up the damn plows?"

"We can't push him with this. What the hell's the matter with you? We'll wreck his Goddamned car."

"Look, I'm going to plant the tip of the front plow dead center of his rear bumper and hope for the best. Besides, I don't think he gives a shit and I certainly don't."

"Well, he will later when he looks at his car. Then we'll be fucked. Why don't you call in for a wrecker?"

"Goddammit!" Dwane was obviously getting frustrated and angry as he leaned across and grabbed the lever that operated the front plow.

Bob's look was still one of disbelief, but he was getting angry himself. "All fucking right!" he barked as he pushed Dwane's hand away and raised the plows himself. "I'm still the wingman in this truck! Who the hell's in that car anyway? It ain't this Nevis guy is it?"

"No." Dwane backed the truck diagonally across the road and approached the rear of the Buick. "I'll explain it later," he added.

"Yeah? Well, I'll be here waiting."

Dwane inched the truck forward. "Put it down a little," he ordered.

"I can see it!" emphasized Bob as he complied.

With the plow centered on the rear bumper Dwane gave the truck a little throttle. The Buick's wheels were spinning and finally the car began to move. Suddenly, the car shifted sideways a foot or two. The plow tip scraped its rear, then slipped up into the base of the trunk. A sizable dent appeared, shown clearly by the truck's headlights.

"Jesus Christ!" remarked Bob, shaking his head.

At last the car began to move away under its own power as its wheels grabbed some of the granular snow-covered roadway. The truck, however, was sliding into the same trap that held the car and the big dual wheels started to spin. The Buick moved out onto the road and gathered speed.

"Goddamn!" Dwane roared.

The truck stopped, its wheels still spinning. Frantically, Dwane tried to back out of the icy area, but to no avail.

"Son-of-a-bitch! I wanted to follow them," Dwane proclaimed in total frustration.

The Buick disappeared up the highway into the swirling snow.

"So now that we're stuck ourselves, you mind telling me what the hell we were just doing?"

Dwane took a few deep breaths and tried to calm down before he answered. "There were four in the car including the driver. Two men, middle aged, a young woman maybe twenty-five, and an older woman about sixty. The driver said they were going skiing, but he doesn't seem to know exactly where. There's even a ski rack and skis on the car."

"So, what's your point?"

"I can tell you right now that none of those people would know a pair of skis from a pogo stick! And what's more, that's the fourth rental car we've seen tonight!"

"Yeah? So they're not going skiing and that's why they didn't give a shit about the car. I'm sure the rental company still does. Is that it?"

"I will tell you what is it," Dwane replied with methodical calmness. "Three of those people I never saw before, but the old woman I recognize. She's Delores Stang!"

"Who the hell is Delores Stang!"

Dwane shook his head in frustration. "Christ! About two years ago Leonard Stang and a couple of his boys got blown away in some night club in downtown Chicago. Well, Leonard Stang was organized crime. High up! And that's his wife in that car we just pushed out of this ditch And she's in deeper than he ever was!"

"Well that's just fucking great! I seem to forget how handy it is you being a walking encyclopedia on fucking criminals!"

Dwane opened his door. "Come on, let's get some sand under these wheels. Now I'll call Mars!"

\*     \*     \*

Walt Conover sat at a table in his den carefully examining the nearly completed model of a P-38 fighter aircraft. Several other model aircraft were displayed about the room as well as books, pictures, and other memorabilia that reflected the World War II period.

Grace Conover walked into the room and stopped at her husband's side. "There's a call for you. The City Manager," she added with feigned emphasis.

"Let me guess," mused Walt, looking up from his project. "Someone just called Briggs to complain that one of my guys just plowed their driveway full of snow after they finished shoveling it. Or maybe their mailbox got knocked over."

"He didn't say. But he does sound upset," said Grace.

Conover reached behind him and picked up the phone from a bookcase shelf. Grace remained out of curiosity.

"Hello, Howard," Conover intoned into the phone. There followed a pause during which his expression changed from irritation to concern and back again to irritation.

"No, Howard. I don't know if it's a full moon," Conover said somewhat sarcastically. I haven't been keeping track of my moon phases lately . . . . You what?" Now a little angry. "You could have called me first, Howard . . . . Yeah, bye."

Conover hung up the phone. "Damn!"

"What's wrong," Grace asked.

"Nothing much probably, except I guess some of the guys are putting a little extra effort into their work tonight. I don't know how much of it is true. The thing is, Briggs has been getting a few horror stories, so he's called Chief Mars to check into a couple of them."

"No. My God," Grace observed.

"Yeah, exactly." Conover got up from his chair. "I've got to go out and see what's going on. Maybe I'll stop down and see Mars first."

# chapter 9

Truck twenty-two slowed to a crawl as it prepared to turn right off Court Street onto Lexington. Roland Powell shifted into his lowest gear and carefully turned the wheel as he succeeded in holding the tight turn intact with plows full and heavy with snow.

"Just look at the garbage, will you," observed Richard Wright. "Christ, these people here must be real pigs. Cans, bags, boxes, everything. Most of it's up on the windrow. We're just gonna have to educate these poor fools."

"I wonder where Slimebag's is?" questioned Roland as he finally got the truck pointed squarely down the street.

"Let's get some speed up," suggested Richard.

"You got it." Roland up shifted, stepped into the throttle and prepared to up shift again as the truck gained speed, the wing sending a sheet of snow up and over the windrow, taking most of the garbage containers in residence into the sidewalk to spill or rupture a fair percentage of their contents thereon.

"There's his place coming up now," said Richard excitedly as he leaned closer to the windshield. "And there's his garbage! Three or four bags right beside the road. Beautiful! . . . Hey! And there's the slimebag himself! Hell, he's going to try to get his garbage out of the way. Come on, let's go! Don't let him beat us to that garbage!"

"Relax. The guy's meat!" Roland prophesied.

Roland up shifted again and the truck gathered even more speed. Snow streaked off the plows over the sidewalk and onto some of the front porches of the houses set close to the street in this older section of town.

A thin man in his shirt sleeves slid to a precarious stop and reached to grab as many of his bags as he could. With the thunderous roar of the approaching truck, he looked up into the glaring headlights and became transfixed in time for a long precious moment.

Roland had the accelerator to the floor. Richard anxiously fingered two of the levers before him.

Like a squirrel in the road that had finally made up it's mind, the slimebag suddenly darted for his house, a bag in each hand. Two bags were left by the road. Richard started making maniacal-like sounds in his throat.

The truck engine was screaming now. The wing grabbed the first, then the second bag of garbage. Richard yanked hard on two levers in quick succession and the wing jerked upward.

The Slimebag slipped and fell on his porch steps landing on one of the bags he had managed to save. The contents burst through the thin plastic.

The roadside bags, partially torn, sailed through the night air along with a curtain of white. The Slimebag regained his footing and looked back toward the street only to be buried in a wave of garbage plus an instant heavy snowfall. Inside the truck, Richard and Roland were denied the muted scream that struggled out of the pile.

Richard dropped the wing and raised both fists in front of his face. "We got him! We got the Slimebag good!" Roland and Richard dissolved in fits of laughter.

Plow truck twenty-two careened around a curve, its tail lights and warning flashers quickly disappearing in a cloud of swirling snow.

*     *     *

At Police Headquarters Chief Mars stood in his office donning a heavy winter parker. There was a brief knock at the half open door and dispatcher, officer Kay Rollins leaned into the room.

"There's a call for you," she said. "On the pay phone in the anteroom."

Mars turned towards the door while adjusting his collar. He raised an eyebrow at his dispatcher.

"The caller says he's Dwane Huckins and that you know him," she continued. "He seems pretty worked up and insists on talking to you personally."

Mars frowned slightly, bringing his eyebrows together, and walked toward the door.

The glass fronted anteroom gave a clear picture of what was happening outside. The wind could be plainly heard and the blowing snow made it difficult to see past the immediate area in front of the building. The second, and certainly the third, street lights up and down the street were but dim beacons in a hostile world. Mars entered the anteroom and grimaced only briefly at the scene before picking up the pay phone receiver.

"What's the matter Dwane? You forget our regular phone number?"

The raging winter storm was even closer at hand through the glass of the phone booth where Dwane Huckins stamped his feet and moved around as much as possible, trying to stay warm while he waited for Mars to get on the line. A few feet away from the booth truck thirty nine was parked, its engine rumbling and its lights ablaze.

Dwane straightened as he heard Mars' voice. "Chief? Look, I wish this was a social call, but it isn't and we may not have a lot of time, so just listen."

Mars stood motionless, looking blankly out to the storm, the receiver to his ear. Slowly the frown, then a look of incredulous frustration appeared on his face. "What? . . . I know. I know who he is, but I haven't seen a paper. You say he was here? Tonight? . . . Who saw him? You?"

Mars' expression turned to one of irritation. "Christ, you mean that maniac with all those bikes? For God's sake, Dwane! . . . Okay. Alright. I'll take your word for it. What kind of a car was it? I don't suppose he noticed the registration . . . . Who? Delores Stang? Stang? You mean Leonard Stang? Jesus Christ! Who the hell but you would recognize Delores Stang? Even I probably wouldn't know her if she was standing right in front of me. Are you sure? Are you damn sure . . . ? So what the hell is this? A Goddamn convention? What with . . ."

Mars' voice trailed off and his face got noticeably pale even in the dim light. Finally, he took a deep breath.

"Yeah, I'm still here," he continued. "And while we're at it, I've got one for you."

Dwane straightened in the phone booth. "Nino Valachi? That old bastard? Well, you can bet he's here then . . . . Somewhere." Dwane looked outside the phone booth as if half expecting to see Valachi standing out there in the snow. "Christ, do you know what this means?"

Mars was now pacing slowly back and forth as far as the short receiver cord would allow. "I'm beginning to. So, why did you call this pay phone, or do I know already?"

"Call it a hunch if you want," Dwane replied. "Just for the hell of it you might ask the state to check on the whereabouts of a few other organized crime people."

"I intend to. You trying to tell me my phone's bugged?"

"It's a possibility, under the circumstances. One thing you can bet on. With these people around there's somebody tuned in to the police channels, you, the state police, sheriff's department, and God knows who else."

Mars stopped in mid-stride. "Well, that's just great isn't it. Maybe I can get some tin cans and a bunch of string."

"Use the public works frequency. They probably aren't on to that and your cars are all equipped with it."

"You've got to be kidding," was Mars' reply. "I don't want to even think about mentioning this on your channel and I would hope you're bright enough not to either."

"You may not have a choice."

"Well, right now I do. We don't even know where the hell they are. You say Stang and her group was headed north on Langston Road?"

"Yeah. And so was Nevis . . . on the other side of the lake," Dwane added.

"Alright. Just supposing the meeting site . . . if there is a meeting site, is in that direction," Mars surmised. "That includes the whole damn resort area to the north all the way to the mountains and probably out of our . . . out of my jurisdiction. And don't forget there's a hell of a lot of people up here this weekend for the skiing."

Mars paused and exhaled heavily. "Look, I'm going to get a couple unmarked cars out just to poke around and I'm going to get some state police up here just in case. You keep your eyes open, but don't mention this to anyone else, you hear?"

"Yeah," Dwane answered after a pause.

"I mean it Dwane," Mars cautioned. "I know how damn carried away you can get and this is no Goddamned tea party we're talking about."

There was another pause after which Dwane answered rather sarcastically. "I realize that."

"So, just keep your eyes open," Mars continued. "And if you happen to notice anything . . . I'll tell you what, if you're not near a phone just call the garage on your radio and say that your engine is running rough near such and such a place. I'll keep your frequency open here and we'll take it from there. Like I said, I don't want to advertise this thing and some people around town that aren't nailed down too tight seem to think your channel is very entertaining."

Dwane looked out at the storm and smiled faintly. "Okay. So my motor's running lousy. I got it. Look, a couple more quick things before I go check my engine. A Lear jet came into the airport tonight after it was shut down. Wouldn't take no for an answer. Sometime about sixthirty. You might check it. You might also check any big rental car agencies in the area. I didn't get the number of the Buick because I intended on following the damn thing. But if this is for real somebody must have arranged for a lot of cars all at once."

"Well, thanks a lot," came Mars' reply. "You got any other things for me to do . . . ? Go plow some snow, Huckins."

"You too, Chief," said Dwane and hung up the phone.

Now free of the telephone, Mars paced a wider track about the anteroom. Stopping to rub his face with both hands, he stepped to the glass door and looked outside. Nothing had changed. Trouble and opportunity often come as a pair, he mused idly. Wouldn't it be something if . . . , Justin Mars shook the thought away.

Moving quickly to the inside door, he opened it and hollered loudly down the hallway. "Kay, Greg, Steve. Come out here!"

A moment later the three officers gathered with Mars in the anteroom and warily looked around as though the reason for their unorthodox summons might be plainly seen.

"Greg, run down to the corner store," Mars began. "I think they're still open . . . and pick up a Boston Traveler. While you're there I want you to call the phone company. Better yet, call Bill Eddleson at home. Tell him this is an emergency and I want an expert down here right now to check for a bug or tap on this phone system."

The three officers looked around at each other. Greg Budner started to speak, but Mars continued.

"Then still from the store, call the airport and see what they can tell you about a Lear jet that landed after they closed down this afternoon. I want anything they got, who, how many, descriptions, where it came from, whatever."

"What's going on?" Greg finally got out.

"I'll tell you when you get back. Get going."

Sergeant Budner didn't bother getting his coat, but immediately went out the front door and could be seen trotting down the sidewalk.

Mars turned to his dispatcher. "Kay, get on the radio. Tell the units we got out to come in. Everybody. Sound casual. Tell them I'm going to reorganize the shift in view of the storm emergency . . . . Nothing more. When you've done that, come back in here. When I've finished with this phone I want you to call in everybody that's off duty tonight. No details, just tell them to get in here."

"How about the specials," Kay asked.

Mars thought for only a second. "No. No specials. Not yet, anyway. Get some change for this thing out of the coke machine."

Kay nodded and left the room. Patrolman Steve Allenson nervously awaited the Chief's next orders.

"Steve, I want you to go downstairs and check all the weapons and ammo. Then issue a dozen riot guns back to the rack in the assembly room."

"Yes, sir," said patrolman Allenson, and followed Kay Rollins' path through the hall door.

Mars reached into his pocket and withdrew some change as he stepped back to the phone. Lifting the receiver, he deposited a coin and began punching out a number.

"Grace? . . . Chief Mars here. How are you this evening? . . . Yes, isn't it. Say, is Walt around by any chance . . . ? I see . . . . Oh, I see. Good, then. I'll be looking for him . . . . Oh no, no. It's nothing urgent. I just wanted to get with him about this storm . . . . Oh, I know. It's a tough job. We take most of that with a grain of salt. Well, . . . yes . . . . Well, you take care, Grace . . . . Yeah, stay inside. I wish we all could . . . . Okay, I'll tell him I spoke with you . . . . Fine . . . . Bye Grace."

The cordial smile Mars had held through his conversation with Grace Conover disappeared immediately. He let out a deep breath as though he had been holding it. Mars inspected his handful of change for a moment before jamming it back in his pocket. Replacing the receiver momentarily on its hook he snapped it up again and punched the operator button on the phone. Another long second.

"This is Chief Mars in Melonia and this is a police emergency. Get me State Police Headquarters in Concord."

Officer Kay Rollins quietly entered the anteroom. Mars didn't appear to notice.

"Hello. This is Chief Mars in Melonia. Let me speak to John Griffin . . . Well, where is he?" Mars nervously tapped a foot on the floor while he waited. "No, I can't call back. Look, I don't care if he's taking a crap or what. Go in and get him out of there. This is important!"

Officer Kay Rollins smiled at the floor.

*     *     *

A well dressed man in pin stripe and dark tie, perhaps in his early fifties was seated casually behind an exquisite old desk. He was listening on a telephone styled in the manner of those produced during the twenties. The office was lavishly appointed in fine colonial antiques with a few Victorian pieces dispersed somewhat haphazardly here and there. The effect betrayed a purpose whose aim suggested impressing the largest number of people and the hell with those who might question the odd mix. Actually, the room was quite large, but beyond it's functional business setting, indicated by the desk and wooden files, any additional intention seemed vague, other than providing space to put some real nice stuff.

Two men in more casual winter attire were seated on adjacent stools in front of a small bar in one corner of the room. They were quietly animated in their conversation. On the opposite end wall a door opened and for a moment several voices could be heard outside. The door closed and the fourth man entered the room and walked to the desk where he waited for the man on the phone.

Douglas Niles appeared completely relaxed as he held the phone receiver to his ear, his left hand stretched motionless on the desk. Niles straightened slightly in his chair and spoke in measured friendly tones. "Well, we're glad you enjoyed it, Mrs. Wilson. The schedule on the advanced seminars will begin again the week after next. You should be getting a notice in the mail soon . . . No, this weekend we're closed. A regional meeting of our own personnel. Business before pleasure, you know, heh, heh . . . Fine, we'll be looking forward to seeing you . . . Goodby."

Niles hung up the phone and twisted around to address the two men at the bar. Suddenly, his voice showed obvious irritation. "Have the switchboard take care of any more calls to this number. I haven't got time for this."

If Douglas Niles were asked to stand in judgement upon himself, he would have replied honestly and with little hesitation that he was a good and decent man. Until three years ago most of his adult life had been spent in and around the New York stage, first as an aspiring actor, then gradually, as this career never quite got off the ground, gravitating into the production end of things. Nile found he liked to organize, to create, to have a part in running the show. He was quite good at it.

Oh, he realized where the money came from in some cases, but he considered it an honorable goal to turn what might be dirty dollars into art to be appreciated by all. And besides, he had met and dined with a great many of these so-called underworld movers and shakers over the years. For the most part they seemed decent men caught up in a way of life they didn't invent, almost dictated by the society in which they lived.

Niles knew very well the proverbial tangled web, how it could destroy, and how easily those of lower class and little character seemed ready to fall to the vilest tendencies of the human animal.

But Douglas Niles wasn't like that. And they knew it. He was no thief or murderer. And in an atmosphere where daily pressures forced weaker souls to drug addiction and worse, Niles had held himself above it all. They knew that, and what's more, they respected him for it. To prove it, it had been they who had stood by him when trouble came.

He certainly hadn't killed her. In fact, her death had been a physical blow to his very being. But the police had arrived, already armed with their suspicions, their formulas, and their motive all laid out in a neat package. Conviction was a previously written epilogue, published and certain as the next days sunrise. All that, a mere hour or two after he had found her in his apartment.

Then the lawyers had come. And miraculously, by the following morning it was over. Of course, he couldn't go back. That part of his life, occasionally distressing, but more often artistically rewarding, was no more.

Hallingford Farm. It sounded removed, almost foreign. Certainly, it wasn't his line of work, but then it all boiled down to dealing with people. Organization. A challenging fresh start. He was grateful. It was just what he needed. And besides, part of the plan included a playhouse theater, which would be his.

But that seemed long ago. Oh, things had gone well. Even the air and open space had done wonders for his health. True, the playhouse was still on paper, but it's foundation was part of the next phase slated to begin sometime next year. In the meantime, he had associated himself with a couple summer stock theaters nearby in his spare time. He'd been appreciated, even fulfilled at times.

Then, a few months ago he'd begun to think back. Back to New York, his previous life, and the utter swiftness of those final events. Somehow, he seemed able to see the true nature of his employers more clearly here than he had in the social jungle of the city.

And this meeting. For the first time Douglas Niles felt soiled, and maybe, somewhat trapped. For the first time he was nervous, even fearful of what would come next year, next month, even tomorrow.

One of the two men stood and wordlessly left the room. Niles looked back to the man who stood before him. "What's the radio talk like," he asked.

Maurice Ritacco calmly measured his response. "Normal stuff. Mostly about the storm. The city police called everybody into reorganize their staff because of all the snow. I guess they've got their hands full."

"What about the State Police?" questioned Niles, his eyes still firmly on Maurice. "Are they still talking about Valachi?"

"No, not for the last hour or so. They had him coming into Concord, but they don't think he made it. At least his plane didn't. From what I get they figure it's an even bet he's still in the Boston area somewhere. Hell, they got nothing on him. They just can't figure why he'd be up this way at all."

"Leave it to him," Niles shook his head. "He's not even responsible anymore. We can hope they'll chalk it up to that . . . How is he anyway? I hope to hell he doesn't croak while he's here."

Maurice motioned above. "They took him up to his room about twenty minutes ago and we sent the doctor up to look at him."

Niles kept nodding a bob or two at Maurice's answers as if it might implant the information more firmly in his mind. "What about the rest of them? They all here?"

Maurice nodded again himself. "Hard to believe, in this weather, but everybody's in. And we don't expect any gate crashers," he added with a smile.

Niles did not smile. "You better hope. How's it going out there?"

Maurice answered in a more serious vein. "Well, . . . everybody's acting civilized. The bank types, and some of the other financial people are meeting in the west conference room. There's a few still in the main dining room. More in the lounge and in the lobby by the auditorium. A few have wandered into the health club area and I know there's some closed door stuff going on upstairs."

Niles consumed this information with a slow nod. "What's the final head count?" he finally asked.

"One hundred and forty-one," Maurice said in a manner suggesting he was proud of his ready answer. "Which is about two dozen more than were supposed to come. Don't worry, they're all connected. Most are additional bodyguards, associates, whatever. Then there must be a dozen more women than were originally included. Some of these guys are looking at this as some kind of vacation, or a damn high school class reunion. Everybody's trying to impress everybody else. The women are part of that. I'm sure some of them have got specific instructions."

This time Niles shook his head instead of nodding. "That's where the trouble will start if it does . . . I'll be glad when this is over. How many are carrying weapons, would you say?"

"It's hard to tell . . . at least a quarter. Maybe a third."

The shaking of the head again. "I knew it! I tried to get them to . . ." Niles slapped the desk top with an open hand, and rose to his feet. "Len," he said to the remaining man at the bar who had been listening intently, a paper filled clipboard almost forgotten in his hand. "Mix us some drinks, would you? Bourbon and ginger for me."

"Yeah, that's good," said Maurice offhandedly, as though it didn't make any difference what he drank.

"Sure thing," said Len slipping off his stool and around the end of the bar in a fluid motion.

"What's Bradford Nevis and his bunch up to?" Niles asked.

"I saw him earlier for a couple minutes," replied Maurice. "Cocky bastard. He and his boys were with the Chicago group just before I came in. Laughing, joking, like he didn't have a care in the world."

"I'll bet!" Niles' voice had risen another decibel or two. "You realize that if the law somehow found out about this and who was here, that warrant on Nevis would be their ticket into this place? I don't even want to think about what would happen. It would be a Goddamned nightmare!"

Len brought the two drinks, setting one on the desk by Niles and handing the other directly to Maurice who reached for his. As Niles glanced at his watch and turned slightly for his drink, Len and Maurice quickly exchanged a raised eyebrow glance. It was difficult to tell if they were sharing Niles' fear surrounding his worse case scenario, or their concern was directed toward Niles himself who had used more swear words in the last five minutes than he had in a week.

Niles took a long pull from his drink. "Alright. I want a security meeting in here in half an hour. In the meantime I want everybody on their toes. And I want constant coverage of all law enforcement channels and I want to know the minute anything sounds out of the ordinary." Niles took another quick sip of his drink. "Now, what about the snow plowing situation? Where do we stand?"

Maurice seemed glad to get back to simply answering questions. "I've got someone on the ton-and-a-half doing everything in the complex itself, and the small truck, plus a three man crew with snow blowers and shovels, are keeping the rear parking lot and garage clear."

"Fine," Niles recaptured his nod. "But I'll tell you what. Don't plow the main driveway for a while. I don't want an open invitation for anyone who might be having trouble out on the highway to come wandering in here to use the damn phone or whatever."

"All right," Maurice agreed.

"Now what about the snowmobiles? They ready?"

"All twenty of them," Maurice paused to chuckle. "But I can just see some of these people . . . , hell, why would you even . . ."

"Good," Niles interrupted as though not listening to or caring about Maurice's personal assessments. "If this thing should fall apart, they may be the only way out of here on a night like this." Niles took a couple steps to line up before a small mirror behind the bar, straightened his tie and flattened the hair above his ears with open palms. "Have you seen Endicott since he came in earlier."

"No, but he's probably back out there by now. They sure had a bunch of stuff with 'em when they came. I have no idea what the hell it all is. Took it all over to their unit." Maurice paused in thought. Back on his stool, Len finished his drink and slowly lowered his glass silently to the bar top.

"You know, he's the one here that doesn't make any sense to me," Maurice offered. "Why would he stick his neck out? He just don't fit into . . ."

"Hey, I'm sure you've heard the stories. We all have," remarked Niles as he started searching his pockets for something he evidently wasn't finding. "But we don't travel in the circles these people do. Not that most of them know any more . . ." Niles had stepped back to his desk and was looking through the contents of it's top center drawer.

Maurice moved closer to the desk. "You hear the one that had Endicott staying at that hotel in Paris last fall when those Islamic whackos bombed the shit out of it cause of some peace conference thing . . . I forget exactly what. Anyway, Arab or not, Endicott got his Syrian buddies to . . ."

"I've heard it," interrupted Niles, looking up from the drawer, a small set of keys in his hand. Maurice appeared annoyed at being stopped just as he was getting to the best part of his rumor.

"There's something going on in the auditorium in a little more than an hour," continued Niles. "That's Endicott's party as far as I know. Maybe we'll find out something then. Now let's go out and test the air. Len, keep an eye on things."

Niles walked to the door. Maurice followed, after another glance between he and Len.

# chapter 10

To the rear of the stately colonial tavern stretched a contemporary connecting building which opened into the highly renovated old barn. As one left the old world coziness of the original structure, the expanse of space was almost shocking. Along a courtyard facing glass wall, now heavily draped, a series of indoor rock gardens and small fountains defied the storm outside. Their existence seemed to flaunt man's ability to control his immediate environment rather than display the inherent beauty of the flora.

To the interior of a winding brick walkway bordering the edge of this implied wilderness, the satin draped restaurant tables held a dwindling number of those just finishing their evening meal. Other conference attendees had retired to the luxuriously appointed cocktail lounge just beyond. Farther on, past a greenhoused section of the connector, still others gathered in an expansive lobby area decorated by tasteful groupings of overstuffed furniture. Here, people seemed more orientated toward the business at hand, or at least laying the groundwork for same. The majority of those in attendance seemed attired for a big city night spot or play opening and would have looked alien beside anyone whose fine apparel was based on a more realistic sense of place and time.

Mr. Niles, followed closely by Maurice, could be seen meandering their way through the assemblage, smiling the smile of a respectful staff person when eye contact demanded, but otherwise continuing on course toward the barn and the facilities beyond.

Lorenzo Denecy had managed to shed himself of his companions for the first time since arriving earlier in the evening. With idle deliberation, he walked into the lobby carrying a cocktail. Heading toward a sparsely populated corner of the room, he occasionally nodded a brief greeting, but like Niles, at least for the moment seemed intent on remaining aloof from any protracted conversation.

Lorenzo was the first to spot Carl Endicott as he emerged from the hallway adjacent to the auditorium and entered the lobby. Sans any makeup or disguise, he was instantly recognized by several people.

Endicott had chosen a less blatant example of his own sports-dress wardrobe for the evening and he presented a very dashing figure, obviously appreciated by the opposite sex. Endicott acknowledged the group, but searched out the figure of Lorenzo Denecy across the room.

Only Lorenzo's eyes betrayed his satisfaction as Endicott approached.

Endicott extended his hand and smiled. "Lorenzo, my good friend. It is good to see you. And looking younger than the last time. Your grandson must be good for you."

Denecy seemed genuinely pleased as he glanced quickly into the room to notice several looks in their direction. "How long has it been?" he asked as they shook hands. "Almost two years, I believe. New York no longer holds your interest as it once did. But I understand. As for Vincent, he is about at that point where he no longer seeks direction from an old man."

"He will find his way," Endicott said. "In his own time. You and I can only hope the trip is relatively painless. But I see many of our younger generation with good instincts for, shall we say, a changing business climate. And with your help, Vincent is surely one of these."

Lorenzo was about to reply, but Endicott continued.

"Oh yes, I also saw Frank and Stephen briefly just after we arrived, but not to speak to."

"About now they would be discussing some financial arrangements with a few representatives of the Midwestern establishment," Lorenzo offered.

Endicott laughed briefly. "I'm glad to see you haven't lost your gift for understatement, Lorenzo. Why is it so many of these people seem intent on portraying the true criminal element? Miami, Los Angeles, even New York, one can blame the foreign influence for many of the headlines. But the Midwest? Chicago? They seem determined to continue the Capone heritage."

Endicott paused, but Lorenzo remained silent, sensing he would continue.

"Maybe it's something in the water out there," Endicott smiled. "They refuse to level off, you might say. Their greed always precedes them. It leads to mistakes. I am reminded of something Errol Flynn once related about his childhood. It seemed he found if he fed a piece of pork to a duck, the duck would pass the pork in a minute or two. So Errol hit upon the idea of tying a string to the pork and soon he had a dozen or so ducks thrashing about, with young Errol still holding the end of the string, of course."

Both Endicott and Lorenzo chuckled.

"Yes, Flynn was always a favorite of mine, but then he never learned to level off either. Maybe it's really a matter of style. Errol certainly had plenty of that . . . And you, Lorenzo, I know you've collected a string or two over the years."

Lorenzo smiled. "In today's world we would call them relationships. Relationships of the kind that last longer than string. I remember that game too as a child and the string will rot in the stomach of a duck in a very short time."

Endicott smiled but said nothing. This time it was Lorenzo who continued.

"And what about you, Carl? I know you were very close to Julian, but I admired you as well. At my age I hate to lose touch with a close friend. How are you spending your time these days?"

Endicott hesitated a moment before carefully answering. "I am glad you ask, Lorenzo. There is a developing issue, and possibly an opportunity also, that I believe warrants our attention. I thought tonight would be a good time to say a few words."

Lorenzo raised one eyebrow just a little. "Really. Could you be a little more specific?"

"I would like nothing more than to elaborate," Endicott replied. "However I regret that the nature of my presentation dictates a one shot deal, so to speak. That, plus I believe I am about to say hello to your nephew, Frank."

Lorenzo kept a thoughtful gaze centered on Endicott as Frank approached, his smile in place, a drink in one hand, the other outstretched.

"My God, Carl, it seems longer than its actually been," said Frank as they shook hands. "You still selling guns to bloodthirsty natives, or are you devaluing some two bit country's currency past the point of no return?"

"I just own a few clothing stores, Frank," Endicott smiled.

Frank laughed out loud at Endicott's feigned humility. "Yeah, a lowly haberdasher, that's you. What is it now, the largest chain of it's kind in the country? Say, some of that stuff you came out with last fall . . . , recognize this?" Frank opened his suit jacket with his free hand and turned to model the garment.

"I always said you had good taste, Frank," Endicott observed seriously.

"How did it go with Nevis, Frank?" asked Lorenzo, changing the subject and possibly a little put out with Frank's distraction. "Maybe Carl would like to hear about it. Ten years ago you might have set it up yourself," he added, looking at Endicott.

"Nevis, huh?" remarked Endicott. "Strange bedfellows, Lorenzo."

"So, did he go for it?" Lorenzo asked again.

Frank finished swallowing some of his drink. "Of course. That is, after we allowed him to get to the point where he could believe it. He seems very pleased with himself, but he's not stupid. He'll check it out every way he can think of."

Lorenzo smiled and looked back at Endicott. "It appears we have just divested ourselves of certain holdings in and around the Cleveland area. And possibly offered certain people enough rope to hang themselves. I dare say, a month, or even a year from now, said holdings will be bargain priced and they won't be carrying the dirty laundry they do now."

"I don't know," interjected Frank. "He may squirm out of it yet. He wields a lot of power where he is and that's just where they're trying to nail him. Hell, he's laying the ground work now. Main thing he's got to do right now is stay out of circulation for a while. Him and a few others I noticed here that I didn't expect to. Christ, this reminds me of the old days."

Endicott smiled at them both. "Ah yes, a page right out of the thirties. Let's enjoy it while we can. We probably won't come this way again . . . Well gentlemen, I must mingle. I trust I'll be seeing you both later."

"We wouldn't miss it," said Lorenzo.

Carl Endicott turned and headed for the lounge entrance. Halfway there an attractive young woman in evening attire stepped forward and took his arm. Endicott obliged the gesture and laughed politely at some remark she made as they moved away.

Frank looked back at Lorenzo. "Wouldn't miss what? What's he up to anyway?"

Lorenzo lowered his glass slowly from his lips as he looked after Endicott. "I haven't the vaguest idea," he said.

*   *   *

Jeff Larazas emerged from the bedroom carrying two pieces of luggage which he deposited carefully on the living room floor. Straightening, for a few seconds he seemed lost in a secret concentration.

A few feet away rested a large leather covered, trunk-like case on the coffee table. Suddenly, Jeff turned and stared at the case. A couple quick steps and he was at it's side. Four feet long, two feet high and wide, Jeff reached and flipped the two frontal catches with each hand. After another full second of thought he raised the cover back to rest on it's hinges and peered down to the contents. Just as suddenly, he slammed the cover shut, secured the latches and moved to the vacant fireplace. He grasped the mantle with one hand as if for support. Jeff's face was pale as he raised the other hand to rub his eyes. "Jesus Christ," he said aloud.

The outside door of the condo unit opened and closed. Brian Verrill walked out of the entryway and into the living room. He was still wearing the white jumpsuit. The snow he brushed off wasn't all that evident until it landed on the dark carpet.

"I just brought the other snow machine over," he announced. "Damned if I don't think we're going to be using them before this is over. There must be a foot of new snow out there."

Jeff didn't appear to notice as Brian walked into the bathroom and came out with a large bath towel with which he started to dry his face and hair. While so engaged, he continued with his news from the outside world.

"I'll tell you, I don't like this whole thing one bit. I wasn't this nervous when we were at that Goddamned chemical plant outside East Berlin a couple months ago. Some of those so-called body guards and the like in there ought to be in a cage. Just wait until later on when a few of them get juiced up . . . . And Christ! There's this bank guy there. Does a commercial on television for God's sake. I'll tell you he's shaking like a leaf. If the police ever showed up here half of these people would shoot each other out of pure reaction. Which reminds me, I'm going to carry that Browning, so . . ."

Brian finally looked up at Jeff who remained at the mantel. He tossed the towel toward a chair and ran a hand through his hair, roughly combing it. "You've been looking in that damn case again, haven't you? Why don't you just leave them alone?"

Jeff turned to face his companion. "Hell, I don't even like to be in the same room. And according to Carl, this may be just the beginning. We've been involved in some pretty strange stuff before, but I don't know if I can handle this."

Brian glanced at the case himself. "Yeah, I know. Look, just be glad we're getting the hell out of here tonight . . . That is if we can."

*　　*　　*

A windswept wintry scene enveloped the Public Works garage leaving it to appear as some lone Arctic outpost. The big plow trucks were gone from their places around its perimeter. Only the drifting snow crisscrossed by heavy tire tracks remained. A couple yellow pickup trucks were parked near the office end of the building, however, lights were ablaze throughout the structure.

Charlie Hayward sat behind his desk, the fingers of his right hand poised above the press switch of the radio mike. Don Masse entered the office, took off his snow covered parka, and shook it wildly. Charlie frowned as some of the snow fell on his desk. Don tossed the coat at a wall peg and plunked himself down in a chair.

*Just a second. I'll give you a license number,* crackled the radio over the background sound of rock music from truck number fifteen.

"Shut that damn music off!" Charlie ordered, pressing the switch. "I can't hear what you're saying."

*I said we've got an abandoned car right in the middle of Locust Street. Have the police send the wrecker over.*

"Pull the wing and drive up on the sidewalk to get around it for now," ordered Charlie. "Can you make it?"

*Yeah, maybe, if we take a couple shrubs along with us.* replied Custer over the radio.

"Well, go ahead then. I'll get a wrecker over there if I can get one out. In the meantime, lay on the horn. Someone may come out and move it."

*Don't worry, ain't nobody asleep on this street,* came the reply. The car must be from somewhere else.

"Well, don't waste time there. We got a lot more of this stuff on the way." Charlie pushed the mike aside as a flurry of snide remarks came over the radio. "Who's in the garage?" he asked Don Masse."

"Number twenty-three, Wayne. His wing was hanging by a thread. Frank and Dennis are putting it back together."

"How's Oscar? You get him to the hospital Okay?"

"Yeah, the Goddamned harness let go when he hit. He broke the windshield with his face." Don shifted in his chair as he laughed. "What a fucking mess. He bled all over your pickup, by the way."

"Well, ain't that nice," Charlie remarked sarcastically. "What's the sidewalk tractor look like?"

"Front plow's all smashed to shit," answered Don.

The telephone range. Charlie picked it up.

*Thirty-nine to garage,* barked the radio.

"See what he wants, will you?" Charlie ordered as he picked up the receiver. "City garage," he spoke into the instrument. After a second or two Charlie stood and moved away as far as the cord would allow, his back to the desk.

Don reached for the radio mike and dragged it across the desk to his chair. "Garage," he spoke after roughly thumping the switch.

*Can you break somebody loose to hit a few of these side streets off Craig Road? This Boulevard is drifting something fierce.*

"What's the matter, Dwane? Having trouble handling that new truck?" Don asked, smiling slightly.

*This is thirty-two. We're opened up pretty well over here. We'll go make a pass on everything to the east of Craig.*

*Thanks Scott. Watch out for that north ditch along Ridgevale.*

*No problem.*

Don pushed the mike away and slouched back in his chair.

Charlie was still on the phone. "Okay. We'll be here," he finally said.

Charlie turned back to the desk with a strange look on his face. "Well, you better dig out every damn set of chains we got for the police vehicles," he said, dropping the receiver back on it's cradle. "That was Chief Mars. He's sending everything over here to have 'em put on. Even the two unmarked cars."

"What?" Don asked. That's got to be at least a dozen vehicles between the cruisers, a couple vans, and those other two. Who the hell is driving them all? Don Masse had both hands on the arms of the old wooden chair as though he was going to get up, but somehow this strange news had short-circuited the effort. "They've usually got only six or eight people on at night. What the hell's going on?"

"He didn't elaborate except to say to get a loader over there to plow out the entire parking lot. Right now. That wasn't a request either." Charlie headed for the office door.

Don finally thrust himself out of the chair. "What the fuck's the matter with him? There ain't no traffic out there at all."

"Ask a cop," Charlie said over his shoulder. "There ought to be a bunch of 'em here in a little bit."

On Elmwood Avenue, truck twenty-two struggled to keep a steady speed behind a barrier of heavy snow which streamed from it's plows. As it got closer, the high revs of a hard working engine became distinctly audible above the rumbling of steel on asphalt. Thundering on by, a sizable amount of unidentified debris could be seen bouncing along behind the truck, it having somehow become attached to the frame area near the taillight.

To the left of twenty-two, truck number eight stopped at a side street intersection to allow twenty-two to pass before turning right on Elmwood to empty it's plows.

Inside truck eight both Gale Mooney and Jason Peck were laughing.

"Man, did you see that stuff they're dragging?" Jason asked.

Gale reached for the radio mike and brought it to his lips. "Hey, Duckling, you looked in your rear view mirror lately?"

After a couple seconds the radio came to life. *Hey yeah, what is it?*

"It's behind your truck," reported Gale. "Looks to me like about twenty feet of cattle fence and a mailbox, stand and all. Can't you afford to buy that stuff?"

Jason erupted into another round of laughter, but quieted when the reply sputtered onto the radio.

*Well, thanks so much for the information. Maybe you ought to mention it on the radio.*

"Hey, you asked," answered Gale.

Roland Powell must have held his mike switch down but hesitated with a further reply. Instead, Richard Wright's background remark came clearly over the air. *No Shit! Where the fuck did that come from?*

Gale joined Jason in more laughter as he put the truck in gear and inched a full front plow around the corner to the right.

*     *     *

In the dispatch room at the police station a young male officer, Pete Howard, sat before the radio base station. Officer Kay Rollins leaned against the counter behind him. The laughter of both caught the attention of the telephone service man at the far end of the counter who looked up from a small computer-like device which was temporarily wired into the phone system.

"Can you believe that?" Kay finally asked, reaching for her coffee cup.

"These guys are something aren't they? Standard radio procedure as far as they're concerned, I guess," offered Pete.

"Who are those people on the radio anyway?" asked the telephone man.

"Public Works," Pete answered simply.

"Oh," said the telephone man nodding as though that explained everything.

"Who is that they call Duckling?" asked Kay.

"I know him by sight. Name's Powell," replied Pete. "He's the one that ran over that phone booth instead of some ducks that were in the road. Therefore, Duckling."

"Yeah, I remember that," commented the telephone man. "Even the telephone was a total loss."

Kay was laughing again. The telephone man just shook his head. "Our tax dollars at work," he added.

"So, they're colorful. What can you say?" said Pete. "But I'll tell you. They do a nice job with the roads. Go to some other town after a storm and see what they look like."

The telephone man finished disconnecting his equipment from the phone switchboard. "Well, I can tell you this. This system is clean inside and out and I'm going home and go to bed. I'll tell the Chief on the way out."

"Okay. Thanks," nodded Pete.

The telephone man collected his gear and moved toward the door. Suddenly he stopped. "Say, what's all the commotion around here tonight anyway? And who did the Chief think tapped his phone?"

Pete turned in his chair. "Ask the Chief," he said.

The telephone man gave a final knowing glance to both officers and left.

Again, the radio came to life. *Dwane Huckins to garage.*

*This is the garage,* came Charlie's reply. *What's the matter? You forget your number?*

"There he is again," remarked Pete as Kay moved toward his side.

*I would like to report that this brand new engine is running a bit rough,* reported Dwane.

*Can you get it back here?*

*I'm going to check it out myself. I'll let you know,* came the reply.

"That's it!" exclaimed Pete. "Get the Chief in here."

Kay hurriedly went out the door. Chief Mars came bursting through before it closed. "I heard it on the scanner," was his explanation.

"Goddamn him!"

Mars stared a moment at the radio, then grabbed the microphone and flipped a switch on the panel. "What's your location, Dwane? . . . I say, what's your location?"

*Who's that talking?* asked an unidentified voice over the radio.

Mars slammed the mike down on the counter. "Goddamn!"

Kay Rollins opened the dispatch room door and leaned in. "Chief, there's a call for you on the pay phone. It's John Griffin, State Police and something about the warrant."

With a last quick look at the radio, Mars pushed past Kay and out the door without a word. Kay slowly moved to the counter. She and Pete exchanged a glance. The silence continued.

"Boy, Mars sounds pissed. What the hell did you tell him that for?" asked Bob Garnett.

Truck thirty-nine had just passed the last house on the narrow dirt road and was approaching it's dead end. Dwane Huckins tossed the mike onto the dash and downshifted. "Because I know where it is."

"Where? It sure as hell ain't out here."

The truck jerked to a stop. Bob pulled back the appropriate levers and the plows rose swiftly into the air with the help of plenty of hydraulic pressure encouraged by Dwane's heavy foot on the throttle.

"Just leave 'em up," Dwane ordered. "We're going back."

"Back where?"

Dwane clunked the shift lever into reverse and swung the rear of the truck roughly into the hammerhead turnaround. Quickly, into first gear, he twirled the big steering wheel. "Hallingford Farm," he announced.

"Hallingford Farm? You think that's where all these Mafia guys and that old woman are?"

"Yes."

"Why there? I saw the lights when we went by, but there's always people there."

"Just a feeling. It's the only place around that fits. It's big. It's got the facilities. It can be private if they want it to. Sure, they had some public stuff going on, but not now. Did you see the sign? Closed February ninth through the eleventh ARABI personnel conference. Bullshit!" Dwane up shifted as the truck gathered speed over the frozen dirt.

"So, tell Mars. Or if you don't want to blab it on the radio, we'll go back and tell him."

"Like I said, I want to check it out."

"Check out what? What are we going to do? Knock on the door and say, heh, you Mafia creeps, we know you're in there. They'll probably blow our fucking heads off."

At the main highway Dwane slowed only enough to get the truck pointed out and up the road before pouring the coals to the engine once more. "Nice guys that we are we're going to plow their driveway," he announced with a quick smile.

Dwane fished in his shirt pocket, then thrust a pencil at Bob. "Here, take this. And look under the seat. I think Dennis left that magazine he had in here earlier. I want to get around into the back parking lot if we can. You write down as many plate numbers as you can see. Look for that Buick we pushed and a late model white Cad."

"You got to be shitting me. I don't believe we're doing this."

"Well, believe it. We're almost there."

Through the wind blown snow, the lights of Hallingford came into view. Set well off the road, the complex appeared warm and innocent as any snug lodging on a cold winter night.

Apparently resigned to what was ahead, Bob reached under the front seat and brought a crumpled magazine into his lap. Sticking the pencil cigar style in his mouth, he rested his hands on the levers before him. "You want it to look good, we better be plowing in."

"Good, drop 'em," Dwane agreed. I'm going to take the south entrance and see if we can come out on the north. That way we can get a better look, quicker."

"Wonderful," remarked Bob.

The plows settled. Truck thirty-nine slowed.

"Watch that granite post on the corner. That driveway ain't that wide," Bob added.

"Yeah." Dwane swept the truck around in a wide turn to attack the entrance more head on. Into the driveway thirty-nine settled to a steady push toward the complex.

A hundred yards in and over a slight rise, more of the sprawling main structure came into a northerly perspective. Over the unprotected expanse of open field, the wind had carved curious drift patterns leaving some areas nearly bare of new snow and revealing the older crusty surface beneath.

"Look at that. There isn't a single car in front. They must all be in back," said Dwane, leaning forward over the wheel.

"Or there's nobody here," Bob offered hopefully.

Dwane said nothing as the back parking lot came slowly into view around a long sweeping curve. Outside lights blazed forth across the snow. Then, car after parked car appeared and suddenly, it was all there. Besides the fifty or so vehicles distributed around the perimeter of the lot and in the center of the cleared area, a half dozen men worked with shovels, brooms, and two snow blowers to keep the cars and the parking lot clear of snow as it came down. Evidently no one had heard the city truck coming due to the running snow blowers as first one, and then the remainder of the men looked up in surprise. The first man quickly jumped into a small foreign pickup with plow and immediately pointed it at the approaching city vehicle. Dwane brought the truck to a jolting halt as the pickup slid to stop inches from the huge front plow.

"Christ! Our ass is grass now," Bob said under his breath. "There's that Buick over there. Look at the rear end."

The driver of the pickup jumped out and headed for the driver's side of the city truck. Dwane reached for his .45 automatic from under his coat on the seat and brought it over into his lap. "Relax. We're just doing them a favor, so we don't know from nothing."

"Sure!" uttered Bob without moving his lips as though that might somehow give them away. Bob's eyes were on the cars as he furiously wrote the license numbers he could see onto the open magazine without actually looking down.

Dwane rolled down his window and leaned his head out as far as he could to discourage the guy from stepping up onto the running board. "What the hell's the matter," he asked the man, getting the first words said. "Move your truck and we'll push everything along here over to the right. Give you more room to clear the lot."

The man was taken aback only for a second and his reply was angry. "This is private property. What do you think you're doing here?"

"Hey, this is a bad storm," Dwane explained. "Just trying to help you guys out."

"Well, we can handle it ourselves, so back it on out," the man ordered with an arm motion as though he would push it himself if it didn't move fast enough.

Now, Dwane took the angry tact as Bob kept writing. "Hey, thanks a lot. See if we ever try to help you people again. There's a lot more snow coming in case you haven't heard and you're going to look pretty foolish trying to push it with that thing."

"I said, back it up!" The man yelled.

"The least you could do is let us turn around in the parking lot." The man took a few steps away from the truck and put his hands deep into the side pockets of his coat.

"Dwane . . . !" Bob breathed.

Dwane raised the .45 off his lap and pointed it at the man though the door.

The man turned to his fellow workers who had been watching the scene, a hundred feet distant. "Hey these guys here don't seem to want to move," he yelled to them.

The men immediately left their tools and started in the direction of the city truck.

"Okay! Alright! Jesus Christ! I've never seen people so Goddamned unfriendly. Pick 'em up Bob!" Dwane ordered, racing the truck engine.

Bob dropped his pencil and yanked on the levers, the plows jerked into the air. Dwane jolted the truck into reverse and backed away under the piercing stares of the parking lot crew.

"You think he had a gun in his pocket?" Bob asked after a few moments.

"Hell, yes," Dwane answered, keeping his eyes on the rear view mirror.

"Christ! I guess I don't have to ask if you would have blown him away if he'd brought it out. Jesus Christ!"

Dwane shot a quick glance at Bob, then back to his rear view mirror keeping the truck on the tight course of the path they had plowed on the way in.

Bob reached to the floor and retrieved the magazine. Turning pages in the dark, it was difficult to find where he'd written. "I got maybe six or eight numbers. That's about all I could make out with the snow and the lights. There was a white Cad over on the far end, but I couldn't read the plate."

"Yeah, I saw it."

"You going to make that sweep around the front?" Bob asked.

"No," was Dwane's quick answer. "I don't want to get them any more worked up than they already are. As soon as we get on the road, read those numbers off to Charlie. He won't know what you're talking about, but Mars, or one of his people will . . . No, on second thought, don't. We better wait."

"Jesus Christ!" Bob repeated. I still don't believe we did that."

At last the city truck emerged onto the highway, but Dwane had pointed the truck away from town.

"Where you going now? I thought we were headed back," remarked Bob, his voice getting a bit suspicious.

"We are, but not yet. You can bet somebody's watching and I want them to see us plowing like we're continuing on our run. We'll cut back onto Foster Road," explained Dwane.

Bob nodded his agreement and dropped the plows. The truck got underway. "I gotta admit, you had this thing figured."

After the truck was out of sight of the complex, Dwane flipped on the interior light. "Let's see what you got."

Bob turned a couple pages and found the one he'd used. "Well will you look at this. I wrote all over Suzanne Sommers' tits!"

# chapter 11

Walt Conover brought the Buick to a stop tight up against the newly plowed windrow in front of the Melonia Police Station. Rather than climb over the high snowbank that now separated the street from the sidewalk, Conover walked the fifty feet to the main driveway that eventually emptied in a rear parking lot. As he approached the entrance, first one, then another car, slowed and turned into the drive. Conover noticed the entire lot had been plowed, presumably by his men, and it now contained several cars. Strange, this time of night under the circumstances, he thought, as he proceeded toward the building over a newly shoveled walkway.

At the front door, Conover looked through the glass into the dimly lighted foyer. Chief Mars stood at the pay phone, gesturing in the air with his free hand as he spoke. As Conover reached for the door handle, an officer emerged from the hallway, spoke briefly to the Chief, then disappeared back into the building with movements suggesting some urgency. With the oddness of the situation gathering in his mind, Conover entered the building to await the attention of Chief Justin Mars.

At the sound of the door, Mars whirled to deliver Conover a blank look as he continued on the phone. "So, you're telling me everything is closed? There's nothing coming north at all. Great!"

Over the course of a lengthy pause Mars continued to look through Conover as though not really seeing him. When he spoke again it was accompanied by the fidgety stance and hand motions. "Like I said, I don't have an exact location, but we know he's here and we know there's more than just him . . . Look John, when I find out, and I'm going to directly, we'll have to move on it as best we can. Hell, I don't dare wait till the weather clears . . . Yeah, I'll just bet they are. Well, if you can't make it tonight we sure as hell aren't going to see anybody from the Bureau either . . . Yeah, I'm glad to get those other two names. It sure would be nice to nab them along with . . ."

Mars turned back to Conover who hadn't moved from his position a few feet from the Chief. This time he seemed totally aware of his presence. "Look John, I've got to . . . yeah. Oh, by the way, I just got the word my phones are clear, so forget this line . . ." Mars laughed briefly. "Yeah, keep in touch. Bye"

Mars hung up the phone and took a deep breath. Conover started to speak, but Mars beat him to it. "Hello Colonel. Hell of a night, ain't it?"

Conover consciously released tension on both eyebrows and allowed them back to a more normal position. "Yeah, sure is. I've been out poking around. The late start's my fault, I guess. It appears we're holding our own, though. I stopped by to see about whatever trouble any of my men have been getting into . . . but it seems you've got something else going on . . ."

Mars scrutinized the older man as if making some decision of his own before he spoke further. "Would you believe the weather's even worse to the south of here? And I guess its not much better to the west or east. The only possible way in here right now is from the north and God knows there's nothing up there."

Mars paused a moment and shook his head. Conover let him continue in his own way.

"Wind's blowing fifty-sixty miles an hour to the south, I guess. Its drifting like hell. Can't see twenty feet in front of you I'm told. Highways are just plain closed. Never happened before that I can remember. They doubt if they can get anybody up here for several hours, if then. What State Police there are, in any other direction, are few and far between and on duty anyway, which means we don't dare call them by radio."

Mars paused again. Conover just raised a single eyebrow in response. He didn't really know Mars that well except as another department head and small talk companion at an occasional meeting.

"I realize this doesn't make any sense to you," Mars acknowledged. "Not yet anyway. Why don't you come in my office and I'll fill you in."

"As the saying goes, I thought you'd never ask," Conover replied.

Mars stepped to Conover's side and put an arm around his shoulder as if to guide him. Surprised by the Chief's action, his first step was a little awkward, but Mars seemed not to notice.

"You know, Walt," Mars continued, "you always impressed me as being bored to tears half the time. Let me see if I can liven up your evening."

\*     \*     \*

Gale Mooney swung the truck hard right out of the intersection, guiding the full plows around to empty against the freshly piled windrow. Jason Peck pulled a series of levers before him and the plows rose into the air.

*Garage to thirty-nine,* sputtered the radio.

*Yeah, Charlie,* answered Dwane.

*I take it you're coming in? I just got a call from the police.*

*We're on our way.*

"There they go again," remarked Jason. "I wonder what happened. You s'pose they had an accident?"

"You got me," answered Gale absently as he brought the truck to a stop in reverse and shifted back into first gear. "Drop 'em. I'm going to hit this corner once more."

*Thirty-two to thirty-nine,* sounded the radio.

*Go ahead.*

*I'm coming up behind you. What's going on?* asked Scott Roy.

*We're headed for the garage.*

*I know. Why?*

*I can't go into it now.*

*You found that guy I saw earlier, didn't you.*

*You could say that.*

*We'll follow you in.*

*Be my guest.*

*Well, don't bother trying to get into the garage,* warned an unidentified voice. *We just stopped to get a couple wing bolts. The garage is full of police cruisers!*

Gale and Jason glanced at each other as truck eight rumbled along.

"Well, pick 'em up," Gale said finally. "We're not going to find out anything here."

\*     \*     \*

Douglas Niles stood at the lounge bar, another drink in his hand. Before him the foreman of the parking lot crew recounted the story of their confrontation with the City Plow truck. Close by, the bartender wiped an area he'd already done several times, thus making sure he remained within easy earshot. Maurice Ritacco sat on a stool by Niles.

Otherwise, the room was virtually empty.

"Hell yeah," said the lot foreman, "they were in plain sight of the parking lot before we even saw them."

"And the driver said they were just trying to do us a favor, huh?" observed Niles.

"Yeah, and I really think he meant it," said the foreman.

"I can accept that," agreed Maurice.

Niles eyed them both for a moment. "Let's hope so," he said softly.

Then to the foreman, "But you say, he gave you a hard time when you told him to leave?"

"Well, he wanted to turn around in the parking lot at first. Said we were real unfriendly," the foreman smiled.

Niles wasn't smiling. "So, as a result, they left angry," he said pausing to nod in the affirmative. The foreman started to speak, but Niles continued.

"Alright. I guess you better plow everything. If we don't, we could be trapped here for whatever reason. If somebody should wander in for help, or to use the phone, we'll handle it up front and take our chances."

The foreman hesitated briefly as if missing his cue to leave, but the lengthening silence quickly made the point. He hastily nodded and walked swiftly from the lounge.

"What do you think," Maurice asked.

Niles exhaled noticeably before answering. "I'm trying not to . . . Probably I just worry too much." After another pause, he turned to the bartender. "Give me the phone."

With a fluid motion, the bartender swept the instrument from behind the bar and placed it before Niles. Niles grabbed the receiver and pressed a single button.

"This is Niles. What's the radio talk like? . . . Nothing? You mean nothing at all? Those units haven't checked in to headquarters once since they went out again? . . . Well, let me know the minute they do."

Niles put the phone down slowly.

"How much longer till the Endicott show?" asked Maurice Ritacco

*     *     *

Walt Conover's old Buick punched its way through the freshly plowed windrow along the street and glided into the driveway, its body leaving a slight wake in the new fallen snow. Conover emerged behind the creaking door and slammed it shut behind him. The only lights on in the house were centered on the second floor. Grace must be in her office with her endless real estate paperwork, he thought. Conover high stepped through the snow, heading for the back door.

Inside, Conover silently navigated his way through the darkened kitchen and hallway until he switched on a single standing lamp next to a long oak table in his den. Carefully sliding out it's shallow drawer, he removed a mahogany case and quietly placed it on the oak. Opening the case, Conover paused a moment to gaze at the nickel plated forty-five caliber automatic. Beside the gun a small plaque stated, "Presented to Major Walton Conover by his Comrades in Arms, July 18th, 1952".

Conover lifted out the gun, then rummaged in the drawer, producing two loaded clips plus a few stray shells. Putting the ammo in a side coat pocket, he placed the case back in the drawer and closed it. Turning away from the table, he checked the loaded clip in the gun, then shoved it back in place. Conover looked up to see Grace standing in his way.

"Going hunting, Walt?" she asked, following the path of the gun as Walt slowly put it in his other coat pocket.

Conover smiled slightly. "I thought you were upstairs. Would you believe me if I said I was going to see you before I left again?"

"Why, of course. You were going to tell me why you were leaving with a gun. Has plowing snow suddenly become that dangerous?"

"I never could fool you mother, could I?" Conover offered.

"They say it's sometimes hardest to see those closest to you. But not for me, Walt. You've always been very clear to me. I've usually liked what I've seen. Usually. What's this all about?"

Conover paused a moment to collect his thoughts. "It seems Melonia has been honored by a visit from a few heads of organized crime, who for whatever reason, have seen fit to have a meeting at the Hallingford Farm Complex tonight of all nights."

"What? You . . ."

"Anyway, a couple of my guys found out about it and now Mars feels he has to move tonight. Bradford Nevis, you know that union boss out in the Chicago-Detroit area, is there and there's just been a federal warrant put out on him on some rackets thing. Mars doesn't dare wait and the State Police can't get here for awhile because of the storm, so the Chief has got his whole force ready to go in and get this guy . . ."

"Well, that's got nothing to do with you. You're not . . ."

"I know," Conover interrupted. "Just let me finish. Some of the big Public Works trucks may be used to blockade the roads in and out of the place and

I've got to be there, nothing else. The gun is a just-in-case precaution. That's all. I don't plan on going that near the place and there probably won't be any trouble anyway, so don't worry."

Grace seemed unimpressed by the benign efforts planned by her husband. "It never ends, does it? The Philippines, Korea, even Vietnam. And now here? I just can't believe it."

Conover stepped forward to embrace his wife, but she backed away.

"At least I won't have long to wait this time," Grace exclaimed, her voice rising. "Walt, I know you'll never accept it, but you're just too damn old for this. We both are!"

This time she accepted his arms, though rigidly she refused to respond. Thankfully, Conover was able to look past her so she could not see the sudden emotion he felt sure his face betrayed. "It's not like that," he said after a moment when he thought he could trust his voice. "It's not like that at all."

"If you should get yourself killed, Walton Conover. Even by accident! At this point in my life I could not forgive you."

"Grace . . ." Silently, Conover wondered how long he should stand there with his wife before making his way out the door.

*   *   *

Karen's Diner, one of those originally trailerable affairs of gleaming metal and rounded corners, was nestled in a pine grove just off the highway. Tonight, as always, it was open. A few four wheel drive pickup trucks with plows and a couple cars populated the recently plowed parking area to one side. Nearer the street rested a yellow city plow truck, it's lights ablaze, it's engine running.

Inside, the seats were nearly all taken by working types taking a break from their involvement with the storm. Their talk permeated the air along with the clanking of dishes and the sizzle of the grill. On two stools at the counter, Pat Gant and his wingman, Dean Smith, were working on a quick meal. Pat had measurably more food on his plate than Dean as it was Pat who was constantly punctuating his dialogue with his fork in the air as he spoke alternately to Dean and a temporarily idle waitress who leaned against the appliance counter behind the bar.

"I'm telling you," Pat stressed to his wingman, I saw it in a bonafide newspaper and not one of those supermarket rags. This was a legit story."

"Alright, alright," mouthed Dean as he continued eating.

"This woman weighed close to five hundred pounds. Didn't even know she'd been pregnant for three-four years and for some reason just never had the kid. Hey, you know . . . I'll bet . . ." Pat eyed the waitress as though her presence had prodded his sudden insight. "Hey Doris, you're a woman. Maybe you'd know . . . I'll bet there's a link between the physical and the subconscious. In other words, if a woman, any woman, is too stupid to know she's pregnant after nine months maybe she just doesn't have the kid, like this one. Is that possible?"

Doris viewed Pat with clenched teeth. "I don't think so," she said slowly.

"Okay, whatever," Pat dismissed the idea. "Anyway, the kid's been pounding on the walls and biting stuff, see? The woman's sick as hell, thinks she's gonna die. Well, some people get together and truck her off to the hospital. As soon as they see her, into the delivery room she goes. And no sooner do they get her legs spread, then whamo! It's like some dam bursts. Anyhow, the kid's like thirty-forty pounds, all green and blue and freaky looking. Eyes wide open. Fingernails and toenails all grown in circles like springs. Hair everywhere. And there's like twenty-thirty gallons of afterbirth slimed all over everything. The stuff had gone sour and there's these bubbles of gas that keep bursting all over it. In a few seconds everybody's puking their guts out. The kid's crawling for the door and . . ."

"Jesus Christ!" exclaimed Dean. "If I end up puking, it's going to be in your lap, I'll tell you that."

"That's got to be the most disgusting thing I ever hear," Doris said, a pained look on her face as she turned and walked toward the kitchen.

"Hey, I'm just . . ."

A blast of cold air and the sound of stamping feet emanating from the foyer door turned Pat and Dean on their stools. Simpson Dunbar, and his fledgling wingman, Dustin Eaves, entered the diner. Eaves immediately spotted his fellow workers and waved happily in the air.

"Hi guys. How's it going? You been around your run once yet?" asked Eaves, still loudly knocking any remains of snow from his boots.

Pat and Dean eyed each other at Eave's blossoming personality.

Dunbar's mood, however, seemed considerably more serious as he motioned the pair to come over to the door. Pat ambled the few steps to Simpson. Dean followed. Eaves stood by, grinning.

"I've created a fucking monster here," announced Simpson, tossing a sidewards glance at Eaves. "Look, obviously you ain't been on the air, so I thought I'd let you know. There's something going on at the garage. I don't know what it's about, but Chief Mars has been on our frequency and somebody came on the radio and said the garage is full of cops. I think everybody is making some excuse to head in."

"Sounds like fun," said Eaves. Nobody seemed to notice.

"You sure you ain't having another one of your flashbacks?" Pat offered with a smile.

"Maybe we're all under arrest just on general principles," said Dean.

"It wouldn't surprise me."

"Hey, suit yourself," said Dunbar, surprisingly without a retort to Pat's remark as he turned to Eaves. "Come on, let's go. We might as well plow our way in. This stuff ain't letting up any." Dunbar turned for the door. Eaves shrugged, smiled at Pat and Dean and followed.

"Yeah, Okay. Thanks," said Pat to Dunbar's back, his mood suddenly pensive.

"Wonder what the hell's going on," said Dean.

"Well, let's go find out." Pat reached into his pocket, selected a couple bills from the half dozen in his hand, and strode to the counter.

Outside, truck forty-one was just pulling away, its plows down, as Pat and Dean emerged and headed for their truck. With the wing of number nineteen up tight against the door, Dean preceded Pat through the driver's side. In another few moments the truck had backed into the now empty highway. With it's plows clanking to the pavement, it too headed for town.

*   *   *

From above, the area surrounding the Public Works garage might have resembled a huge playpen where small boys had been given far too many toys to keep track of. It seemed nearly all of the big city plow trucks were parked haphazardly in the yard, along the street, or pulled into a line beside the gas pumps. Dispersed in and around these were various police vehicles which completed a curious, certainly never before duplicated mixture. With engines running and lights ablaze, any passerby would have had a hard time explaining such an assemblge.

In the garage the strange composite was defined with people, the neatly uniformed police on one hand, and the more disheveled and diversified members of the P.W.D. on the other. The garage was jammed with as many vehicles as it would hold, it's center lane now populated with five police cruisers that had just been dressed with tire chains. As members of both classes of personnel simply stood in small groups, or navigated the tight quarters between blue collar yellow and official black and white, the big rear door rose upward to the rafters. One by one, the cruisers backed out into the snow to be replaced by chainless others of their kind.

In the garage anteroom Walt Conover walked in from outside as Charlie Hayward came out of his office.

"Walt! Do you know what the hell this is all about? I'm beginning to think everybody does but me. The crews are coming in and the cops won't say anything except, talk to Mars. Where the hell is Mars?"

"If he's not here he will be shortly," replied Conover.

"Well, I ain't seen him," insisted Charlie, both hands in the air. "And if we don't get back out there we're going to lose it. It's not supposed to stop snowing until sometime tomorrow."

"I know, Charlie. I know," Conover said, more calmly. "Look, call Division Three and see if they can divert a couple trucks through town to keep the main drags clear. Tell them . . . tell them we're having a nonstorm related problem here."

"What non-storm related problem?" Charlie insisted.

"We're all going to find out in a minute," Conover said through gathering frustration. "Just call the State, Charlie."

Charlie turned for his office with hands in the air again and nearly stepped into Dennis Atherton coming through the outside door. Charlie moved around Dennis as Conover spied the big payloader operator.

"Dennis."

"Yeah, yes sir," said Dennis awkwardly, unused to being directly addressed by the Director of Public Works, particularly at this time of night.

"What are you doing right now?" Conover asked pointedly.

"I . . . well, I just came up from tidying up the yard after . . ."

"Fine," Conover interrupted. "I want you to grab somebody in the garage and put the chains on my car. They're in the trunk. Key's in the ignition."

"Yeah, sure . . ."

"I hate to ask but I'd like you to do it right outside here where its parked. I don't want to get it caught up in here and maybe . . ."

This time it was Dennis who interrupted. "No problem. No problem at all, Colonel. I'll just go get Don."

Dennis strode past Conover toward the garage as a group headed by Dwane, Bob, Scott, and Lester entered the anteroom from the side entrance hallway.

"Is Mars here?" asked Dwane walking directly to his boss.

"I just walked in myself. He may be in the garage," Conover answered.

"Have you talked to him about this?"

"I have. I understand you verified what we're up against. Good work."

"We? I'm glad you put it that way," said Dwane with some satisfaction. "We want in on this. There's no way Mars can get enough people together to handle it."

"Handle what?" asked Bob Garnett, looking from one to the other. "And there you go again with this 'we' shit."

Conover started to speak, but Scott Roy broke in first. Charlie eyed the conversation from his office doorway.

"Look, we could block every exit and entrance to that place with our trucks," suggested Scott.

"As a matter of fact, I had kind of the same notion," Conover nodded. "But you've got to understand, this is not my party. It's up to Mars. In the meantime, get me a number of how many would want to volunteer for something like this."

"Well, we've got four trucks standing right here," said Dwane, glancing around.

"For Christ's sake! There's probably seventy-five, eighty cars in that parking lot. That's got to mean at least a hundred-fifty people in there," argued Bob.

"You're kidding. That many?" breathed Lester Hartwell.

Even Conover looked a little surprised, but only for a moment. "Well, I can tell you this much. Mars is thinking about using a couple trucks to block the highway north and south of the main entrance. But that's not going to be enough. There's more ways than that in and out of there and if we block the main road, we'll snarl up what traffic there is from moving anywhere."

"That's why we've got to get in closer and block everything. Hell, keep 'em on the property," Dwane insisted.

"And maybe just get a piece of the action?" Scott asked.

Dwane shot him a quick disapproving glance.

Conover surveyed the group and raised his hand. "Alright! Listen up. This could be, hell, this is going to be dangerous. We don't know what to expect. We don't know how many may just sit tight, or how many will try to get out anyway they can. The point is, I don't want anybody involved here that has any qualms about it in any way. And frankly, everybody ought to have some."

Dwane gave the group only a second or two before pressing his question. "Well, have we got at least these four trucks, or what?"

Bringing up the rear of the group that had come in from the side door were Gale Mooney and Jason Peck, Roland Powell and Richard Wright. Until now, no one, not even Richard had spoken, being too interested in the revelations spilling forth from the others who were presently casting questioning looks at those silent four.

"Hell, at least I got nothing to worry about. I ride with the 'Great Destroyer' here," Richard announced, clasping his arm around his driver. Roland glared back, perhaps more put out at Richard's alluding to his badly scarred driving record in front of The Boss than anything else.

Seemingly satisfied, the eyes shifted to Gale and Jason.

Gale was also looking at Jason who was still smiling at Richard's remark. "I don't know. It sure goes against my better . . ."

"Oh, come on!" Jason exclaimed as he realized his new north country hero was about to turn it down. "Man, no matter what goes on it's gotta be safer than where I come from!" Jason Peck probably never realized the precise moment during which he became 'one of the guys'.

Gale paused another moment, then nodded once. "Count us in."

"Alright!" applauded Dwane.

"You understand that if Mars agrees it will only be to use the trucks as road blocks. Nothing else. I'm sure he'll insist, as will I, that once in place, you leave the truck and get back to be picked up, or if that's not possible, get on the floor. You've got to assume these people are armed."

"Yeah, sure. Agreed," said Dwane.

Conover studied the faces before him. "Well, we haven't much time, so get me a count of the rest of the men that are here. And make sure you tell them what's involved. I'll get with Mars in a minute and I imagine there will be a quick meeting in the garage."

Most of the men moved toward the side door through a moment of silent contemplation just prior to the surge of conversation that would ensue at any moment. Scott and Lester, then Dwane, stepped to the coffee machine.

Conover turned to see Charlie standing in his office doorway, a strange look on his face. "Charlie, did you . . ."

Charlie disappeared into his office as Chief Mars, followed by Sergeant Budner, stamped their way through the outside door leaving more fresh snow on the concrete floor. Conover moved to face Mars. Charlie reappeared in his doorway.

"Chief, I strongly suggest you include some of my men in this thing. I've already spoken to a few and . . ."

"Goddammit, Walt," Mars interrupted, "I told you before this is police business, I can't openly endanger private citizens. What I need is your departments' cooperation like we talked about."

"Justin, I know it's police business," Conover stated, feeling a little awkward using Mars' first name, but doing it to compliment Mars' use of his. "And you've got our cooperation. But there's more ways out of that place than you realize, so it's just going to take more trucks in a little closer. Hell, there's still some traffic out and about and I don't imagine you want any of these types getting hold of any private transportation and maybe the people in it." Conover had calculated the last remark to soften Mars and the Chief's wordless exhale of breath confirmed it's effectiveness. Over that brief second Conover wondered why he seemed to be pushing so. After all, these were not soldiers under his command and perhaps he shouldn't be so quick to allow them into harms way.

"I know. I know," said Mars. "I've been thinking about it on the way over here. There's no way to do this by the book. I just hope it doesn't blow up in our face."

"How much help have you got outside of a few men from the sheriff's department? Anything new with the State Police?"

"No. I may have a couple guys coming in from the north, but basically we're it," Mars admitted.

"Well, like I said, what we're talking about is using the plows to blockade all the ways in and out. Hell, there must be at least six or eight which they've probably got plowed and ready," Conover explained.

"Alright," Mars said finally, shaking his head. "Let them go ahead if they want to. But, I'll coordinate it. Make damn sure of that!" he added emphatically.

Conover nodded. A few yards away next to the coffee machine Scott mouthed a forceful, but soundless "Yes" with clenched fist. Charlie retreated to his office again. Dwane appeared beside Conover.

"What about that Lear jet?" he asked. "Did you check it out?" Mars glared at Dwane. "And to think, without you we probably wouldn't have known anything about this at all. I don't know whether to thank you or kick your ass."

"Want to flip a coin?" Dwane chided.

"The plane," Mars said simply instead of answering the question. "Three men, none over fifty, so that lets out Valachi, not that it makes any difference now because we know damn well he's probably here. Anyway, they were on their way up to Waterville to cover that big ski thing this weekend. Media types . . . the Lear is leased by Cable Sports Productions. It all checks. Still . . . I don't know. I get the feeling they tossed some money around. The plow operators . . . I talked to one of them on the phone. He didn't have much of anything to say which is rather strange considering . . . Hell, it doesn't matter now. That plane isn't going anywhere soon and I can't afford to keep an officer over there just hanging around."

Dwane nodded. "Like you say, it probably doesn't . . ."

"Walt," said Mars, dismissing Dwane. "I've got to get with my officers in the garage and then I'll have a few words for your people, so have them in there in say . . . fifteen minutes."

Several Public Works men, including Custer and Bill Board gathered on the north side of the building near an outside floodlight. The value of a more or less private meeting place seemed to outweigh the wind and snow. Scott and Lester came out of the side door and joined the group.

"Leave my truck. Get on the floor," Scott repeated in disgust. "Who the hell does he think he's kidding?"

"I'll tell you one thing," offered Gale. "I don't mind going in on this, but I'm not doing it unarmed. I'm going to take a quick run home and pick up a gun. I don't intend to be a sitting duck behind the wheel of that truck."

"Wait a minute." interjected Bob. "Just because Dwane is carrying a gun doesn't mean that everybody should. It could be just asking for trouble and I never figured you for that."

"I'm not asking for anything," replied Gale quickly, a slight edge to his voice. "But it's stupid not to be prepared. And I do happen to know something about guns as you well know."

"Fine. Okay. Fine," Bob shrugged.

Jason turned to Gale. "Well, don't forget me. We got plenty of guns in New York, at least most of the people in my old neighborhood do . . ."

Gale didn't look directly at Jason, thinking that he had no intention of supplying Jason with a gun. Dwane came out the side door and moved the few steps to the group. Jason's next comment was towards him.

"And I'll bet you I know somebody else that's at this here meeting that nobody's mentioned. Old man Denecy! Lorenzo Denecy. I bumped into him once coming out of some restaurant over in Queens. Right into him. Almost knocked him down. I thought his motherfuckin bodyguard was going to blow me away. Man, that old guy's got eyes that could kill a rat."

"I'll bet he is here," agreed Dwane.

"You find out anything else in there?" asked Bill Board.

"Mars is going to go along with us blocking all the exits. Hell, it's a natural. But anything more we do we're on our own."

"Anything more?" Bob looked at Dwane, his tone suspicious. "What do you mean, anything more?"

"How the hell do I know? What I do know is we got some of the worst scum in the country right here in town, and if I get a chance to do something more than block off some driveway, I'm probably going to do it."

"Like probably get your ass shot off," warned Bob.

"Well, I'm just not going to sit around. Look, there's nobody here that would blame you if you don't want any part in this. Am I right?" asked Dwane looking at the other faces around him.

"Hey, no way you get rid of me, fellah," Bob answered angrily before anyone else could say anything. "Who the hell's going to keep an eye on you if I'm not there?"

"I understand you're carrying a gun?" Scott asked Dwane.

Dwane scowled at Bob. Scott took that as a 'yes'.

"Son-of-a-bitch! I guess I better run home myself," said Custer.

Bill Board looked at his wingman with amazement. "You? You are kidding, of course. I never heard you mention anything about guns in my life. You'll probably shoot me and then I'll have to wring your fucking little neck."

"Don't worry about it," assured Custer. "It's like Gale said."

"I'll tell you, anybody that figures on carrying anything better keep it out of sight of the police unless you have to use it. Mars will go bullshit," said Dwane.

Gale Mooney made a move to leave. "Well, I'm not standing out here freezing to death any more. Jason, you stay here. Custer, we live pretty close to each other. I'll drop you off, then pick you up on the way back. It'll save time."

Wordlessly, Custer nodded and headed off with Gale toward the line of parked private vehicles. Jason glanced after them, but said nothing.

"Hey, what about us?" Richard asked, seemingly of everyone that was left. Then he turned to Roland. "You own a gun, Duck?"

"Yeah, a twenty-two, but I ain't bringing that."

"Hell, the only weapon you guys ever needed was your truck. Christ, I pity the poor bastards," said Bob.

"Well?" Richard asked Roland.

"Well what?" said Roland, obviously getting quite annoyed. "You said it yourself inside, right in front of Walt, I might add. I'm always fucking up anyway. Let's see what I can do if I really put my mind to it."

"Mister man, we are going to be dangerous," Richard stated flatly, looking at Scott. "What about you? You getting a gun?"

"I don't know . . ." Scott replied thoughtfully as he turned to Dwane. "You tell Mars about all those snow machines that were delivered up there?"

"He knows," replied Dwane.

"You know, that's where the action might be. Maybe I'll wait to see how Mars is going to play this," said Scott.

"What are you talking about?" asked Jason. "What snow machines is that?"

"A whole truck load of them went up there last week." Explained Scott. And on a night like this they may be the only way out of there. Those guys aren't stupid. They're probably got some drivers and with all those rental cars over there they've got to have some other transportation around here somewhere. When they find out the cops are sitting on their doorstep you could see those machines headed for the lake and from there they can go anyplace. The only thing that might stop them is another snow machine."

Jason seemed extremely interested in this last piece of news. "No shit! Maybe Gale would want a piece of that instead. But man, I can't believe some of those guys even riding on a snow machine."

"Some of them will, that's for sure," insisted Dwane. "They're not sitting there for nothing. Hell, they may already be staked out by the ones that don't want to be caught there under any circumstances . . . Look, I've got to get with the guys in the garage." Dwane headed back for the side door.

"Scott, you thinking of going out there with yours?" Bob asked before following Dwane.

" . . . I don't know. It might be a good way to get killed," Scott said seriously. "Hell, maybe we ought to sneak Lester into the main building so he could let a few of his farts. That ought to wipe them out," he added in a lighter vein.

There were a few chuckles, including Lester's. Scott suddenly turned and headed around to the rear of the building. The remainder of the group was about to disperse when truck forty-one, followed closely by number nineteen, pulled in and stopped next to the side door. The group moved to confer with the new arrivals.

# chapter 12

From the auditorium stage Carl Philip Endicott surveyed the scene slightly below him. The scattered tables appeared arranged for a dinner show where an audience might be entertained while consuming the evening meal. Endicott studied the faces of those seated and the few in the process of settling into place. It appeared the mood of some was that expecting a curious interlude, maybe even to be amused. Occasionally, he detected a smiling glance or derisive look in his direction after sharing some private remark. A joke perhaps, at his expense? Endicott met these fleeting confrontations with calm attention and a visual hint of his own subtle understanding. They were nervous, he thought. Good.

Three smartly clad waiters stepped smartly among the tables delivering drinks and after dinner refreshments to the privileged two-thirds of the total Hallingford attendees. Endicott rested his elbows atop the large leather case planted squarely on the table before him. The case was drawing nearly as many questioning looks as Endicott himself. Was it a prop of some kind? A display? What?

Everyone was seated now. As eyes occasionally betrayed their impatience at waiting, Endicott's countenance remained unchanged. A successful capacity for swimming against the social rule was never portrayed more strikingly than it was in this room, he thought. For a moment he marveled at his power in getting them here, for each had only a small piece of the puzzle and that, they didn't understand. True, they would not have responded to a simple order to come. That orchestration had been much more complex. But part of the decision of each had centered on him and the things they didn't know. To varying degrees, each knew that Carl Endicott would somehow define this night.

Lorenzo Denecy sat quietly watching Endicott. Stephen Langella was by his side, a pen and small pad of paper on the table in front of him ready to record whatever was required. To the other side of Lorenzo, Frank imparted a few hushed statements to Vincent who leaned close to hear.

A few tables away Bradford Nevis cast a quick disdainful look in Endicott's direction before saying something to one of the Los Angeles group next door who smiled and nodded. Beside Nevis, Stanley Fagner looked blankly around the room. John Elvio toyed with his cigarette lighter on the table.

A late arrival in the person of Nino Valachi gathered some attention as he was assisted to a rear table by his two companions.

Delores Stang exhibited an icy cold presence as she sat motionless at her table between her bodyguards. The younger woman was not to be seen. Finally, they simply waited, the sporadic conversation filtering into silence, even the displeasure gone from their eyes as if they realized that Endicott would continue to feed off it and punish them as long as it was there for him to see.

"Ladies . . . gentlemen," Endicott began slowly, straightening behind the case. "My name is Carl Philip Endicott. Some of you know me only by way of my activity in the world of men's fashion, my chain of stores and perhaps a rumor or two relating to something more. Others among you may feel you possess more inside information. And perhaps you do. But I will not bore you with an autobiographical sketch. I will, however, illustrate certain points that I am sure will not bore you and that may indicate precisely how I have contributed to your financial wellbeing over the years and may indeed have touched your very lives."

Endicott smiled slightly. A few people in the audience shifted uneasily in their chairs. Endicott leaned forward, his arms resting on the case once more, his face becoming hard.

"Miguel Navious!" he said with some force. "A name I am sure some of you have heard. A certain Latin-American connection who has coordinated many profitable business dealings originating to our south. A man who has accurately foretold the actions and reactions of more than one South American government. A man without whom little is accomplished in this region. For those of you who may be interested . . . Miguel Navious belongs to me!"

There was a flutter of conversation within the group as reactions ranged from shock to intense interest. Endicott did not wait for silence before he continued.

"A few more names if you please. John Albert Rainie; southwestern United States, Roman Dirsch; eastern Europe, Christos Mottala; the Bahamas, Kendal Grabonski; Europe again. And how about the names of Hebert

Lieubman, Frederick Devillefane, Ernest Jargerman, Hans Weider, Lawrence Spaulding . . ."

Endicott stopped to allow these names to sink into the consciousness of the group and their animated reaction to choose its initial course. One of the few not so disposed was Lorenzo Denecy who continued to watch Endicott intently.

"You own these people too, Endicott?" came a challenging voice buried somewhere in the group.

"Hell sir, I am these people!" Endicott answered directly.

The uproar rose in crescendo. Endicott raised his hand for quiet, but continued immediately.

"It is always helpful to have friends in the banking community. However, it is sometimes more expedient to have a controlling interest. Southwest Mutual Trust, Atlantic Citizens Deposit, World Corporation International . . ."

Endicott reached into his pocket and withdrew a sheet of paper which he held up to be seen. "I have here a list of bank accounts numbers that should be of interest to some of you. Those of the Swiss variety seem to out number the others. When I am finished it will be available for any of you to inspect."

This time Endicott leaned on the case and waited for the undivided attention of his audience. Finally, he had it.

"My purpose here has been to illustrate that we are partners, you and I. One might even say that I work for you. Or rather we work for each other."

Endicott smiled once again. There was silence.

"However, my primary objective tonight is to tell you all that there is a new game in town. And it is one that I am sure you will agree we had best get involved in. Ladies and gentlemen, I speak of the modern day phenomenon of International Terrorism."

\*     \*     \*

At the city garage, Public Works personnel and uniformed police were gathered around the area outside the tool crib. Although the two groups had, to some degree, segregated themselves from each other, a few interdepartmental conversations proved that indeed both were employees of the same city and some cross-over acquaintances did exist. Beside and beyond the Michigan payloader, pulled close into the area, stretched a group of a half dozen police cruisers ending at the big equipment door to the rear of the building. Along the east wall still resided the now silent salt trucks as well as the backhoes and assorted other pieces that normally would not see service this time of year. Through the high windows could be seen the yellow flashing lights of the idling plow trucks, now all returned more or less to their respective births around the building.

Chief Mars turned away from three of his higher ranking officers and stepped atop the payloader bucket to get a better look at those around him. "Alright, listen up. This is going to be a short as I can make it," pronounced Mars. Conversation subsided over the next few seconds as the Chief gathered the attention of everyone.

"At the Hallingford Farm complex there is going on right now a meeting of what may be every notable Mafia-organized crime head in the country. There may well be a hundred and fifty or more of these people and their associates in attendance."

A swell of conversation echoed in the big room as most of the Public Works people were unaware of the real scope of the gathering.

"Quiet down," Mars ordered. "There is at this meeting one Bradford Nevis, erstwhile union leader. You may have heard of him. Anyhow, there is, as of this afternoon, a federal warrant out on this guy. And we want him. It is also likely that at least a couple, maybe up to four other wanted individuals are there as well . . ."

"Motherfucker!" came an explanation from deep in the body of the Public Works, which drew instant laughter from the rest of the group. The more disciplined police contingent just eyed each other and shook their heads.

*     *     *

In the front office at Hallingford Maurice Ritacco sat at Niles' desk looking at the winking lights of the radio frequency scanner in front of him. Behind the bar, Lenny selected a can of soft drink from the cooler and snapped the lid. Douglas Niles opened the hall door and walked into the room.

"Anything?" Niles asked, looking at the scanner.

Maurice shook his head. "I set this up just to make sure the other one was working right. Nothing. It's just like they're off the air. It doesn't make any sense. Once in a while you get something from the State Police, but its way south of here and it's mostly storm related. The reception's pretty lousy."

Niles thought a moment, then walked to the bar. "Len, take the jeep and go out and look around. Drive into town and see what's going on. Keep your eyes open for anything unusual. I've got a bad feeling about this."

A hundred yards away in the auditorium Carl Endicott continued to hold the rapt attention of his audience.

"So-called political acts of terrorism are currently taking place around the world. England, Europe, the Middle East, the Far East. Aircraft highjackings, kidnappings, bombings, etcetera. It's all around us and its going to continue. This government, any government, can be paralyzed by unpredictable acts of war perpetrated by various organizations for a host of reasons."

"So far we have only seen the tip of the iceberg and although political terrorism has been going on in this country for many years, the United States has until now escaped the large scale single catastrophic act of terrorism involving great loss of life."

Endicott paused to assess the effect of his words. Certainly his audience didn't know where he was going, but they remained attentive, curious.

"I will suggest to you now," he continued with emphasis. "That is where we come in."

\*    \*    \*

"Can the commentary and listen!" barked Chief Mars. "If we're going to get this done we need everyone's cooperation. It appears this storm is even worse to the south and the east. Most highways have drifted in the high winds and are impassable. Therefore, we can expect little, if any, outside help from the State Police. We can't just sit on this thing because despite the weather these people may leave anytime. I am led to believe their vehicles in the back parking lot are being kept free of snow and all the interior roads may well be plowed."

"In all likelihood they are monitoring police radio frequencies, so we are using the Public Works frequency and I will ask Colonel Conover to direct that no unnecessary chatter be aired for the duration."

"We haven't got time to plan this operation in detail, but roughly, this is how it's going to go. At a . . ."

At that moment the loudspeaker on the wall above the group sputtered to life and an excited voice came over the air. *Chief! Chief! Dickerson just called from the Whalen house just down the road from Hallingford. He says a vehicle just came out of the main drive and it's headed this way. It's a red jeep and it's got a radio antenna on it. One occupant.*

"Damn" roared Mars. Then turning to an officer close by, "Tell him we receive."

The officer stepped quickly to the nearest police cruiser and grabbed the radio mike. Conversations again commenced amongst the group.

"Quiet! Knock it off!" barked Walt Conover from his place beside his men.

There was silence.

"Greg! You and Kelly," Mars snapped after locating his sergeant below him. "Take the white Ford unmarked that I came over in. It's parked out front. Get up to the Prescott and Main intersection before this guy comes through. Hang back, and when you see him coming, take him out! Ram him! Don't kill him, but I don't want him to get a chance to use that radio!"

Greg Budner, standing a few feet away, looked amazed for only a moment before lunging toward the anteroom door. The officer in the police cruiser jumped out and scampered after him. Public Works personnel and police alike looked at each other with surprise at the realization of just how far Mars was sticking his neck out. A new tension permeated the garage.

"Alright! Listen up here. We're not through yet," said Mars, gathering their attention once more.

*     *     *

Endicott scanned the faces before him, attempting to personalize his dialogue to each and every listener. "Law enforcement in this country on all levels realizes only too well that they will be unable to effectively discourage the terrorist activity they know is coming. And this at a time when public sentiment is dictating a strong law and order stance. I certainly don't have to tell you that the federal judiciary is actively pursuing cases and attempting to curb activities that would have been ignored only a few years ago."

Endicott paused briefly, wondering if anyone in his audience was getting close to what he was driving at.

"Shortly before the outbreak of World War II a direct offer was made to President Franklin Roosevelt by the Cosa Nostra to go into Germany, secure the person of Adolph Hitler, bring him to this country and sit him down in the Oval Office where the facts of life could be explained to him."

A voice from a rear table broke the momentary silence.

"That is true! That is true!" stated Nino Valachi, waving a hand in the air.

Many of the group turned to glance at the old man. Lorenzo Denecy leaned forward in his chair, not taking his eyes from Endicott.

"That offer, though many felt it could have been accomplished, was refused. Twenty years later the same basic offer was made regarding Fidel Castro. It too, was refused. I suggest to you that today we are presented with a golden opportunity, and for the sake of our own future preservation, we dare not let it slip by."

*   *   *

On Prescott Avenue the white unmarked police vehicle slid to a stop in the snow rutted street about a hundred and fifty feet from it's intersection with Main Street.

"This looks about right," said Budner. "We'll be able to see him coming through the gap between those houses there," he indicated off the right quarter of the car.

"I hope he hasn't gotten by us," said Kelly. "Maybe he took Lane Road."

"I don't think so," said Budner, his eyes trained to the north. Make sure your shoulder harness is tight. I'm going to try to nail him in the front wheel area. I hope we don't disable this thing. We're going to need it."

"Boy, the Chief is taking a hell of a chance. This ain't exactly procedure . . ." Kelly paused a moment in thought. "What are we supposed to do with this guy anyway?"

"Well, let's see what he looks like after we get through with him. I don't want to hurt him bad, but I do intend to bang him up enough to keep his hands off the radio until we can get to him. No doubt he'll be feeling rather poorly . . . after his accident. So, we'll probably have to put him on ice in an effort to facilitate his full recovery." Budner smiled at his own choice of words.

"Which means that our ass will be hanging out about as far as the Chief's," observed Kelly.

"The way Mars just came out with it in front of everybody I get the idea this will just be a minor detail by tomorrow morning."

"I wonder if that's good or bad," mused Kelly.

"Where the hell is that guy?" asked Budner impatiently. "Jesus, I hope to . . ."

"Here come some lights now," Kelly said excitedly, his angle between the houses a little better than Budner's. "Wait till he goes under that street light . . . Yeah, that's him! Or some other poor bastard in a red jeep."

Budner shut the parking lights off and inched the car forward. As the jeep approached the intersection, the police vehicle started to roll, it's rear tires spinning as it gathered speed.

As the jeep moved into the intersection, the white Ford shot out of Prescott Avenue. Obviously intent on navigating the snow covered street, the jeep driver didn't see the approaching car until the last moment. The jeep tried to swerve, but the heavy chrome front bumper of the older car caught the jeep just behind the front wheel in a resounding crash. The Ford stopped almost dead in it's tracks. The jeep was propelled sideways across the road, coming to a stop against the snowbank.

The lone streetlight at the intersection bathed the area in a soft glow through the swirling snow. Budner and Kelly were out of their car and running toward the jeep almost before it came to a stop. The damaged sheet metal of the driver's door snapped and complained as Budner wrenched it open. Half conscious, Lenny tried to step out of the vehicle, but started to fall to the ground. A trickle of blood ran down his cheek from a nasty looking bruise on his forehead. Budner grabbed him by the front of the coat and stood him up against the jeep.

"You all right?" Budner yelled close to Lenny's face.

Lenny mumbled something as he tried to focus his eyes on the sergeant.

"Yeah?" said Budner. "Well, you should have been more careful. You're under arrest!"

*     *     *

At the city garage Chief Mars steadied himself on his perch atop the payloader bucket. "The Colonel tells me we have some Public Works volunteers here that will be placing their trucks to block all driveways and roads in and out of Hallingford . . . Is that right? Let me see some hands?"

Several Public Works personnel raised their hands immediately. Mars glanced quickly to where Conover was standing. He was not there. Mars looked about the room for the P.W. Director as the anteroom door opened and Simpson Dunbar, Eaves, Gale, Custer, Pat and Dean Smith entered the room and squeezed into the crowd. Looks and nods were exchanged between those present and those just arriving. The newcomers got the word quickly and raised their hands. Not seeing Conover anywhere, Mars became suddenly aware that every Public Works employee present had raised his hand.

"We . . . we can't use all of you, so you'll have to decide . . ." Mars shook his head in frustration. "I want to emphasis once again that Public Works participation ends with the placement of these blockades. When that is completed I want you guys on the floor of your trucks or better yet well back of the perimeter that we will set up."

"Units from this police department, along with those of the sheriff's office and a few officers from the surrounding communities, will place themselves at all exits from the property to stop any vehicles that may try to break through. And again, I remind all law enforcement personnel that there will be no discharge of firearms unless you yourselves are in imminent danger of being fired upon. Do I make myself clear?"

Mars paused to take a breath and clear his throat. There appeared to be no lack of understanding among the officers concerning Mars' order.

"Okay, when it is acknowledged by me that all units are in place, I want two Public Works vehicles, the bigger the better, to block the main highway to the north and south. At this point they're going to know what's up, but before they can organize any meaningful resistance, if that be their intention, a few officers, led by myself, will attempt to penetrate the complex to locate Bradford Nevis in particular."

Conversation had once again started among Public Works crews. Some were now moving about, presumably involved in some last minute preparations. Charlie Hayward stood well to the rear of the group, his expression betraying disbelief at what was going on.

Mars turned to an officer below him on his left. "Get Budner on the radio. Find out what happened to that jeep."

Then, squatting down to his right, Mars spoke to his police captain in a more or less private venue. "Where's Conover? Did you see him leave?"

At a young looking fifty-eight, Dan Warner had been one of the few senior men who had stayed when Mars had arrived. Easy going, indeed totally unflappable, Warner was a fine officer and his continued presence, along with his steady one-speed approach to any given situation had been appreciated by Mars. An occasional drawback, however, was Warner's somewhat different sense of humor which could pop up at the most inopportune moments.

"Yeah, as a matter of fact, I did see him headed for the back door a couple minutes ago," answered Warner.

"Goddamn!" said Mars with feeling. "Ten to one his car is gone. I've got an idea he's up to something. I don't' know what in hell it is with these public works guys. Christ, if we don't keep a tight rein on these people this could end up being a friggin circus."

"By the way," Warner offered. "Did you know that one of them—I don't know who—holds the National Northeastern Driver's point record for a single accident by colliding with two busses and a train? Couple years ago as I recall. I think you were at a police chiefs' convention."

Mars looked strangely at his captain for a second.

"I suppose you think that's funny," Mars said, his eyes mere slits.

"Well, I just thought it might . . ." Warner let his voice trail off, but allowed the hint of a smile to remain as he looked at his chief.

*     *     *

Several of those seated in the auditorium at Hallingford Farm were showing signs of restlessness. Endicott's delivery had speeded up noticeably and his voice exhibited something of a sharp edge to it.

"We are, all of us here tonight, representative of a viable third party, strategically located between law enforcement and the general public on one hand, and the various entities of international terrorism on the other. We are in a perfect position to resurrect a variation of the old protection game to a level never envisioned before. If we do nothing, the advent of increased terrorist activity in this country will bring forth such a ground swell of anti-crime sentiment that law enforcement will stamp you out one by one."

Conversation swelled within the group. Endicott pushed on.

"Unable to deal effectively with the random terrorist group that will continue to strike without warning, you, and the distasteful element you represent will present a much easier target and your hides will be nailed up in the halls of justice just to prove that law enforcement is indeed doing something!"

Several in the Miami, Chicago, and west coast groups rose to openly challenge Endicott. John Elvio started to rise, but was pulled back into his seat by Nevis. Vincent Denecy leaned over and said something to his grandfather who did not answer, but kept his eyes on Endicott. Frank Denecy smiled and calmly lit a cigarette. Looking somewhat worried for the first time, Stephen Langella glanced from Lorenzo back to Frank.

"However!" Endicott said loudly above the commotion. The conversation faded somewhat at that single spoken word. "What if, I say, what if it became known that organized crime, or more specifically that shadowy element referred to as the 'underworld', was taking steps of it's own to deal with such terrorists themselves, totally unsolicited, unrequested, and unasked for? I suggest a formed and named entity created, controlled, and operated by us that would effect startling results that any government law enforcement body would be unable to duplicate, limited as they are by the very laws they purport to uphold, and the political considerations they must keep in mind as a result of any action they take. I suggest to you that the media would take to the concept like a rat to cheese. They would, unwittingly at first, and uncaringly at last, become our press agent. Hell, they knowingly encourage terrorism itself by their intense coverage of these acts and their creation of a worldwide platform from which these political lunatics can extol their demands and ideas. The international media will certainly not object to relating our anti-terrorist exploits in the cloak of a Black Knight, if you will, soiled by past deeds, but unable to tolerate the wanton acts of these modern day madmen."

During Endicott's dialogue, those standing had slowly taken their seats, seemingly captivated by their speaker's enthusiastic delivery, if not the content of his theories. After a brief silence, laughter was heard from a couple locations in the group.

"All due respect, Endicott, but you got to be nuts," came a remark from the audience.

"Am I?" asked Endicott, his eyes wide. "Think about it!"

"Hey Endicott, I don't even own a white hat," someone said.

"Sorry, I left my cape at home," from someone else.

There was more laughter. Even Endicott smiled. Lorenzo Denecy leaned back in his chair. There was a sparkle in his eyes also, however, it could not be perceived to result from something he thought was funny. Most of the audience settled quickly after the momentary release, their mood thoughtful. Endicott continued.

"A successful action along these lines would take the pressure off the organized crime structure that indeed the public has come to accept as part of the American scene. Law enforcement itself would welcome the respite. After all, their actions reflect what the public wants and public priorities are often dictated by a media led politic, or sometimes the other way around. At any rate, it's a vicious and unwieldy circle simply begging for some disciplined outside direction. I suggest we give it some."

"Just how do you suggest this so-called anti-terrorist force gets off the ground?" asked Bradford Nevis. "I don't happen to know any international terrorists at the present time."

John Elvio and Stanley Fagner chuckled at their boss' remark.

Endicott smiled. "I thought you'd never ask. The international terrorist network is complex, but at the same time simple. In this country many splinter groups are controlled and funded by either the Soviet KGB or their surrogate, the Cuban Intelligence Service, the DGI. The Irish, the Italian, and particularly the Palestinian and Moslem groups have further variations, but we need not go into details now. What I will tell you is that organized crime factions around the world at this time possess the capability of formulating the finest global counter-intelligence network in existence, far superior to that of any single government including our own."

\* \* \*

Maurice Ritacco sat at his desk in the small office a microphone in his hand. Amidst an assortment of clutter in front of him, a small red light winked atop a small radio transmitter.

"Base to Len . . . Come in Lenny . . . ," repeated Maurice for the dozenth time.

After another couple seconds of motionless waiting, Maurice disgustedly tossed the mike on the desk, snapped up the phone receiver and pressed a single button.

"I can't raise him. Maybe it's the weather, but hell, he should have been back by now . . . Yeah."

Maurice dropped the phone back in place. A moment later, Niles strode into the room.

"Issue three of the handheld units to the best of our crew out back," Niles ordered. "I want them to cover the east, north, and south side areas of the property. You keep in touch with them here. I want to know about anything that's going on."

"I don't get it," said Maurice, standing. "So what if the cops busted in here. We haven't done . . ."

"You ever read the statutes on harboring wanted criminals? We run this place. We're the proprietors of record, at least for the moment. We can't very well pretend we don't know who these people are, and I'll tell you, Bradford Nevis isn't the only one here currently wanted by the authorities. Niles turned for the door, then looked back at Maurice.

"I'm going to check the Bronco myself. I think we're screwed."

\* \* \*

The restless energy and tension of those assembled in the city garage strained against the verbal restraints of authority. Even the police contingent had slipped noticeably out of their more disciplined format. Mars, himself, had relinquished his perch on the payloader, and for the moment, occupied the front seat of the nearest police cruiser. With the driver's door still open, Mars had one foot on the concrete as if that retained some semblance of control while he held the radio mike close to his mouth.

Even Charlie Hayward had wandered into the mix and seemed ready to exercise what control he could to calm the raucous atmosphere. From the police standpoint Captain Warner was about to do the same.

Mars moved quickly out of the cruiser and reclaimed his spot atop the payloader bucket, then knelt as Warner, and another officer, Lieutenant Titus approached.

"Just talked to Greg," said Mars. "Their radio went out when they smacked the jeep. They got the driver at the station. He hasn't said much, but Greg thinks he was supposed to look around then check in with Hallingford by radio. We've got to move now!"

Mars stood immediately leaving his two officers to look at each other. Commotion in the big room had quieted somewhat at Mars' reappearance, and as he turned to them, silence came quickly as they could sense things were coming to a head.

"All right! Let's have your attention!" Mars shouted. "If we wait any longer they may get the idea somebody's coming. So we've got to move things up a bit. We'll coordinate the rest of this on the way. Let's roll!"

The men of the Public Works reacted as though they had been holding their breath. "Let's get 'em," someone yelled amidst other more creative calls to arms as they brushed past the slower reacting police and out of the garage in all directions. Mars and his two officers looked at each other in amazement.

"Jesus Christ!" Mars uttered to no one in particular.

The big rear equipment door was still clanking upward as the first cruiser escaped underneath with the others on its heels. The twin front doors were also rising as the Michigan payloader and the road grader fired up in the cramped area. The loudspeaker on the wall crackled past the sounds of anxious engines with various bits of clipped transmissions.

Finally, Chief Mars jumped down from the payloader bucket, its operator causing it to jerk slightly under his feet as though the iron beast was flicking off a fly. Mars' expression was still one of reluctant comprehension as he moved away from the big machine.

"Chief! Justin!" Captain Warner shouted from the driver's window of the nearest cruiser. "We'd better get going if we don't want to get there last!"

Outside, the wind and snow served to heighten the excitement of P.W. crews climbing into their trucks with style and flourish approaching that exhibited by those ascending into bomber aircraft during World War II. The yellow and blue flashing lights signaled a celebration of combined purpose as the property flushed its curious mix of vehicles into the street. As the strange caravan began to rumble away, the heavy steady beat of classic rock, certainly from Custer's speaker, pierced the night air. A lone private vehicle coming from the opposite direction was forced to climb into the fresh windrow in order to avoid the procession.

# chapter 13

By sharp contrast was nature's peaceful scene along the woods road just north of the Hallingford complex. Several unplowed inches of deepening new snow across it's narrow breadth remained unmarked by man, his machines, or even small animals. All that was about to change, however, because approaching were the two small parking eyes of Walt Conover's Buick.

With the sound of snow crunching beneath its wheels the car came to a stop, it's front bumper bobbing slightly into the white, leaving a couple shovel fulls resting up against the grill.

Conover got out of the car and looked around. After a moment, he continued down the road for several yards then stepped into the pines. A few rear lights of the complex could be seen through the trees on the far side of an open field. The sound of an engine back on the road made Conover stop.

The four wheel drive pickup, its plow down, followed the Buick's tracks to within inches of its rear end as if half expecting it to jump out of the way. Engine off, lights out, the driver opened his Hallingford lettered door and stepped out into the snow. Tossing the beam of a flashlight quickly around, the man then approached the car.

Conover's tracks gathered first attention as the light traced their direction into the darkness. Then back to the car, the light swept it's interior. The man opened the driver's door, leaned inside, and quickly noticed the two-way radio nestled under the dash of what was otherwise a nondescript automobile. A low garble of voices was coming from the radio. The man reached to fumble at the dials on the instruments face.

Conover took one last careful step and slowly planted each foot deep in the snow. Looking down at the man's back, he cocked a tight right fist close to his cheek.

"Hey," Conover shouted loudly.

The flashlight thumped to the floor of the car as the man whirled out of the car, bringing another dark object around in his right hand. Conover let go with the punch catching the man full in the face. Down he went, his head striking the door opening on the way. Something clattered on the sill, then dropped into the snow packed tire track close to the slumping figure. Shaking his stinging right hand, Conover pointed his light downward with his left and retrieved the gun.

"I must be getting old," he said to himself. "I never saw it."

Moments later, the Hallingford man was slumped in his truck, his wrists handcuffed around the window opening of the driver's side door.

Conover stood outside, breathing heavily from the exertion of getting his adversary to his present location. The man raised his head and looked at Conover.

"Who the hell are you?" he said through a rapidly swelling upper lip.

"Colonel Walt Conover, United States Marines, retired," Conover answered proudly. "I want to know where the majority of the people are located in that place right now. What's going on in there?"

"The Marines?" the man snickered as he tried to lick his damaged mouth. "Why you fuckin' old fool. You don't stand a . . ."

Wham! Conover kicked the truck door into the man's exposed wrist. Predictably, he yelled out in pain.

"I asked you a question! Shall I break your arm before or after you answer it?" Conover pulled the door back open a foot.

"Okay! Okay . . . , they're probably most of 'em in the auditorium about now. Hell, I don't know. I've been outside most of the time."

"Anybody in the Health Club Lounge end of the place?" Conover asked.

The man hesitated. Conover pulled the door open again.

"Wait! . . . I don't know. I don't think so. That ain't been used much since they had some reunion thing in there a few weeks back."

Conover held up a set of keys and shone the flashlight on them. "Which one of these fits that outside door off the patio?"

The man tried to focus on the keys. "It's that brass Yale key."

"If I'm locked out I'll have nothing better to do but come back here and pass some more time with you," Conover warned.

"They're going to kill you, old man."

Conover leaned on the door. As the man gasped, he released the pressure. At that moment a portable two-way radio came to life on the seat of the truck.

*Base to north side . . . come in north side . . . North side come in!*

Conover reached past the man, grabbed the radio, turned, and threw it against the trunk of a large pine beside the road. As an afterthought, he reached back into the truck, pulled the horn pad from the steering wheel, then tossed it over his shoulder in the direction of the radio.

"I do appreciate your concern," Conover remarked as he trudged off through the snow.

*    *    *

Carl Endicott had just talked down another series of comments and objections from his audience. The strain of the occasion was becoming evident on his face as he continued.

"I didn't come here tonight armed only with some vague vision of the future and your eventual demise! Nor did I come only to tell you of a carefully laid out course of action designed to preserve the social fabric of this country from which you grow richer every year. No, ladies and gentlemen, I knew you would want more than that and indeed I have it here to give you."

Endicott slammed his open palms atop the leather case before him. His audience quieted immediately at this reference to the strange case. Endicott continued at a more rapid pace.

"October ninth, nineteen eighty-four. A British Airways Boeing 747 took off from Heathrow Airport in London bound for New York. An hour later flight 117 was blown out of the sky over the North Atlantic. All three hundred and six people dead, more than half of them Americans. It's still making the news as you may have heard."

Endicott appeared angry now. Brian, who had been sitting at a table off to the side by himself showed some concern for his boss as he stood. No one else noticed.

"It was first thought that the IRA might have been responsible," Endicott continued. "However, within a week, British and French Intelligence determined that a claim from a group calling themselves the Sacred Army of Islam was valid. Furthermore, the names and photographs of two men, one Rufel Arlasian, and one Sticio Taumsiel were attributed as being personally responsible. The search for these men has been world wide since that time as I'm sure most of you are aware . . . Now I ask you, what do you suppose would be the reaction of the news media, and in turn everyone else, if they were presented with proof that these men had been dealt with?'

Endicott paused for a reply, piercing the gaze of everyone in the room, one by one. There was none. Carl Endicott slid his hands down each end of the case to hidden mechanisms near its bottom.

"Then I suggest we find out!" he snarled. "Ladies and gentlemen, may I present Rufel Arlasian and Sticio Taumsiel!"

Endicott lifted the case upward and threw it off to his right where it skidded across an empty table before knocking over a couple chairs. There was a collective gasp from the crowd accented by louder reactions from the few ladies present. Delores Stang started to choke, her eyes bulging. A moment later, she slumped to one side against one of her bodyguards who seemed unaware of the pressure. All over the room, the men were equally shocked and several stood up immediately for no apparent reason.

Carl Endicott placed his hands atop two clear plastic spheres, each well over a foot in diameter, which rested on a platform that had served as the bottom of the case seconds before. There, leering out at the audience through the clear material were the severed heads of Rufel Arlasian and Sticio Taumsiel. The base of each sphere, near the open neck area of the head, was clouded in a pinkish red, presumably from the blood still oozing from the fatal wound when the head was encased. Endicott's eyes were wide and flashing as he watched the reactions of the group.

"Step up and say hello. Meet the scum who said goodby to flight 117. They won't bite you now!"

With that, Endicott placed his hands behind the heads and pushed them forward off the table. The heavy spheres hit the raised stage with resounding thuds, and then again, as they bounced to the floor where they began to roll down the aisle between the tables. Several men were swearing loudly amidst more female screams as those near the path of the heads left their chairs.

At that moment the auditorium door burst open and Douglas Niles stepped into the room. Obviously surprised at the uproar going on, at first, Niles did not see the heads.

"Can I have your attention?" Niles shouted, still uncertain. "Your attention, please!"

Some of the group looked to Niles. Others were moving about, their attention still on the heads. Brian had moved to Endicott's side. Endicott yelled for order in the room. As some resemblance of control was once again established, Niles opened his mouth to speak when he first heard, then saw, a head rolling in his direction, its substantial mass pushing a chair aside as it came nearer.

Niles' face turned white. First, he looked behind him toward the door, then to Endicott on the stage, and then back to the head. No one seemed ready to explain things to him, so Niles moved to the side of the aisle where he sought shelter among the tables and chairs. The second head appeared on the floor in front of him.

"Well, what is it?" asked Endicott, angry yet concerned. "Speak up, man!"

"I . . . I'm not . . . er . . . positive . . . , but I feel I must report that our security may have been breached."

"What? What are you talking about?" demanded the man closest to Niles.

"The police may be on their way here right now! I can't say for sure, but I can't get hold of . . ."

Niles' voice was drowned out as pandemonium ensued. Brian grabbed Endicott's arm as his boss smiled faintly at the confusion before him.

"Come on, Carl! I'll get the . . . the heads and let's . . ."

"No!" Endicott interrupted. "Leave them be! This is a fitting place for them to make their debut. I'd love to be here when . . ."

Endicott's voice trailed off, but he quickly regained his direction. "Brian, get with Jeff, take only what we mentioned and go back to the plane. Leave the van. Take both snow machines, but don't be seen at the airport with them."

"What about you?"

"I'll be along," Endicott answered. "But if I'm not at the plane thirty minutes after you arrive, fire up and go. Now move! Side door," he added, pushing Brian away.

Several men had already drawn guns as they moved out of the room. Frank Denecy spoke loudly to Lorenzo, who though standing, had not made a move in any direction. Vincent and Stephen Langella waited impatiently for a decision.

"For Christ's sake, Lorenzo. Lets go!"

"Why? Why should we run? They have nothing on us," Lorenzo insisted.

"Goddamn!" Frank roared. "Do you want to spend all of next week up here explaining that? Who knows what they'll try to pull."

Endicott caught Lorenzo's eye as he moved to a door located at the back of the stage. He briefly raised a hand in parting.

"Yeah, you may be right," Lorenzo agreed finally.

The auditorium was fast emptying. Someone kicked a chair aside in their haste and it tumbled into one of the heads which rolled away on the floor, now all but forgotten.

The two bodyguards of Delores Stang bent over the older woman who was still slumped in her chair. One of them held and briskly rubbed her hand. The other removed his hand from beside her neck and stood. "She's dead," he said. "Leave her there."

In the reception area outside the auditorium people were running back and forth through the complex gathering their things and preparing to leave. Most were heading toward the long hallway leading to the garage and rear parking area. Maurice Ritacco ran up to Niles who was still pale as he came out of the auditorium.

"I've got the rest of the guys down cranking up the snow machines. Christ, I never thought we'd be . . . anyway, they'll take the ones that reserved a seat down the lake and right through town to the car dealership. It ought to be easy. On a night like this nothing else can . . . Say, what's the matter? You look . . ."

"Len's on his own, wherever he is," interrupted Niles. "Bring the Bronco around to the side and let's get the hell out of here!"

"Look, I turned the radio hand sets onto the P.A. system. One of the boys is stationed a half mile down the road. Relax, the cops ain't . . ."

"Just do it!" Niles interrupted again. "These people are worse than I ever dreamed!"

*    *    *

Walt Conover stepped up onto the outdoor pool patio and made his way past a small cabana building to a rear door of the main complex. He was breathing heavily once more from trudging up the hill through the new fallen snow. The sound of snow machine engines idling filtered over the snow laden night air. Conover turned the key in the lock, opened the door and stepped cautiously into the building.

To the right, the dimly lit indoor pool could be seen through a floor to ceiling glass partition. On the left of the wide hallway extended a translucent wall of colored glass brick. For a moment Conover stood motionless as he heard excited voices coming from the end of the hall and above. Drawing the .45 from his coat pocket, he stepped quickly back outside and closed the door.

Conover leaned flat against the building. The door opened. Two men emerged and continued out onto the patio.

"Hold it right there!" Conover ordered, moving out of the shadow cast by a distant light on an upper level.

One man stumbled and fell as he tried to turn around. The other just stopped and whirled, a gun in his hand. Conover fired. The slug from the .45 caught the man high in the shoulder sending him down beside the first man now on his hands and knees in the snow.

"Don't bother getting up," Conover ordered as he withdrew another set of handcuffs from his coat pocket and moved toward the men.

Back inside, another man stood motionless in mid-stride after hearing the shot only a few yards away. Seeing the knob turn on the outside door, he quickly ducked inside the lounge.

Conover re-entered the building, now holding the .45 waist high. A short distance down the hall, he too stopped, as more commotion sounded ahead on the stairway coming down from the second floor. Conover looked around and noticed the lounge entrance. It was unlocked. He stepped inside and closed the door.

The indirect lighting of the lounge had been left at a low level suggesting only a temporary suspension of use. The warm illumination seemed to offer a quiet, cozy, private space momentarily shielded from the outside world. Conover couldn't help but notice some of the decor of the room, still in place from that last exclusive function. A banner on the far wall welcomed The Twenty-sixth Bomber Group. World War II armed service posters, along with other period memorabilia was displayed about the room. Models of military aircraft hung from the ceiling. Conover moved closer to inspect one of these.

Only partially did he perceive movement from the corner of his eye as the figure of a man rose from behind the end of the bar swinging a long slender bottle. At the last moment Conover jerked sideways to avoid the blow. The bottle missed his head but slammed into his upper arm as he turned. The .45 was jarred from his grasp. Conover watched it slide across the polished floor, ending up beneath a pool table several yards away.

The figure flashed by him and another split second elapsed before he realized the man was after the gun. Conover lunged at the man's back, his fingers luckily catching into the suit coat collar. Both men staggered off balance into a table and chairs and finally crashed to the floor.

The younger man was on his feet first. Conover was slower to stand, but quickly put a table between he and his adversary while he shed his heavy coat and thrust it aside. For the first time the other man took stock of Conover as he moved from around the table. With tailored suit and half his opponent's years, he smiled, then finally laughed aloud.

"I don't know who you are, old man, but I don't need a gun to kill you," he said, assuming a casual karate stance.

Conover countered with a prize fighters stance and stepped into the open. The man laughed again and plunged ahead. Conover threw a left jab which missed. His right failed to block a vicious karate blow to his neck. The man's second swing parted the air above Conover's head, but the older man was going down from the first attack. Catching himself on one knee, Conover rolled to one side, backhanding a chair between he and his opponent so he might have time to regain his feet.

The man laughed again at Conover's feeble attempts. "Could have had you there," he chided. "Give you one more chance."

Now standing, Conover held his neck briefly as he circled widely toward the wall. The younger man pivoted in place waiting for the right moment. Suddenly, he lashed out again, this time hitting Conover high on the forehead. Stumbling back, Conover bounced off an old jukebox, then to the wall. The younger man stepped forward, but a flash of light hit him in the face. The jukebox had come on! Conover straightened, still with one arm across the curved top of the machine as it clicked and clacked and shook an old 78 RPM record into place. As swirling lights now pulsed a greenish glow into the room, the first strain's of the WW II vocal "Tangerine" filled the air.

The younger man had seemed fascinated for a moment by this mechanical marvel, probably never having seen one so old. Then, dismissing the interruption he mouthed an obscenity and came forward swinging a backhanded left for Conover's head. Maybe it was the better light this time, for Conover successfully ducked aside and the blow landed squarely against the heavy chrome molding that encircled the front of the jukebox. The man yelled in pain, withdrawing his hand. The record skipped and resettled, now at a higher volume. Seeing his chance, Conover started a right hand near floor level and slammed it into the man's ribcage while he was still off balance.

The younger man staggered back only a couple steps before recovering. Conover moved away from the wall and regained his stance. The man bore in, seemingly unhurt, but this time Conover's straight left took him by surprise and landed flush on his face. Instantly, the man swung a right which found nothing but air as Conover powered a straight right of his own into the man's neck, jolting him again.

The two men separated slightly, the younger one taking new stock of a job he had thought would be much easier. The flamboyant karate stance was now forgotten in favor of a basic street fighting attitude.

The music continued. Conover seemed to gain strength and resolve from it as memories of long ago flooded to the fore. A hard determined expression was evident on his bloodied face.

Down the road from Hallingford, a man on a snow machine sat hidden from the highway behind a thin line of small trees and brush along the top of the high embankment. To the south, a quarter mile of road could be traced through a long downhill curve by widely spaced streetlights, now blurred in the falling snow.

The rumble of many engines and the faint glow of approaching headlights was evident now in the distance. The man on the snow machine stood astride his mount so he might see better over the shorter brush. The crescendo of engines had quickly risen to a dull roar. Above the lengthening line of headlights, a river of yellow flashers blended artfully with the telltale blue of the police cruisers. Now closer still, a pale illumination began to flood into the hiding place of the snow machine and its driver. The man quickly pulled a portable radio unit from a large coat pocket and raised it to his mouth.

"Maurice! Hey, Maurice! Here they come! Christ, there's fucking truck loads of 'em!"

The pool lounge was fast becoming a sea of scattered and broken furniture. Both Conover and his younger foe rose from the floor a few yards apart. As his opponent stood, he grabbed a chair and swung it at Conover as he advanced. Without time to secure one of his own, Conover stepped back and concentrated on catching some leg or rung before it reached him.

With the chair locked between them, the two men stumbled into the pool table, each trying to hold or damage the other through the bars of wood. Suddenly, the chair was thrust aside and Conover was first to get a firm grip on his adversary. With his right hand clamped firmly into the man's full head of hair, and his left holding his collar, Conover gained his footing and whirled the man in a wide arc, slamming him into a wall rack holding a dozen or more pool cues.

The man bounced forward and sprawled face first on the pool table. The cues cascaded out of the rack en masse.

As though someone had literally placed a weapon in his hands, Conover gathered three of the cues to him. When the man pushed himself erect off the table and started to turn, Conover was already into his swing. Grasping the three cues as one would a baseball bat, he guided the heavy ends straight into the face and neck of his enemy. The tremendous blow sent the man skidding down the side of the table and into another group of chairs where he crashed to the floor, still and unmoving.

Totally exhausted, Conover held onto the pool table for support as the last line of the song faded away leaving the jukebox only with it's glowing colored face to penetrate the room.

Suddenly, as if it had waited its turn, a speaker over the bar came to life. Conover turned his head toward the sound. *Maurice! There's at least a dozen police cruisers! I'm running alongside of 'em in the lower pasture. Those trucks I told you about? Maurice? . . .*

It sounded like a squadron of ancient giant aircraft, the winding engines of the caravan speeding up the slight grade. On a parallel course, a hundred feet to the side past a barrier of broken stone wall and occasional tree, a lone snow machine streaked along, keeping pace with the convoy as it raced toward Hallingford. The machine's driver and a wingman in a plow truck locked glances for a moment before the driver turned away to again raise his radio to his lips.

Kneeling down, Conover swept a pool cue beneath the table. Picking up his .45, he painfully stood as the speaker came to life again. *Maurice! It's the Public Works Department! They're coming with the cops!*

Conover straightened and smiled. Walking to the door, he opened it, and went out into the hall.

*   *   *

The view through the windshield of truck twenty-two revealed a police cruiser only slightly ahead of the raised front plow. The cruiser's tail end slid from side to side precariously, but always saving itself just in time as though it knew one really false move would leave it dead meat for the city plow. The lights of Hallingford were visible ahead on the right. The sound of the truck's engine filled the cab.

"Hey, gimme a cigarette, will ya?" yelled Richard Wright.

"I thought you quit," replied Roland, fighting to keep the bouncing truck going in a straight line.

"Well, I didn't! And give me a match."

"Son-of-a-bitch!" Roland reluctantly released a hand from the wheel, grabbed a cigarette pack and matches from his breast pocket and thrust it at Richard.

"Christ! You're shaking like a leaf," observed Roland as Richard fumbled with the pack.

"So what! I like shaking like a leaf. Keeps my blood circulating," answered Richard angrily.

"Anything else you want before we plunge into the jaws of death?"

"Shut the fuck up!"

As the Hallingford Complex began to come into full view the waving beams of headlights could be seen near the rear parking lot.

Richard grabbed the mike. "They're moving out!"

An authoritative voice, presumably that of Mars, barked a reply over the air. *The first two trucks block the front drives. The second two go past, take Hampton Road and block the north access. Next two take Perimeter Lane around to the south. Anything left stay on the highway . . .*

"There's something headed for the road now," Richard yelled into the mike.

"Is that Mars in front of us?" Roland asked, downshifting.

"Yeah, I think so . . ."

"Gimme that mike." Roland was talking before he had it to his mouth. "Chief, we're right behind you. Go past the first drive and we'll get that car coming out."

*Negative! You just stay . . .*

Other transmissions began to crowd the air. "Didn't get that, Chief," smiled Roland, tossing the mike toward the dash. "You ain't my boss anyway," he added.

"That looks like one of their small pickups with a plow. Christ, he'll probably make it to the highway!" warned Richard.

"Wanna bet? Hold onto something and get ready to drop the front plow," ordered Roland.

"You're shittin me! I'm fucking doomed!"

"Hey, this is what we came for ain't it? No way they're getting . . ."

"Let's do it!" Richard yelled, getting set in his seat.

The Hallingford grounds were ablaze with lights now as several cars were on the move. The leading contingents of the police and Public Works vehicles slowed as they approached the circular main drives.

The small pickup sped toward the highway, it's plow up, obviously interested only in escape. Truck twenty-two careened into the driveway and headed straight for the smaller vehicle. The pickup tried to turn out of the drive but to no avail. The front plow of the city truck slammed to the ground a moment before the two met head on.

The big truck shuddered only slightly while the front end of the pickup and its plow all but disappeared into the curl of the big plow. As the city truck slowed to a stop, the little truck stood on its nose for a moment before it twisted awkwardly and crashed to the ground on it's side along the right door of the big truck.

Richard looked down at their prey. Swearing, along with heavy movement, could be heard from below, just as the latch popped on the passenger door and it started to open upward. Richard turned to Roland for a moment before looking back. As the head and shoulders of a man appeared beneath the door, Richard had the wing jack rising while the city truck's engine raced to supply hydraulic pressure. With the rear pivot point of the wing now five feet high, Richard released the wing which reached out and crashed down on the door, slamming it shut and driving the truck's occupant back into the cab.

Truck fifteen pulled into the north drive at high speed with plows down, throwing chunks of snow and half frozen pieces of lawn in every direction. With no obstacles in it's path the truck kept on going creating a plowed lane for the two police cruisers which followed closely behind. Finally, a hundred feet from the front of the old tavern, it ground to a halt. Immediately, Custer's door opened and the long blond haired wingman stood out of the truck, steadied by one foot on the window frame of the door. Raising a microphone to his mouth, Custer's voice echoed forth from the loudspeaker mounted atop the cab.

"This is Captain Leonard Atwell of the New Hampshire State Police! The weed of crime bears bitter fruit, you fucking cupcakes! Come out with your hands up!"

Out on the highway, other trucks rumbled past, heading for Hampton Road a couple hundred yards north and those Hallingford exists which emptied there. To the south, two more trucks, the lead one plowing, could be seen proceeding down Perimeter Road for the same purpose. In each case the trucks were followed by a police cruiser, while most of the cruisers had penetrated the front of the property.

Chief Mars approached truck fifteen, bounded over the wingpost and stepped up on the running board next to Custer.

"Give me that," he roared, grabbing the mike from Custer's hand and bringing it up to his own mouth.

Captain Warner and Lieutenant Titus arrived close behind their Chief. Warner held an extra short barreled shotgun which he thrust at Mars. Mars took the gun, but hesitated a moment before stepping down from the truck.

"Here, give 'em hell," he said putting the mike back in Custer's hand.

"But keep down! Let's go," he said to his officers, jumping to the ground.

No sooner had Mars and company gotten over the plowed windrow and into deeper snow, than a car came around the drive from behind the complex. The three raised their guns, but suddenly the vehicle veered away and struck out toward the highway over the windswept lawn.

It was never fully understood exactly how Dennis Atherton had gotten the big Michigan payloader up to Hallingford so fast. But there he was. As the car gathered speed in an attempt to make it over the plowed windrow and into the highway, the loader crashed through a group of manicured cedars and turned to face the vehicle. The eight foot wide front bucket of the loader engulfed the front end of the car as it tried to stop. Into the air the bucket rose as the loader inched forward. Three police officers had gathered as close as they dared, one of them motioned frantically for the loader to stop. At last, with the car locked in a near vertical position, the doors started to open and passengers half jumped, half fell to the ground.

Lieutenant Titus was the first to speak. "Well, I guess the front's covered."

"Some of the Public Works guys are armed, you know," Warner said to Mars.

"Don't tell me that," Mars retorted angrily. "Don't even say it out loud! Now, lets go!"

As the three turned back toward the complex shots rang out from the tavern, and a second later, a window on the second floor was broken from inside the room. Another shot, and a flash of gunfire was seen from the window. Captain Warner was first to fire twice in rapid succession, taking out most of the remaining small panes of the window.

"The front door! Now!" ordered Mars and the three ran toward the building.

At their backs, Custer's voice once again boomed into the night. "Sergeant! Get ready with those gas canisters. I ain't waiting around all night. I've got to get in there and take a shit!"

Beside truck twenty-two, a head poked up through the narrow opening in the passenger's side window of the small pickup next to the cutting edge of the city wing plow which laid across it. The head twisted around until it looked up at Richard.

"Let me out of here, you son-of-a-bitch! Get this thing off me!"

"Fuck you," said Richard Wright.

The head disappeared to be replaced a moment later by a hand holding a gun. There was not room for both the head and the gun, so without any precise direction, the gun pointed blindly at the truck.

Richard's eyes opened wide as he yelled to Roland. Bam! The bullet struck the vent window a foot from Richard's head. The truck's engine raced and the big vehicle moved forward in the snow. The wing scraped along the door, snapping off the rear view mirror just before it slipped the last few inches, pinning the arm to the side of the window frame.

The scream could have been heard anywhere on the property. And it continued with all the breath the pickup's helpless occupant could put behind it. Richard stared down at the arm as the gun fell from quivering fingers to clatter across the metal door and to the ground. The pressure against the arm continued. Even the pickup shifted slightly in the snow. Richard yelled something back to Roland as it was evident the arm was now almost totally severed. Roland let off the throttle and the truck settled. The screaming had stopped.

With a flashlight in one hand, a police officer rushed up and collected the dropped gun. The officer motioned Richard to lift the plow and slowly the wing rose into the air. Free at last, the half severed arm flopped down into the pickup cab. The officer glanced up at Richard, then down into the smaller truck with his light.

"Jesus H. Christ," was all he said.

There was time only for Richard and Roland to exchange one wordless look before the cab was filled with headlights. Two cars, one behind the other, were headed down the drive in an attempt to make it to the highway. Roland stepped on the accelerator, winding the engine to build hydraulic pressure.

"Lift 'em! Everything!" yelled Roland as he slammed the transmission into another gear.

Richard was already on the levers and the plows jerked into the air. "He's going left!"

"I see him," acknowledged Roland.

The lead car veered off the driveway into a windswept area revealing nearly bare ground. The big truck started to move, it's chained rear wheels slashing their way to the ground. Roland cranked the wheel left and the leading edge of the big front plow swept a wide arc in that direction. The forward point of the plow caught the vehicle just below the hood ornament and the hood folded backward in several snapping cracks like a beer can being crushed end to end. The hood flew from it's mounts, followed by the windshield as the plow point continued into the firewall and the passenger compartment beyond. Both vehicles ground to a halt.

"You got him!" yelled Richard jumping up and down in his seat. "And to think, we're on fucking overtime! Man, what I wouldn't give for a video of this."

Two police officers ran in from the left shaking their heads at Roland and Richard as they shone their lights into the car.

The second car was turning right, in the direction of the overturned pickup. The lone officer still there drew his own gun, and with one in each hand, leveled them at the oncoming vehicle. At once, a police cruiser came up the drive, forcing the car farther out onto virgin ground. With most of the new fallen snow having been windswept from the area, the chained tires of the cruiser gave it an advantage. As the car began to slide, the cruiser turned into it and both vehicles came together and slid to a halt side by side. Immediately, the officer driving the cruiser shoved a riot gun into the open passenger window of the car inches from the face of the badly shaken man in the seat.

"Just relax, guys. And let me see your empty hands," ordered the officer.

Two more large sedans, close in tandem, were now headed for the highway. Taking benefit of the open, unoccupied space between the front entrances, the two drivers expertly held to their bumper to bumper strategy. Though police fired several rounds at tire level, the lead car, prodded by the second, successfully made it into the highway. With nothing immediately available to give chase, police could only radio ahead with general descriptions.

Police had yet to penetrate into the rear parking lot which still contained about half of it's original total of vehicles. A few cars were only now being occupied. A few more were preparing an assault on the main highway. The big Denecy Lincoln could be seen skillfully maneuvering it's way through the congestion toward a rear exit drive.

Inside the complex, the elegantly appointed surroundings were fast becoming totally evacuated. Two men, closely followed by two more, jogged down the winding corridor through the restaurant and into the lounge. Each was already garbed for the season outside. One carried a snub nosed .38 loosely in his right hand. In the lounge, a finely suited middle aged man clutching a briefcase under one arm, hesitatingly stepped forward and attempted to speak with one of the fleeing four. Instantly recognizable as the star of many television commercials promoting certain banking interests, the man spoke in a desperate tone, almost whining.

"I . . . I can't locate my people. Take me with you. I've got money!"

The four jogged past with hardly a notice. A few yards away the last man slowed and turned long enough to answer.

"We all got money, you fucking asshole!"

# chapter 14

Outside, confrontations were now developing over a wider area as many of Hallingford's weekend guests attempted to avoid apprehension at all cost. Two police cruisers had approached the rear parking lot, thus preventing any additional cars from attempting to exit directly to the main highway. Another group of officers were now inside the complex. The only unhindered activity was centered farther down the slope near the renovated carriage barn and garage where snow machines could be seen collecting passengers, then heading through the woods toward the lake.

Elsewhere, in Melonia, it was becoming obvious to many that the city was strangely devoid of snow plows at a time when snow was accumulating to unusual depths on streets and thoroughfares. A few people were realizing why. But knowing that something extraordinary was taking place was only part of the puzzle. Without any background or explanation, it was difficult to tell exactly what.

Scanner junkies still in operation at that late hour, had, for the last twenty minutes, been locked on the Public Works frequency. A continuous stream of phone calls was widening the listenership even further. After a reasonably quiet approach to Hallingford the airwaves had suddenly become alive with some clipped and broken, but dramatic and incredible pieces of dialogue. This, coupled with one or two strange remarks earlier in the evening, would have had a few curious eavesdroppers out the door, that is, if they had been sure of where to go, or could have made it down the street. But then, they would have missed the audio show and maybe something really startling. Indeed, those familiar voices, often occupying a background setting where they provided an occasional amusing exchange, were presently otherwise engaged.

*There's another one on the highway headed south. Frank, you . . .*
*I see him. He ain't getting any farther than this.*

*Hey, those guys are shooters! Watch . . .*

*Fuck!*

*Dennis! We need the loader over here! Two cars headed out that lower pasture road toward you!*

*This is Sergeant Howe! Stay clear of them! Let . . .*

*Custer! Yell at Don in the other loader to move that car out . . .*

*Look out! Here comes another one across . . . guns out the window . . .*

*Forget the one headed north. We're on his ass!*

*Hey Fly!*

*I see their lights. Come to Papa, you slime!*

Truck thirty-nine pulled off Perimeter Road into the southeast Hallingford access drive. Several widely spaced foundations awaited future condos along the open grassed slope to the left. The city truck slowed to select a path between the jutting concrete, punched through the recently plowed windrow and churned it's way up and over the frozen turf. A full view of the rear portion of the Hallingford complex appeared a couple hundred yards distant. At that moment two snow machines headed off to the east, their singular headlights casting bouncing patches of light against the treeline before them. Back on Perimeter Road, the yellow flashers of Scott Roy's number thirty-two could be seen continuing north.

"This is far enough," announced Dwane Huckins from the passenger seat in thirty-nine.

Bob Garnett set the air brake as the radio came to life.

*Thirty-two to thirty-nine. This thing's been plowed all the way. We're going to hang out here and nail anybody coming around from the north.*

"Yeah, Okay," replied Bob, pressing the mike button, but leaving the instrument secured on its hook.

"Who's with Lester," asked Dwane.

"Wayne, I think."

"Wayne? I thought they blew him up earlier."

Bob didn't reply to Dwane's remark as his driver, turned temporary passenger, withdrew the .45 automatic from his coat pocket and released the rear of the wing to fall, allowing exit from the passenger door.

Dwane nodded at another handgun on the seat of the truck. "You want me to show you how to fire that thing again?" he asked with forced levity.

Bob was not amused. "Just try not to get yourself killed. Now, get the hell out of here."

Without another word, Dwane got out of the truck and headed up the windswept slope toward Hallingford. Bob had the wing going back into an upright position as soon as Dwane had cleared the truck.

Lieutenant Paul Titus finished handcuffing the second of the two men into the oak balustrade near the bottom of the stairs. This one was still conscious. The first, with arms secured around the lower ornate upright was much less so.

Titus glanced at Mars halfway up the stairs and both joined Captain Warner at the top. The three men stood listening to the voices coming from one of the rooms down the hall.

"That's got to be about where those shots came from," said Warner softly as he leaned close to his chief.

Mars nodded and the officers moved quietly down the hall to either side of the door in question. Titus stepped back and motioned with a foot as though proposing to kick the door in. Mars shook his head, pointed at the door, then made a grasping motion toward him. Titus looked disgusted with himself because he hadn't detected that the old door opened outward.

Mars reached along the wall and took hold of the knob. It would not turn. Stepping back, he brought the shotgun up to a ready position.

"You in the room!" he shouted. "This is the police! Come out with your hands in sight!"

The conversation stopped immediately. Suddenly, several shots boomed forth from within the room and splintered holes appeared in the old door. The last slug crashed through the wall a foot from Mars' head. The volley apparently over for the moment, Mars stepped in front of the door, leveled the shotgun and fired four quick rounds about chest high in a tight pattern. With the middle of the door now in tatters, he shielded his face with his left hand and brought the gun muzzle inches from the knob and lock. Wham! The metal parts disappeared as shrapnel struck the opposite wall. The door started to swing into the hall. Mars stepped to the side and kicked it open all the way. Dan Warner, followed by Mars and Titus moved into the room.

A big heavy set man, over six feet tall, stood facing the threesome as they came through the door, guns leveled. The man's upper chest, neck, and face were a mass of bleeding wounds. Splinters of wood could be seen sticking out of the bloodied areas. His one good eye stared at some vague point in space past the three officers. Taking one slow, seemingly careful step backward, he then crashed to the floor like some huge falling tree.

Past him, just inside the smashed window, slumped another unmoving figure of a man, his upper torso wedged awkwardly between the floor and the sill. An occasional swirl of snow blew through the window propelled by the draft out into the hall. Big white flakes settled onto the face of the first man and quickly disappeared in the red shining liquid.

The third man in the room seemed unaffected by the sudden violent death of his two companions. In a finely tailored pin-stripe suit designed in a bygone era, Nino Valachi leaned nonchalantly on the fireplace mantle as he held a half empty champagne glass.

"Not bad for hick cops," Valachi observed in a sharply edged voice. "But they were stupid. I told them that a man of my age has learned to accept one more minor inconvenience. Ah, but the young. They are so impatient!" Valachi paused to look down at the bodies. "Now they have all the time in the world, yes?"

"Read him his rights and cuff him," ordered Mars, apparently unimpressed with the old man's cool exterior.

Titus handed his riot gun to Warner and moved toward Valachi, motioning him to raise his arms and turn around. Valachi understood very well and obediently obliged.

"Watch your manner's, kid," he said over his shoulder. "Treat me nice or I will have a dozen lawyers sitting on your face, ha ha. I will anyway."

After a search of his person, Titus brought the arms down into the small of his back.

"Would you consider in front, no?" Valachi asked in a kindly tone. "This is very uncomfortable for me. As you know, I am not in good health."

Titus paid no attention to the request and turned Valachi around to face Mars again.

"Nevis. Bradford Nevis," snapped Mars. "Where is he?"

Valachi's eyes narrowed. Then he turned his head and spat on the floor. "Nevis? He is gone across the snow, I think. I hope you catch him. He is a crook, ha, ha. He gives us all a bad name. He has no respect."

*   *   *

Plow truck nineteen was traveling over forty miles per hour, a high speed considering the road conditions on the highway north of Hallingford. The engine noise filled the cab. The big front plow bounced up and down, throwing it's weight around and making it difficult to keep the truck on course. Pat Gant had both hands on the steering wheel, making constant corrections as the front end jumped in and out of the snow rutted road ahead. Dean Smith held a double barrel shotgun before him in front of the plow levers.

A scant seventy feet ahead of the city plow, a large dark sedan was having equal difficulty staying on the road while trying to get away from the thundering beast on its' tail.

"I wonder which gangsters we got in front of us," yelled Pat in the noisy cab.

"Fucked if I know," answered Dean, his eyes staying on the car ahead.

"What the hell are we doing this for?" asked Pat after barely managing to correct out of a sudden skid.

"Same answer," replied Dean.

"What are we supposed to do if we catch 'em?"

"Hell, stick the plow in their back window. Run 'em off the road," was Dean's quick, but somehow unenthusiastic answer.

"Yeah, I love it!" said Pat loudly, after a moment.

At once there was a loud clink of metal striking metal.

"Holy shit! They're shooting at us!" exclaimed Pat, backing away from the wheel. "I saw a flash from the rear window!"

Another muffled report sounded from the vehicle ahead and a bullet hole appeared in the truck windshield midway between the two men. Pat ducked down and peered under the rim of the steering wheel. Dean crouched behind the plow levers. The truck slowed perceptively.

"Raise the Goddamn plow, will you?" Pat shouted.

"It's up!"

"Maybe we ought to . . ." Pat started to say.

His voice trailed off as he and Dean looked at each other from their hunkered down positions.

"The hell with this!" exclaimed Dean, suddenly angry. "I ain't gonna take the time right now to decide if I really want to try and kill somebody or not. Let's get 'em!"

Suddenly, it was all decided. Pat straightened up in his seat, downshifted, and slammed the accelerator to the floor. The engine screamed. Dean opened his window.

Thinking they had succeeded in scaring off the city truck, the occupants of the dark sedan had also slowed down to a safer speed. Before they realized the truck was again resuming it's pursuit, their advantage was gone.

"Get closer! Get on their ass!" Dean ordered.

"Keep your fucking shirt on. You sure you know how to use that thing?"

Dean flashed Pat a disdainful look. "Don't make me laugh. I got so many ducks last fall I didn't know what to do with 'em."

"Ducks?" Pat seemed incredulous. "You mean you got birdshot in there?"

Dean opened the door as far as the raised wing would allow. Not quite far enough, he jiggled the lever control which lowered the rear of the wing a bit. "Fuck no! Triple O buck!"

"Oh," replied Pat.

Dean hooked his right leg through the window opening of the partially open door, and with his left foot on the sill, stood up through the space between door and cab. With both arms free as he kept pressure against the door, Dean leveled the shotgun at the swerving car ahead and squinted into the wind and snow.

The distance between the two vehicles was now down to fifty feet as a hand holding a gun stretched out the rear window of the sedan and pointed at the truck. Wham! This time the report was plainly heard and inside the truck another slug had thudded through the windshield closer to Pat's head.

"Shoot! For Christ's sake, shoot!" screamed Pat.

Boom! Holes appeared over the upper rear deck of the car as well as a few through the rear window. The gun holding hand disappeared inside. Boom! This time a large portion of the rear window disappeared. Headlights of the city truck revealed violent movement in the vehicle.

"You got 'em! You got 'em!" yelled Pat.

While still locked into his position above the half open door, Dean broke the double barrel and ejected the empty shells. Holding the gun away from him against the wind with his left hand, he fished two more from his shirt pocket with his right and reloaded. As Dean was about to level the gun the car slid to the right, bounced off the plowed windrow, then back into the road as the driver fought to gain control.

Half frozen, Dean hastily decided to abandon his precarious perch. No sooner had he retaken his seat, the car was in trouble again. Now into a sweeping curve to the right, the sedan never made the effort, plunging through the embankment and down over a steep slope into some trees.

The city plow thundered by.

"Goddamn! I never got to touch him!" complained Pat, grabbing for the radio mike. "Chief, we got one off the highway for you about three miles north."

\*     \*     \*

The swirling snow had settled into a series of deep drifts around the east flank of the vacant condos. Nevertheless, the buildings offered the only cover this side of the carriage barn. Near the restored hundred and fifty year old structure, a pair of mercury vapor lamps high on the naked trunk of a towering pine cast an orangery hue down over the fresh blanket of snow.

Dwane struggled through a particularly high peaked dune and into the shadow of the last condo. The barn was just a hundred feet beyond and the sound of idling snow machine engines along with an occasional loud voice, could be heard. At once, the engines rose in pitch and three of the machines were in the open, headed for the woods. Dwane ran through the old crusty surface along the leeward side to the corner of the condo and raised the .45 to shoulder height.

The machines were speeding away. It would have been an impossible rear quarter shot. But here came two more! As they passed directly before him, thirty yards distant, Dwane followed the first, then the second machine, with the gun. Another second and they too were out of range.

"Goddamn!" Dwane exclaimed into the crisp night air as he lowered the gun. Oh, how he had wanted to fire. But if he couldn't be sure of hitting one of the forward engine compartments, damned if he was going to take the chance of shooting someone without singular provocation.

But here was that sound again. Dwane turned the corner and moved along the thirty foot width of the building. There, out in the open, on the other side of condo sat three snow machines, the farthest of which could be heard idling as it sat unattended. Dwane glanced quickly around, there was no one about. Raising the gun, he fired a shot into each of the first two machines. Both shuddered visibly as the slugs slammed into the hard engine surfaces beneath the fiberglass shrouds. Maybe the third would explode as it was running, Dwane thought, swinging the gun toward his last mechanical victim.

"Don't turn around! Just drop the gun," came the firm but calm statement.

Dwane froze for a moment, then started to turn slowly.

"Another inch and you're a dead man. Now, drop the gun and step forward away from it," came the voice, now slightly irritated.

This time Dwane complied. The tall figure of a man clad in his white jumpsuit stepped to pick up the gun.

"That's far enough. Now turn around with your hands away from your sides."

Dwane did so and strained to distinguish the face of his adversary in the poor light. The heavy mustache, goggles, and black stocking cap pulled low over the forehead failed to ring any bells in his mind. The man raised his own gun at Dwane's chest with his right hand while his left held the retrieved firearm loosely at his side.

"Now, undo your coat with your left hand, then with both, open the collar and let it fall to the ground."

Dwane followed the instructions precisely.

"Move to your left five steps."

Dwane did so, after which the man moved to lift the coat by its collar with his gun toting left hand and hefted it several times off to his side. Finally, he tossed it back to Dwane. "Put it back on and lay down in the snow on your stomach," the man ordered. "Face that machine you were about to disable."

Again Dwane did as he was told.

Putting his own gun inside his suit, the man strode over to, and mounted the idling snow machine while Dwane slowly elevated himself with his arms.

"You're not dead yet! Don't spoil it now," the man warned, leveling Dwane's gun in his direction. "Stay right where you are until I tell you to move."

Giving the machine some throttle, the man traveled a short distance to where a group of small leafless trees protruded from a landscaped knoll. As Dwane watched, the man hung his .45 by it's trigger ring around a stubby branch. The weight of the gun dropped the branch close to the ground, but it held. The man turned his full attention back to Dwane.

"Listen to me! Do you remember flight 117?" the man asked, raising his voice to be plainly heard across the twenty yard distance. "You hear me?"

"Yeah, yeah," Dwane acknowledged finally. "I remember it. What about it?" he added with some confusion.

"In the auditorium you will find something indicating the intent of some of us who gathered here tonight."

The lights of the snow machine came on, and with a twist of throttle, it shot up over the knoll and out onto the field. Dwane was already on his feet, running toward the suspended gun. Then it was in his hand. The bobbing lights of the snow machine were still within range, but Dwane showed no desire to try a shot as he stood and watched the snow machine get farther away.

Mars, Warner, and a third officer stood in a lower hallway outside the open door of a ground floor room. Mars had a radio hand set to his mouth.

"Are you sure that's Nevis' Cadillac in the parking lot . . . ? Damn!"

The garbled reply, though emanating from a hundred yards away, was lost to anyone more than a couple feet from the radio.

"Anyone down?" Mars asked. " . . . Good. Any ambulances here yet except ours? . . . Well, there's over a dozen on the way. Some from twenty-thirty miles away so . . . Yeah, set 'em up in the parking lot unless they can get right to the scene . . . Yeah. Mars out."

As Mars lowered the radio, Lieutenant Titus emerged from the room guiding Magan Anthony, still in a formal evening gown, before him. Magan smiled sweetly at the chief. Mars glowered at her.

"I understand you came with Nevis. Where is he?" Mars asked.

"In an emergency, he and his two Neanderthals had arranged to leave on those . . . those snow things. I guess you provided the emergency," Magan replied simply.

"Where were they headed?"

"I have no idea."

"And they just left you here, huh?"

"I wasn't included. Not that I would have . . . , or could have gone,"

Magan said, raising her naked arms to emphasis her inappropriate dress for such weather. "Besides, I have nothing to hide . . . , as you can see, Chief . . . Chief Mars, is it?"

"You got something you can put on over that," Mars asked thinly, his growing irritation obvious.

"Not at my fingertips. That wasn't my room," Magan looked at all four officers. "You boys won't let me get too cold, will . . ."

"Get her with the others in that conference room, Paul," Mars ordered abruptly. "The County will be here soon to . . ."

A tremendous crash sounded and the building itself trembled. Captain Warner and the other officer started down the hall just as another officer rounded the corner and jogged up to meet the group.

"Public Works just put their fucking road grader into the reception area," breathed the heavy set officer, nearly out of breath. "There's a twenty foot hole in the side of the building."

"Goddamn!" roared Mars. "I swear, some of those guys are going in with the rest . . . Well, get back out there," Mars cracked at the recent arrival. "And see if you can keep them from getting killed."

The officer was a second late in taking his eyes from Magan Anthony, but just in time to avoid an angry repeat of the order from Mars. "Yes, sir," he managed to get out before turning and retracing his steps down the hall.

Lieutenant Titus followed with his charge. Mars shook his head, jammed the radio back on his belt, and turned to Captain Warner.

"Dan, take Riggs here, and anybody that's free outside and go see what's left in the carriage barn. I'm sure it's no accident there wasn't any plowed road to it."

"Alright," nodded Warner. Look, Budner and Kelly should be out on the lake by now. Maybe they . . ."

"Yeah, maybe," interrupted Mars, turning and walking quickly off in the opposite direction.

                    *      *      *


Simpson Dunbar wrenched the transmission into reverse, released the clutch, and bore down on the accelerator. The chained dual rear wheels thrashed in the snow while the entire cab vibrated on it's mounts. The truck went nowhere. Then, violently into low gear. The same result. Dunbar threw the shift lever into neutral, forcibly settled back in the seat, and reached for the pint bottle of scotch between his legs.

"Son-of-a-bitch!"

"Want me to see if I can lift it with the plow?" asked Dustin Eaves.

"No. We'll just fuck up something else. The truck's a mess as it is," said Simpson in disgust as he reached for the radio mike. "This is the Fly," he proclaimed. "We are down on the second driveway off Hampton Road on the north side. We are in need of a payloader."

A few silent seconds passed.

*You mean you're stuck?* came the crackled reply. *Jesus Christ, Fly.*

"I've got a Goddamned car upside down on top of the truck!" stated Simpson. "There's dead guys in it, I think,"

*Jesus Christ!* repeated the radio voice. *I'll be down, but it'll be a few minutes.*

We'll be here," said Simpson, tossing the mike back onto the dash.

The light colored, full sized Oldsmobile reposed across the front plow and cab of truck forty-one. The hood of the car extended rear of the steel cab top protector of the truck. The front plow frame and hood of the truck was buried up into the rear window and roof of the car. The car's inverted windshield was suspended a foot away from that of the truck.

The man's face pressed flat against the glass to the clear side of the initial impact point where the bulged and distorted area seemed close to collapse under it's own weight. The eyes were open and lifeless, their blind attention turned downward into the truck like stilled pendulums. A dark heavy path of blood ran from the shattered glass into the unbroken surface. Fresher offerings, mainly from a sliced vein in the neck, continued to drip and collect in a growing pool which expanded along the windshield frame. The man's neck was obviously broken, the torso behind, twisted at an unnatural angle. Beyond, on the crumpled roof, the features of another body were vaguely evident. The solitary yellow flasher left functioning atop the passenger side rear view mirror of the truck cast a stabbing pulsing beat into the car, illuminating the dreadful scene like the final fluttering frames of an old film coming to a stop.

"I think there's something moving in back there," exclaimed Eaves, extending himself over the plow levers to get a better look into the car. "Why don't you shoot 'em just to make sure."

"You're a bloodthirsty bastard, ain't you Eaves," observed Simpson Dunbar. "I might get to like you after all."

"Well, why don't we get out and take a look?" asked Eaves. "Maybe the two of us can roll it off. I can't stand to look at that much longer."

"Does get on your nerves after a while," agreed Simpson.

Dunbar reached under his coat on the seat and withdrew an old Colt single action revolver and inspected it closely, finally pulling the hammer back to half-cock. "Alright, let's go see what we can see. Gimme that flashlight."

Dunbar opened his door as he took the light from Eaves. "Leave the wing alone. Slide over here and get out this door." Stepping down onto the running board, and then to the ground, he held the door for Eaves.

"Actually, it's not these guys here I'm wondering about," confided Dunbar in a low voice, leaning close to his wingman. "We better check out whoever's in the car that slammed into that tree behind us."

                              *    *    *


Chief Mars walked swiftly through the cocktail lounge and into the reception hall. Suddenly, a gust of wind hit him in the face and he stopped momentarily to survey the damage wrought by the P.W. D. The heavy expensive drapes, along with much broken glass, littered the floor. A large section of outside wall hung crazily to one side, pinned down by sections of mortared brick strewn amongst broken two by fours and plywood. Every second or third blast of wind carried snow into the room which melted into little pools of water here and there as heat from other parts of the complex flooded toward the area. The road grader was nowhere in sight. Mars shook his head and stepped through the debris.

The auditorium door was slightly ajar. Voices could be heard within. Mars lowered his shotgun, slowly opened the door with the end of the barrel and moved into the room.

Only a few dim emergency type lights set flush in the ceiling illuminated the large area. Maybe the grader had something to do with the power being cut. A man, forty feet away, with his back to Mars walked toward another individual standing next to a table on the stage platform. The first man appeared weighted down with something in his arms.

"Alright, don't anybody move!" ordered Mars.

Dwane Huckins stopped in mid-stride and looked back over his shoulder at Mars and his shotgun. Walt Conover glanced up from the table, and with his hands out away from his sides, slowly turned toward the door.

"Hello, Mars," said Conover.

"You two!" exclaimed the Chief, recognizing both men and lowering his gun. "What the hell are you doing in here? What's that you've got?" he asked, walking toward Dwane.

"My new bowling ball. All I have to do is drill the holes. Here, take a look." As Mars approached, Dwane turned the sphere in his arms until the head was looking almost straight up.

Mars bent to get a closer look in the dim light. "What? . . . What is it? Is that real?"

"Chief Mars, meet Rufel Arlasian," Dwane said, somewhat enjoying Mars' astonishment.

"Rufel Arlasian?" Mars repeated after a moment. "You mean that Rufel Arlasian? My God! . . . Where did you get that?"

"Over by the door where you came in. If you'll excuse me, this thing's heavy." Dwane struggled up onto the stage and deposited the sphere next to its companion. Mars followed.

"Sticio Tamsiel, I believe," said Conover by way of introduction of the second head, his hand resting on the clear hard surface.

Mars looked from one to the other. "I know who they are . . . but I still don't get it . . . But this is big, really big," he added after a moment.

"Somebody's trying to make a point, that's for sure," agreed Conover.

Dwane started to speak, but Mars' attention was on Conover and his battered face, turned for the moment into the light.

"Jesus, you been auditioning for the same treatment? You look like hell!"

"I guess the welcoming committee here isn't what it used to be," Conover answered. "By the way, there's a couple guys cuffed to the patio rail out back. One of them's got a slug of mine high in his left shoulder. The guy responsible for this," Conover indicated his face, may still be in the bar across from the swimming pool. I haven't been back to check."

Turning away, Conover lifted the upper part of the leather case from the floor and lowered it over the heads, experimenting with how it fit together. Mars shook his head, but said nothing. His expression said it for him.

Dwane broke the silence. "There's someone else here you ought to meet. Dead, of course, but at least this one's still warm."

Mars looked quickly around, not knowing what he expected to see at this point. Dwane stepped off the stage and moved out amongst the tables and chairs, now in disarray.

Delores Stang reposed face up on the floor, one arm flopped askew over her chin, her eyes wide open. Mars shoved a table aside and knelt over the body.

"Delores Stang," stated Dwane. "Remember, I told you earlier I . . ."

"Yeah, I know who she is . . . was."

"I took a quick look at her," Dwane went on. "No bullet holes. She may have been sitting in a chair and just keeled over. Her arm was like that."

"Her friends left in a hurry, I guess," Mars observed.

"Looks like she might have been trying to keep somebody from cutting her head off," offered Conover innocently.

Mars stood and turned to the two men. He couldn't see Conover's face well in the light, but he chalked the remark to his continuing dry sense of humor.

"Well, one thing's for sure, by tomorrow this time you're going to be the most famous police chief in the country," Dwane said brightly. "You really ought to get a haircut."

Mars didn't smile as he took a moment to assimilate the statement. "Really. Well, for your information, this whole thing hasn't been all that profitable so far. Oh, we can cover ourselves coming in, and those . . . those heads will be . . ." Mars paused to think of the words he wanted. "In your wanderings around here tonight I don't suppose either of you has seen or heard anything of Bradford Nevis?"

# chapter 15

The sound of snow machine engines seemed to be getting closer as it filtered down amongst the old virgin pine. Scott Roy sat astride his machine on the far side of a small embankment several yards from the woods road which led to the lake. Taking a radio hand set from his ear and stuffing it into a pouch behind the handle bars, Scott jammed his helmet down on his head and punched the starter button. The engine growled its presence. The machine lurched a couple feet forward, then settled into a throaty idle.

Scott still wasn't sure exactly what he was going to do. He knew there were a few Hallingford machines that had made it out onto the lake and headed north. Coming up from the south he'd seen them a mile or two distant. He prayed they'd be more as he'd selected his hiding place beside the trail. Scott knew he was a superior rider to anyone he was likely to meet. His vague plan was to somehow overturn, disable, or at least slow down as many as possible. Scott forced himself to take several deep cold breaths as he found himself unconsciously cranking the throttle. Why was he this angry anyway? Why the hell had he been this way for the last six months or more? Forget it! Somewhere in the back of his mind was the thought that this would undoubtedly be the only time in his life where he'd have personal license to actually make all out war on someone else. No matter what the outcome, the idea of it served to heighten the certainty that he could not let such a chance slip by.

The engine noise was louder now and bouncing spears of light were flooding through the trees. At once, on his right rear quarter, a single machine exploded through the fresh snow as it hurtled over a rise. Suddenly, as Scott twisted on his seat, it was past him, skillfully snaking it's way through the trees toward the lake on a northerly tangent.

"Damn!" he said aloud in a moment of indecision while he contemplated turning around and going after the lone machine. But then, the others were approaching.

Three machines were coming down the gently sloping woods road at high speed. Scott readied himself. The first two carried a passenger behind the driver. The last bore a single rider. Scott flicked the headlight on and opened the throttle. The machine lunged over the embankment and into the air before slamming down into the snow a few yards from the trail. The beam of the headlight caught the trailing rider full face for an instant as he shot past. Scott slid his machine behind the man who hunched low over his handle bars, somehow knowing this was not a friend on his tail. In a moment, the whirling track of Scott's high performance machine dug in and held as he accelerated on his prey. Noticing light flashing over his shoulder, Scott snapped a quick look to his rear. There were two more machines coming hard behind him.

Gale Mooney hadn't heard Scott's and Dwane's somewhat plausible reasoning for thinking some of Hallingford's attendees would make a run for it on a snow machine. Nor had he known anything about the recent delivery of a truckload of the vehicles to the site. Regardless, it was hard to imagine any big city bozo, hardened criminal or not, attempting such a getaway.

Gale hadn't thought much of some of the gungho attitude displayed at the garage. He knew most of the younger guys simply didn't realize what they might be getting into. Not that he was afraid for himself. He tried not to dwell too much on the fact that he clearly wanted to go, even knowing he'd have to explain it to an angry Doris later. But Gale felt responsible for Jason. After getting him to come out of his shell, he certainly didn't want to get him hurt, or even killed.

So when it became obvious that every truck was heading for Hallingford, Gale thought it a better course to submit to Jason's plan involving the confrontation of fleeing criminals on Gale's big snow machine. Fine. He and Jason would spend an uneventful hour or so waiting around on the lake shore until it was over.

Yeah, sure. So why did he still have the shotgun? And why had he carefully formulated the lie to Doris about dropping the gun off to somebody on his plow run to look at in lieu of a possible trade. And why was he sitting here hoping the last snow machine hadn't already fled the scene. And why did he feel the adrenaline . . .

"They're coming this way, all right," Jason yelled from several yards away over the snow covered beach where he peered up into the darkness of the woods. The sound of the machines was getting louder. "They're following the tracks of these others," he added, pointing excitedly in the snow at his feet.

Gale sat on the rear of his machine loading shells into the ancient Winchester ten gauge, long barreled lever action shotgun. "Well, come on. Get over here!" he barked at Jason.

Jason ran back to the machine and seated himself behind the handle bars. Punching the starter button, the engine of the big Arctic Cat quickly settled to idle.

"Wait on the lights," Gale ordered. "Don't turn 'em on till they pass in front of us."

"Yeah, Okay. Take 'em by surprise, huh?"

Gale finished loading the Winchester and cradled it across his legs. "I must be crazy letting you talk me into this with you never being on one of these things until last fall."

"You said I was doing great," Jason said back over his shoulder.

"I know, I know. Just remember I'm on the back of this thing."

"Don't worry about it."

"And remember what I said. I don't want to shoot anybody unless I see a gun and unless I have to. I just want to stop their machines and leave 'em out here for the cops to collect later."

"Well, that ought'a do it," remarked Jason glancing around at the barrel of the Winchester. "You take that thing off some tank?"

"I hope your ears can handle it cause I'm going to be yelling directions at you at the same time. Just don't jump when it goes off."

"Here they come!"

Three machines flashed out of the woods, their lights streaking the snow before them. Out over the beach they came and onto the lake. Closing behind their tight single file came another machine which looked and sounded different from the preceding three.

"That's Scott behind them!" yelled Jason. "I think he saw us!"

"That's him alright! Crazy bastard!"

Jason laughed loudly as he turned the lights on and cracked the throttle, jerking the machine forward.

Gale reached for Jason's shoulder. "Wait!"

Two more machines were suddenly on the beach, quickly passing in front of the waiting Arctic Cat, then on to the lake.

"Go. Go!" yelled Gale.

The big machine leaped out of the snow, turned a tight circle, and headed off in pursuit.

The first two of the machines in front of Scott Roy streaked north across the lake in tight formation. The lone rider hung back by fifty yards, and in gradual weaving arcs, seemed to be protecting his friends from the approach of the stranger to their rear.

Scott accelerated steadily on the trailing machine, his headlight catching the face of it's rider as he continued to glance back over his shoulder. The next glance was accompanied by a sweeping right hand holding a gun. Bam! The sound and the flash brought a lump into Scott's throat as he swerved to the machine's left side. As he did, the rider brought the gun around in anticipation, but quickly, Scott was back over his tracks again. This guy was no novice, Scott acknowledged to himself. The two machines, retraced the maneuver again, then again, Scott obediently playing the wagging tail to the dog ahead. The rider whipped his gun first right, then left, only to find his target ahead of the move.

Meantime, Scott had been closing the distance, making the movements sharper and quicker. Frustrated, the rider fired blindly to his rear. Now! Scott took advantage of the man's momentary inattention and a second later, when the man looked around, his expression was one of stark terror. Scott had opened the throttle a mere twenty feet to the rear and all the lone rider saw was two skis high in the air and a whirling steel barred track coming to eat him alive.

The track hit first, slashing and clawing it's way into the back of the soft seat and beyond. Like the jaws of a wild animal trying to gulp its victim, the steel teeth lunged forward onto the man's back as the ski tips crashed onto the handle bars and out over the fiberglass hood. In one last jerking thrust of showering sparks, Scott was up and past the mangled snow machine and it's driver as it pitched and rolled in the snow, it's driver gone, it's headlight tracing a short bouncing path in the night until it was finally still. Scott didn't cast a look to his rear. He didn't think about what had occurred beneath the pounding track of the machine as he guided his charge to a soft landing and took off after the two snow machines now a hundred yards distant.

Gale's big Arctic Cat with Jason hunched low behind the windscreen closed quickly on the two snow machines ahead. Now fifty feet behind, Jason guided the Cat off to the right and away from the blowing snow wake that streaked from the rear of the trailing machine.

"Not too far! I hav'ta see!" yelled Gale close to Jason's ear.

Jason responded by bringing the machine closer in to the contrail of snow where the headlight revealed the flapping black trenchcoat of the passenger on the fleeing snow machine. The man was hatless, his eyes narrow slits against the wind, then against the bright light of the Cat, as he turned to take a long look to his rear. Now facing forward, he pounded on the shoulder of the driver.

"Get closer." Gale yelled.

The distance closed to thirty feet. Now twenty. Gale raised the Winchester against the wind, it's barrel extending to Jason's left. Suddenly, the black coated man twisted his torso around as far as he could and stretched out a right arm. In the Cat's light a glint of steel reflected briefly in his hand as Gale pulled the trigger of the Winchester.

A tremendous "Boom" sounded over the roar of the machines as a ball of fire exited the barrel of the shotgun. The gun recoiled skyward and Gale reached a left hand to Jason's shoulder for support. A brilliant flash appeared at the lower rear of the machine ahead and debris joined the stream of white as it cascaded back, just to the left of the Arctic Cat.

The snow machine jerked slightly in it's path. The passenger's gun had disappeared as he flailed the air. Now turned almost completely around, the length of his coat caught in the wind and whipped up over his head, further pulling him backwards. At once, with a loud thud, the vehicle lifted in place. For an instant, the foot wide steel enforced track floated rearward, then in a flash, like a wet towel snapped at a naked ass, it returned, catching the man full in the face.

Now, nearly beside the Arctic Cat, the machine pitched left and rolled, the body of the driver somehow still connected by a coat sleeve as it was thrashed over and over. Quickly, the scene disappeared to the rear as the Arctic Cat sped off toward the remaining snow machine.

Scott Roy closed on the second machine in line which now sped off to the right in a separate course from it's leader. Without warning, headlights flashed on approaching objects, and in a moment, the speeding machines were past the first bob house. Scott accelerated, bringing his machine close in on the left of his intended victim as more of the structures loomed ahead. In an instant, the two machines narrowly cleared on either side of another bob house which flashed by between them. Again, Scott crowded the other machine, this time getting the attention of both driver and passenger for one long fatal moment. Before looking back ahead, the driver instinctively swerved away from Scott.

It was too late to avoid the hulking shape before them as the snow machine disappeared into the eight by eight foot structure. For a split second they were swallowed from view, then the diminutive fish house literally exploded.

First the machine, followed by the driver, passenger and assorted debris, exited the far wall as separate objects, tumbling in space. But not for long. A second bob house, stationed a scant dozen feet from the first, had collected all travelers, their remaining force serving only to topple the little building over in the snow.

Scott sped past in triumph as he raised a fist into the air. The passenger on the machine he had recognized as Stanley Fagner. Just maybe, that meant . . . Scott opened the throttle and set his sights on the lone remaining snow machine, now fifty yards ahead.

"Take him! Keep to his right!" Gale yelled as he worked the lever on the Winchester and slammed another shell into position.

For half a mile, the machine ahead had traced a slow weaving defensive pattern in trying to keep it's pursuer at bay. Now, apparently, it's driver had decided to make a run for it as the machine straightened out and gathered speed.

"We must be doing sixty now!" Jason shouted back.

"It's now or never! My hands are about frozen! Move!"

The Arctic Cat responded. Gale leaned close to Jason's back, the Winchester crossed between them while he tried to keep his hands out of the wind. At twenty yards and closing, the Cat's headlight revealed more of the two men ahead and at that moment the now familiar right arm of the passenger swept to the rear.

"He's got . . ." Jason yelled, hunching lower behind the handle bars.

Boom! Gale fired, and as the long barrel of the Winchester recoiled upward, most of the back of the passenger's coat disappeared in a puff of fluffy fragments which swept by the Cat as a tiny cloud, gone as soon as it was perceived. For a second, the man's back appeared to gain a reddish hue as he was flung forward onto the driver's shoulders before disappearing to the left in an explosion of white.

The machine swerved across the path of the Arctic Cat, then straightened as the driver gained control and headed back on his original course.

"Go get him! And lets finish this!" ordered a voice Jason had never heard before. Gale snapped a fresh shell into the Winchester and held it up and ready. There was no thought of cold hands now.

Closer, until the driver cast a quick sideways look and veered off to his left.

"Stay with him! He'll turn back!" Gale yelled.

Faster went the Cat to stay with it's prey on the outside of the turn, then suddenly, the driver took his last chance to regain his intended direction. Back across the bow of the Cat he came, but Jason was ready. At the last moment, the driver realized he'd never make it as he frantically turned to avoid the unyielding trajectory Jason would not give up.

For a long second the two snow machines were but a few feet apart, the Cat slightly ahead. Before the driver could react, Gale had lowered the Winchester. It's muzzle almost touched the forward engine cowl. Bam! Most of the fiberglass disintegrated in the cold a moment before fire enveloped the entire front of the machine.

Now miles from Hallingford, Scott wondered if the driver ahead knew precisely where he was, or where he was headed. In this northern, more confined part of the lake, the swirling wind tossed snow about in blinding pockets, separate little storms to be pierced and escaped from, one after the other.

Scott had already seen the now familiar face of Bradford Nevis turning to leer at him once a long minute ago in the beam of his headlight. That was just before Nevis had fired his little hand gun for the last time after which he'd thrown it back in Scott's direction.

Scott knew Nevis had fired previously, probably a half dozen times. He couldn't remember. Didn't really care. The farther they went, as long as they kept on going, Scott had definite plans for the machine ahead.

The weaving pattern had begun, but now it was different. Instead of Scott following the machine, he was cutting it off from making a turn. A moment ago as they'd passed before him, he'd seen Nevis pounding the shoulder of his driver with a closed fist. Why were they afraid of him, Scott wondered? Why didn't they just stop? What could he have done? Maybe it was just the nature of these people who always had things to hide, he thought.

Scott knew they were very close as he tried to see through the white gloom. Then, there it was, an approaching black nothingness, an edge. Scott steadied himself, his eyes ready for the first reaction of the machine ahead.

Nevis turned one last time to glare into the headlight behind him. Scott knew he had no idea of what as to come.

But suddenly, the driver knew, and at the same time cut the throttle and swerved heavily to the right. Unprepared for such a move, Nevis started to lose his balance, his arms flailing, reaching, as the machine slid sideways, throwing up clouds of snow.

It was as if they'd sailed off into space, as white was now black. With a final explosion of icy spray, Nevis, his driver, and the snow machine were gone.

Several yards to the left, Scott Roy hit the water straight and true, the rear of the machine settling only slightly. The surface ahead shone like diamonds on black velvet, the headlight reflecting off each little wave that got larger and larger the farther he strayed from the ice shore to his rear. To each side of the machine, water sprayed out from the skies, steady, silent, hopeful even comforting as it verified his progress in a foreign medium. Water split to the inside of each ski clattered into the undercarriage in a constant barrage like hail on a tin roof, loud and threatening. Of course, he'd done this many time before. But never at night. And certainly never for the distance he knew was before him.

Slowly now, into the turn. Not too much . . . A little more throttle . . . Spray to the left was almost gone, seemingly transferred to the right. The racket underneath changed pitch, even above the whine of the engine. Easy now, don't slide . . . And God, don't loose traction!

Scott could feel the sweat running down into his eyes. He could feel the left rear of the machine settling. Sinking? Shift your weight! No! More RPM, now before . . . No! Well, maybe a little . . . But God, don't cavitate! Scott dreaded the sound of the engine suddenly winding free . . . That would be it! Period! Finish! . . . No! Calm . . . Steady . . . Easy does it . . . The waves are getting bigger . . . Jesus! Goddamned if there won't be a life preserver on this thing from now on . . .

Scott almost laughed aloud at the thought . . . Stop it! . . . Look ahead . . . Where the hell's the edge of the fucking ice!

\*     \*     \*

He was in a charitable mood, so he only slipped two Hershey bars up the sleeve of his suede jacket. The third he waved cheerfully at the counterman on his way out as he slapped down a dime. Busy with someone else, the man nodded his okay.

Reaching the door, it eluded his grasp as it opened before him. She'd been looking behind her at some friend on the sidewalk. When turning back, she bumped right into his chest.

"Oh, . . . I'm sorry," she said, with an intake of breath and sudden smile, looking right at him.

He stood transfixed while the smell of her wafted into him. Then she was gone, walking into the store, her hair bouncing smartly, the hem of her coat revealing graceful calves, slim ankles, polished high heels . . . She was the most strikingly beautiful woman he had ever seen. Bradford Nevis was fifteen, but that face had never left him. Never . . . never . . .

. . . Cold vicious air assaulted his face like a fistful of needles. Choking . . . gasping pain. His heart pounded. Bradford Nevis opened his eyes, arms flailing under tremendous weight. A throaty cry passed between his lips, no words, just sound. It was dark, black, well almost.

He felt something! Then it was gone. Frantically, Nevis thrashed in that direction. Ice, thin and fragile like slippery glass, collapsed under his touch as if mocking him.

And then light flooded the area. Nevis lunged toward it. At last, something solid enough to support his forearm and get his head clear of the water. Each breath, hard as gravel, rasped from within. But he could hear something else! He knew he could. The sound! The light! Desperately, his mind made the two as one.

"Help . . . help . . . ," Nevis croaked across the void.

Scott Roy removed his helmet and turned the ignition key. Now there was only the sound of the wind. From a distance of thirty yards, he watched Nevis cling to life.

The sound had stopped. The light remained! There must be someone behind the light! Maybe it wasn't . . . But, maybe it was . . . "Please, please! Help me . . . Anything you want . . . I'll . . . , please . . ."

Scott hadn't moved, hadn't taken his eyes from Nevis. He could see his face clearly, illuminated in the light against the dark background. "No way. I couldn't get to you even if I wanted to . . . I figure you got about ten more seconds . . ."

Nevis choked out another word or two. Scott started his machine and the engine settled to idle. Possibly the ice broke under Nevis' arm. Maybe the sound of the engine starting had swept any last hope away. Maybe he finally passed out. But in a moment, he was gone.

Scott continued to stare at the spot where the face had been as he reached into the pouch before him, withdrew the radio hand set, and raised it beside his head. "This is Scott Roy. Nevis is down. I repeat, Nevis is down," he spoke firmly, but calmly into the instrument before placing it back into the pouch.

# chapter 16

Activity in the Hallingford parking lot continued, dominated now by a growing police presence. A few cars belonging to conference attendees remained untouched and in place. Others sat skewed about, their escape abruptly curtailed by some previous action. Occupants of a dark Lincoln stood against the car, loudly objecting to the restraints recently placed upon them by two officers who remained in close proximity. A half dozen people were being shepherded out of the main reception entrance which was now pretty much in shambles. Three police cruisers, lights flashing, were parked center lot, their rear seats full of people who clearly didn't want to be there, or even with each other. A large van, displaying the Melonia city seal, proceeded slowly into the area, ready to transport prisoners to the nearby county holding facility.

Nearer the complex, Chief Mars stood between the open door of another cruiser and the white Cadillac in which Brad Nevis and company had arrived. A cord stretched from inside the police vehicle to a microphone Mars held to his lips. Captain Warner and Dwane Huckins joined Mars who looked at them both, shaking his head in frustration.

"Where are you Scott . . . ? Where is Nevis now?" Mars said into the mike, then brought it down to his side. "Goddammit!" he said loudly to no one in particular raising the mike again. "This is Chief Mars calling Scott Roy! Give your location!"

Mars paused another moment, then thrust the mike at Dwane. "Here, see if you can raise him."

"He's on his snow machine. My guess is he's got Nevis out on the lake," related Dwane, reluctantly taking the mike.

"Here, let me see that," interjected Warner, reaching for the mike. "Budner and Kelly are supposed to be out there somewhere. Maybe they've seen something. I'll . . ."

At that moment, the mounting whir of revolving tank tracks gained the attention of the three, which escalated considerably with the sound of a car horn followed immediately by a loud crash. First Mars, then Warner and Dwane trotted out between the vehicles to see a police cruiser and Bombardier sidewalk plow head to head, the front of the car raised in the air halfway up the vee plow of the tractor.

"Son-of-a-bitch!" roared Mars, turning to glare at Dwane. "I don't know where the hell Conover went to, but I want a stop put to this foolishness, or so help me I'm going to start throwing some of your guys in jail along with the rest of this crowd!"

Dwane rolled his eyes away and for a second almost broke out laughing. "Christ, that must be Oscar," he said under his breath.

*     *     *

Truck thirty-two blocked the narrow road. Under the partially raised wing was jammed a car, two-thirds of the width of it's roof peeled off at hood level from the windshield almost back to the rear window. The crumpled metal rose into the air ahead of the wing and creaked in the wind, held only by its rear roof pillars and left doorpost. Lester Hartwell stood on the truck running board of the open passenger door and looked down into the exposed interior of the car. In his right arm he cradled his favorite hunting rifle, an old Savage model ninety-nine.

Wayne Harrington knelt on the dash of the car where the windshield used to be. Holding a large ball peen hammer, he waved it menacingly at the two occupants of the car. The running lights of the truck revealed a man in the front seat and one in the back. Both appeared unhurt, but were still lying down in the position they must have assumed when the plow took the roof off. Shattered glass covered the man in the front who glared up at Wayne, but for the moment as silent.

The man in the rear had been anything but silent, and now struggled up on one elbow to continue his whining dialogue. "Oh, my God! I told them I didn't want to come here. I'll be ruined! Oh my God, my God . . . Please let me go, please! I've got money . . . I'll pay you more than you make in a year . . . ten years!"

"Go where, asshole?" Lester barked down at the pudgy faced man in the expensive suit. "You don't even know where you are! Where do you think you'd be crawling off to dressed like that in this weather?" Lester waved his rifle at the snowy landscape. "Maybe you could make it to that tree over there. You wanna try?"

Wayne laughed from his perch. The man in back flopped back off his elbow and continued mouthing his despair.

"Shut up, for Christ's sake! Just shut up, Franklin!" shouted the man laying in the front seat.

Wayne directed his next sneer at him. "Who is that guy, your gynecologist, you pussy?"

Angered, the man started to get up.

"Go ahead! Bring your face right up here," warned Wayne, raising the hammer. "I'll knock you colder 'an a cunt!"

The man thought better of the invitation and slouched back on the seat.

"I asked you a question!" Wayne insisted. "Who is he?"

"Him?" asked the front man in disgust. "He's a banker! All clean and pure, ha, ha," he laughed with emphasis.

"My, my," observed Lester. "What will the stockholders say? Exbanker, I think."

The man in back elevated his vocal despair at the remark.

"Goddamn! Where the hell are the cops, anyway?" asked Wayne, shifting his position on the car. "I don't want to be babysitting these guys all night."

"Well, you don't have to be sitting there with that stupid hammer, you know," said Lester waving his rifle. "If they try anything I'll just shoot 'em."

"So, call again on the radio and see what's going on," Wayne insisted.

Lester leaned back into the truck while keeping an eye on the men in the car and grabbed the mike off the dash holder. As he brought the mike to his mouth, he reached back to the radio and turned up the volume.

"Hey, listen to this," he said.

*. . . don't know where they've been, but four, maybe five more just came off the beach where the others did. It looks like they're headed south down the lake towards town!*

\*       \*       \*

Over the past twenty minutes the wind had subsided considerably as evidenced by the absence of continuous blowing snow. When limited to that which was falling from above, a lighter, finer variety gave indication that the storm was at last winding down. On the open expanse of frozen lake the effect was quickly realized. Distant lights were more clearly defined, as opposed to being fuzzy points identified only by chance. Even horizons of a mile away could be discerned against a sky now a shade or two this side of black as ink. To the south particularly, the glow of Melonia reached upward, it's orangery hue powered at this late hour by it's many street lights and little else.

A quarter mile from the western shore a four wheel drive Chevy Carry-All sporting the Melonia police insignia stood at rest, it's lights ablaze, it's interior illuminating the three men who stood immediately outside by the open driver's door. Ahead of the vehicle Officer Kelly stood in the glare of the headlights looking down at a wrecked snow machine lying on it's side, it's front cowl shattered, one ski bent awkwardly at right angles, it's cleated track missing altogether. Several yards away, what appeared as a small snowdrift casting it's shadow to infinity along the flat plain, featured a man's forearm sticking straight up, the rigid blood stained fingers of the hand assuming a beckoning gesture. Kelly turned away and walked back to the vehicle. Sergeant Budner, Gale and Jason were momentarily silent as they leaned close to the open door.

*. . . confirmed four snow machines left the vicinity of the last condo on the north ridge just as they approached. Took off heading for the lake, r*eported the radio voice from within the vehicle.

Gale was the first to turn away from the vehicle and look toward the west. In a moment a group of lights bounced their way to the ice, then stretched out in single file as they proceeded south along the shore.

"There they are! There's four all right," exclaimed Gale, glancing around at Budner. "Get us back to my machine, then head for shore. Maybe we can turn 'em around and . . ."

"Forget it!" ordered Budner. "They're probably headed for Lansing's dealership where some of their own cars are. And we've got that covered! Besides, I would think you two would have had enough of this tonight. Christ Almighty! How many more bodies are we going to find lying around here anyway?"

"Can't we do this later," asked Jason, turning from the sight of the fleeing snow machines. "That one ain't going anywhere, that's for sure."

"Goddammit! If we don't find 'em now, while there's still some sign of your tracks, we may not see 'em for a week. Now, I've still got some risers and flagging left in back from the sled dogs last week. The least we can do is stake them out."

Gale stepped back to Budner, resigned to the fact that he and Jason would not be taking off after any more snow machines. "Well, I suppose the driver of this one could be wandering around here somewhere."

"What? You mean that wasn't the driver?" asked Budner.

"Hell no," explained Gale. "Then there's the other machine up ahead and I'm damn sure neither one of those guys are up and around."

"Jesus!" Budner shook his head, then turned to Kelly. "You better get on the radio and see if the Fire Department can spare a sled and a couple paramedics in case we find somebody still breathing out here." Budner looked back at Gale. "I'll tell you one thing for sure. You better hope we find that handgun you mentioned. Who had it? That guy over there?"

"Him and the guy on the other machine up ahead. They both did. Hell, you don't think we did this just for the hell of it do you?" Gale fastened Budner with a critical look.

"It doesn't matter what I think," replied Budner simply.

"Well, the only one that's got any of my holes in him is up ahead. This one here just fell off the back of the machine when I nailed the track," stated Gale in a emphatic tone.

"Oh," Budner nodded a little sarcastically. "That certainly explains why he's dead, doesn't it? Fell off his machine."

Gale was getting angry, but Budner put up a hand as he expelled a deep breath. "Look, I hope this thing sorts itself out for your sake. I really do . . . From what I hear there's just a few other things been going on while we were out here cutting off the lake route . . . a little late as it turns out . . . . which is the basic Goddamned reason I'm not in the greatest of moods . . . Anyway, it's going to take a metal detector out here tomorrow to find something like a gun."

"Well, I ain't' worried about it," insisted Gale, much calmer after Budner's last comments. "They're here somewhere."

"Hey, we almost forgot about Scott," said Jason, ending the short pause.

"Who?" asked Budner.

"Scott Roy," said Gale. "He was chasing the three machines ahead of the two we were after."

"Why the hell didn't you say so," said Budner, showing some excitement. "He's the one that called on the radio about Nevis!"

"Yeah? Well, I'll bet you none of those guys got away from Scott," nodded Jason. "He can be a crazy bastard," he added.

"Where have I heard that?" again the sarcasm. "And compared to who? You guys? Jesus Christ!" Budner shook his head for the umpteenth time as he turned toward the open driver's door. "Come on, get in the truck . . . Never in my life did I ever think I'd be stumbling around out here in the middle of the night looking for stiffs spread all . . ."

Jason and Kelly had gone to the other side of the vehicle. As Gale reached for the rear door, Budner was looking down at the Winchester.

"Drop that lever down, will ya? That thing makes me nervous," said Budner.

Gale scowled, but brought the gun up, snapped the lever down, and with some flare, caught the ejected shell in the air with the same right hand.

"What the hell gauge is that?" Budner asked, looking at the huge cartridge.

"Ten," intoned Gale.

"Ten . . ." repeated Budner.

From the north, the headlight steadily increased in size, it's growing presence now joined by the high winding sound of an engine. Gathering the attention of those surrounding the Carry-All, the snow machine sped past, fifty feet to the west, heading south.

"Speak of the devil," remarked Gale.

# chapter 17

Charlie Hayward was alone in the garage. Sitting behind his desk in the small office, he'd been listening to the amazing dialogue coming from the radio base station. An hour ago he'd taken the phone off the hook. First, there'd been calls from people wanting to know why their street hadn't been plowed. Then, increasingly, there were questions from those who couldn't believe what they were hearing over the Public Works frequency and what the hell was going on.

Well, the hell with them. The hell with them all! If nobody else cared that the streets were all but impassable to anything other than a four wheel drive vehicle, why should he? As to what was going on . . . , the fact that he knew, made it all the more incredible. He'd thought he knew the men. But never in the world would he have believed they'd so cavalierly go off . . . , all of them, to pit themselves against some of the country's nastiest crime figures. And what in God's name was Walt thinking of when he'd actually endorsed the whole thing? And Mars! Of all people, he should have known better . . .

In his heart, Charlie hoped none of the men had been hurt . . . or worse. But in his strangely growing anger it would serve them right, he thought, nodding silently.

A rumbling sound from outside in the street had Charlie standing from his chair to peer ahead out a window. A state plow maybe? No, by God! It was a private plow! A dual wheeled ton and a half struggling up the street. And right behind it, another one plowing in tandem. Charlie sat back down. Now he'd seen everything.

A minute later he was staring at some indeterminable point in space as he rapidly turned a pencil end for end on the desk with his right hand. When the radio came to life again, it startled him. Charlie clenched the pencil tight in his fist.

*They're still following the shoreline. Looks like they'll get off the lake at Center Landing if they keep going.*

*We're on our way back, just passed Clayton Avenue. They'll probably take Tyler Street from the Landing. We'll be there first!*

*Delay that, Public Works! We know their destination and we've got it covered.*

*Delay that yourself. They'll never get that far!*

*This is Chief Mars speaking and this is police business! I'm ordering you to stay out of it!*

*Hey, who's impersonating Mars on our frequency? Ha . . .*

*Whoever you are I'll have your . . .*

*Never mind Center Landing! They just turned toward the east shore.*

*Hell, they could come off somewhere around the city garage!*

Unconsciously, Charlie had been softly pounding his fist on the desk while he listened to this latest spurt of radio talk. On hearing that last remark, his eyes widened slightly and the pounding stopped. Coming here? They were coming here? Charlie thought, dwelling on those final two words. Like hell they were! Maybe fate . . . maybe even God had fashioned some final challenge just for him. Maybe . . .

In a single fluid motion Charlie was on his feet, sending the chair to bounce against the back wall. Throwing the pencil across the room, he came around the desk, and with a few purposeful strides, was out the office door.

Through the anteroom and down the hallway, he stopped momentarily at the side door to glance at an array of long handled shovels leaning against the wall. Reaching past a few dirtier examples, he grabbed a shiny new pointed specimen, and together with a push broom, went out the door.

The shovel went in the back of his truck up near the cab. With the push broom he took a few quick swipes at the accumulated snow on the windshield and hood. Tossing the broom aside, Charlie got in and started the engine. Lights, wipers, in gear, the truck bolted ahead, through the windrow the private trucks had just plowed and up the street.

The four snow machines slowed as they approached the shore and finally came to a stop near a private dock frozen in the ice. A break in the concrete retaining wall which skirted the shore in both directions was apparent near the base of the dock where snow covered steps led up from a small beach. Once on solid ground the landscape sloped sharply upward to its crest which bordered the street a mere couple hundred yards from the city garage. To either side of their intended path stood private homes, now darkened, any inhabitants therein totally unaware of the group now gathered near their property.

Each machine carried a driver and passenger. The driver of the first machine turned in his seat to address the others.

"Just follow me. We're going right through town. Ain't nobody out on a night like this and we know where all the cops are. Hold on tight when we jump off the bank onto the road."

There were a few remarks of impatience echoed from the other machines as their drivers prepared to attack the steep slope.

Charlie had seen them approaching the shore and he thought he knew the one logical place they might choose to get on solid ground.

Twenty years before, the concrete retaining wall which held the shoreline had been part of a city contract involving the installation of a sewer interceptor along the water's edge. Just last summer he had looked at portions of it which now required . . .

With his window down he thought he could hear the engines. Charlie crowded his truck as close as he could in toward the narrow sidewalk and the three foot high stone, and in places concrete, wall which held back the embankment on its far side. With his lights off, he inched the truck ahead straddling the fresh windrow, the four wheel drive occasionally slipping and churning it's way forward.

A street light only fifty feet behind him provided a soft illumination to the area, but Charlie kept his eyes fastened on a narrow gap in the hedgerow along the wall where he expected to see the brighter bouncing beams of snow machine headlights. The engines were getting louder. Maybe he had misjudged . . . He ducked low to see out the passenger window and check up along the top of the hedge closer to him. Maybe they'd just go through . . . No! As he looked back, there they were, shining through the gap. And he was still twenty feet away! Charlie stepped on the accelerator and the truck lurched ahead, it's wheels alternately throwing snow to the rear.

Almost there, the first machine came through the gap and out into the air, missing the front of the truck by less than a foot before clearing the windrow and landing in the street. On the way by, the machine's passenger had shot a quick astonished look right at Charlie. But Charlie had only time to glimpse the machine speeding off down the street while he grasped the steering wheel as tight as he could and steeled himself for what was to come.

The three machines came off the embankment in quick succession. The first almost made it onto the truck's hood, but after slamming it's track into the front fender, it bounced back upside down into the gutter. The driver had flipped in the air, ending up on his back on the hood, the passenger went down with the machine.

Charlie held on tight as the truck shuddered again, rocking back up on two wheels. A ski had smashed through the side window reaching halfway across the seat. Outside, the engine cowling skidded over the top of the truck cab just ahead of the driver. The passenger was thrown a little to the side, landing spread eagle on the windshield where he slid down onto the driver of the previous machine who was just now beginning to stir. Charlie had just become aware of the ski tip inches from his head when it snapped upward, smashing the courtesy light and remaining stuck there. The machine settled against the side of the truck, caught in place.

The last machine clipped the hedgerow to its left as it cleared the embankment and crashed down into the pickup body near the rear of the truck which lifted back up on two wheels for a third time. Both driver and passenger were thrown forward into the road, the snow machine remained in the back of the truck.

Two, three . . . five seconds. Charlie didn't move. One of the snow machine engines had continued to run. Finally it sputtered to a stop. Suddenly, as if jolted from a trance, Charlie was out of the truck, shovel in hand, whirling around, trying to look everywhere at once. Quickly he spotted the driver of the last machine just getting to his knees on the far side of the road. Raising the shovel over his head as he moved, he ran to the man and brought the implement down squarely on his helmet, flattening him to the pavement.

A couple yards away the passenger was also struggling to get up, a gun in his hand. As he raised his head and started to lift the gun, Charlie was already swinging the shovel like a huge bat.

Charlie turned and ran back to the truck, stepping over the motionless form of the driver of the second machine on the way. One of the two men on the hood of the truck was stirring again and about to slide off onto the ground. Charlie hooked the corner of the shovel in his heavy parker and pulled him off the hood. Falling head first to the road, the man immediately started to swear as he reached for the truck bumper and started to get up. Charlie planted a boot on the man's shoulder, shoved him over on his back and brought the shovel point down on his throat.

"Don't . . . don't move," Charlie managed to get out. "Don't even think about it!" he said louder as though realizing he must be more forceful and angry. "Look what you did to my truck!"

The man tried to say something, but instead reached for the shovel handle. Charlie kicked him in the side and put more pressure on the shovel. The man's eyes showed pain, then fear as he looked up.

"If you don't be still I'll slit your throat, I swear!" Charlie yelled down at the man. "This is a brand new shovel!" he added without knowing why.

From the far side of the truck came the sound of metal against metal as if the first machine was settling in place or being moved along the truck. Charlie looked quickly in that direction, then back to his captive on the ground. The noise stopped, then in a moment, started again.

"Goddamn!" said the voice with some difficulty. "I'll kill the sonof-a-bitch . . ."

There came a pain laden cry followed by more harsh scraping against the truck. Bam! The gunshot rooted Charlie in place until he forced another glance toward the truck. He could see no one, but the sound of escaping air accompanied the downward path of the right front of the truck. They'd shot a hole in his tire! The shovel shifted beneath him, but the man appeared as before when he looked down.

Bam! Then again, escaping air, more swearing from behind the truck. The rear tire! What the . . . ? Lights were on in the nearest house. There was a figure outlined in a front window. Was that a hand grasping the top of the truck tailgate? Was that the sound of another snow machine approaching?

The shovel was nearly wrenched from his hands as the man rolled to one side and onto his knees. Charlie instinctively pulled back, securing his grip, but the man was on his feet and coming toward him.

The shovel was a familiar tool he'd used all his life. It's feel, it's balance . . . Now, pry that rock off the side of the ditch before it falls . . . Charlie jabbed straight ahead through the man's guard, planting the point hard against his chest. The man stopped, straightened while exhaling every last bit of air . . .

Now! Charlie yanked the shovel back and around in a tight arc . . . Bong! The dull tone resounded as he brought the business end down hard on the hatless skull, the man crumpled to the ground.

Charlie looked up to see a man standing behind his truck. Leaving the support of the vehicle, he staggered a few steps out into the street. The gun in his right hand loomed larger than anything Charlie had ever seen . . .

To the left he noticed the flash of light through the hedgerow, the straining sound of the engine, louder now, but muffled behind the snowy ridge.

"You fucking . . . son-of-a-bitch!" snarled the man in short gasping breaths. "This . . . is going to be . . . a pleasure . . ."

Charlie remembered his legs feeling like water, immobile and useless. But he couldn't recall bringing the shovel up to cover his chest as if it might . . .

The man took a couple more painful steps toward him wanting to make sure he couldn't miss . . .

With a sudden roar from it's engine as the track ran free, the snow machine parted the hedgerow and hurtled through space. The man with the gun turned just in time to see the twin skis pass over his head before his face and upper torso was engulfed by the whirling steel cleats. A momentary cry was quickly squelched by the sickening sounds of pounded tearing flesh and bone which somehow found their way above the dying engine. With the mangled body spat to it's rear, the machine slammed down onto the street and slid up against the far windrow, it's engine finally stalling.

For a moment, there was silence. Scott Roy stepped off his machine, removed his helmet, and surveyed the scene. Walking past his latest victim, he took a quick look to the inside of the pickup before proceeding toward Charlie.

Charlie didn't speak. For a moment, he wasn't sure he ever would. As Scott stopped in front of him he felt the shovel slip from his hands.

"Where the hell's the other machine? Don't tell me you let one get away?" Scott asked harshly.

Charlie knew he was grinning from ear to ear. At least he thought he was. Of course, that didn't explain the tears he could feel on his cheeks. Scott looked surprised, even concerned, as he stepped closer and placed a hand on Charlie's shoulder.

The sound of rising thunder filled the air. Both men looked skyward as it advanced toward them. From the northeast came the dark shape of an Executive Lear jet, its lights ablaze. It passed very low overhead, then it was gone.

# chapter 18

By mid-morning, the temperature had risen into the thirties under an unusually warm winter sun. The Melonia police station, and the immediate area outside, was a center of activity made even more congested by the previous night's heavy snowfall. Quite recently, the street and sidewalks had been cleared as best they could be until a major snow removal operation would finish the job during evening hours. Parked vehicles crammed one side of the street making it difficult for police to keep two-way curiosity-driven, traffic moving with any regularity.

Newspaper people, television crews, along with an untold number of interested citizens jammed the sidewalk and walkway in front of the building. Many more adventurous souls had ventured into the deep snow on either side in an attempt to better view any significant goings on. Atop a particularly high snowdrift, fashioned in the lee of the large lawn mounted police department sign, a television camera was being operated by a man obviously not dressed in preparation for such conditions.

Captain Dan Warner and Lieutenant Paul Titus stood before the double front doors, in essence, keeping the crowd at bay. Unable, at least for the present, to gain entry to the building, or encourage higher ranked officials outside, cameras were trained on the two officers as reporters fired an endless stream of questions in their direction. Warner smiled at the crowd and seemed quite at ease as he imparted the same limited amount of information in creatively different sounding answers. The younger Lieutenant Titus appeared more on edge and more concerned that some enterprising individual might sneak by them into the building.

" . . . was carried out in accordance with standard police procedures," Warner was saying. "But under the unusual circumstances, we were forced to utilize resources of the Public Works Department to . . ."

"Are you saying that Public Works personnel were deputized?" asked a reporter.

"No, I didn't say that. Initially, Public Works was to perform a road blockade function using their heavy equipment, but due to the intense resistance by several of the subjects, Public Works had to take action in their own defense. I might add that they did this in admirable fashion in the face of some of the most professional criminal types in the country."

"What's the final count on the dead and wounded?" a reporter wanted to know.

"We, at least I, don't have a final count at the moment," stated Warner, turning to this new questioner.

"You stated before that there were no police injuries, but wasn't one of the Public Works people shot and wounded?" persisted the reporter, struggling to the forefront of the crowd.

"Yes, that's true. He . . ."

"Was Bradford Nevis the only one you had a warrant for?" interrupted another reporter who attempted to get a microphone closer to the police captain.

Warner was quick to accept the interruption. He wasn't sure of the other details. "No, he was not," he spoke towards the mike. "But Chief Mars will answer any questions along these lines."

"Was Nevis apprehended or not?" came a loud accusatory question from back in the crowd.

A little irritated, Warner glanced back to find the source of the question. He could not. "Chief Mars will answer that," he said evenly. "I'll have to ask that you be patient until he . . ."

"Why can't we go in there? That's a public building isn't it?"

The question came from a short, very pretty girl who had managed to fight her way to the front of the crowd and now held her microphone high to accommodate the six foot plus captain. Warner looked down at her and couldn't help but smile.

"To begin with, you all won't fit in there," Warner explained patiently. "And secondly, Chief Mars is presently conferring with officials from the State Police, the Governor's office, the F.B.I., the Justice Department, etcetera, etcetera. There will be a written report released as soon as possible . . . Believe me, there's more material here than you ever dreamed. They'll be talking about this for months to come."

This final statement only served to heighten the excitement of the press. Warner turned to Titus and gave him a concealed wink.

Walton Conover and Dwane Huckins stood together talking in the hallway. Both had changed clothes and now appeared in sport coat and tie. From a nearby office doorway, Chief Mars emerged with an older man in a conservative suit. The man nodded at a last remark from the chief and departed past Conover and Dwane who sidestepped to allow his passage. Mars was attired in a dress uniform complete with pearl handled .357 magnum.

"Wow! Is this our very own chief of police? Pretty sharp," commented Dwane in his usual aggressive approach to authority.

Mars ignored the remark. "Dwane, I understand you're back in the police business yourself, or whatever they call it down in Washington these days. Last night have anything to do with that?'

"Actually, no. It's something I've been trying to line up for quite a while. But they know what went on here all right. My first order is not to appear directly on camera."

"All dressed up and no place to go, huh?" Mars chided.

"You might say that," Dwane admitted.

Mars turned to Conover. "Well Walt, I assume you don't have any such reservations. We've got to go meet the press at some point."

"Have I got a choice?" Conover asked.

"Not that I can think of. Just remember, the Public Works vehicles were requisitioned by me. The volunteers were yours. There's a half dozen out of town lawyers here now. By this afternoon they'll be a lot more. The next few days should be interesting . . . By the way, I appreciate you keeping the rest of your guys out of here this morning. Some of them really ought to have some council before they go shooting their mouth off."

Conover nodded his agreement. "They've been told. Hell, there's more press at the garage. Except for Dunbar, most of them are out plowing snow. The city's still a mess, in case you haven't noticed."

"I know," Mars agreed. "We've been getting calls from the few people that hadn't heard what went on last night. And I've been told that there must have been a couple dozen private plows that just started working on the streets after they heard. Some of them started late last night. Kind of a silent tribute, you might say."

Conover nodded. "So I understand . . . Anyway, I thought it best to try to keep the guys out of touch until some of this gets sorted out."

"Well, needless to say, you can count on our support. Say, how is Dunbar doing anyway?"

"Fine," Dwane answered. "I was up at the hospital about an hour ago. They took a slug out of his shoulder early this morning. The other one just grazed his thick skull."

"Good . . . good," said Mars. "I'm sure he's doing a damn sight better than the men that shot him. I suppose you already know that that new kid of yours picked up Dunbar's old .45 and emptied it into the car after Dunbar went down."

Both Conover and Dwane nodded affirmatively.

"Looks like he'll fit right in with the rest of your work force," Mars added with a slight smile.

"Seems as if I heard you took out a couple guys yourself," Conover said in reply.

"You won't hear me say this to anyone ever again, but it seems like we were just mopping up after Public Works."

Conover seemed a bit taken aback by the stark admission. "They did a hell of a job. I'm damn proud of them."

Mars seemed to want to get back on a lighter vein. "Remind me never to get in the way of one of those plow trucks . . . , and how about those guys out on the lake. That Scott Roy of yours. I just wish he had . . ."

Traffic in the hallway had become progressively heavier as Melonia officers made their way back and forth addressing duties relating to the previous night's operation. Sergeant Budner stopped beside Mars.

"Chief, John Griffin wants to know when you're coming down to the squad room to get started. I guess they're getting pretty anxious."

"Tell them to give me another ten minutes. There's something I've got to take care of first."

"All right." Budner turned to go, then looked back. "Oh, we've got that case set up on the table down there. Thing weighs a ton. Couple of the FBI guys seem really curious about it."

Budner left. Mars turned back to Conover and Dwane with a smile. "They're all down there and they think they know it all . . . . You realize, we still might be hanging pretty loose on some of this if it wasn't for what's in that case. This way everybody will have something to think about they sure as hell never figured on and I'll be glad its out in the open. Why don't you two go on down. I'll be along in a little bit . . . And save me some coffee if there's any left, will you?"

Chief Mars headed off in the direction of his office.

\* \* \*

If it hadn't been for the heavy old car and some superb driving, they would never have made it at all. Even so, Tony was still fretting about a small crease in the Lincoln's right front fender which had happened when squeezing past another car caught in a snow bank. Down the narrow drifted rear drive and finally back onto the highway to the south just ahead of a big yellow plow truck that sealed the intersection behind them. It had been close. They'd headed west. Over a series of impossible windswept secondary roads, Tony had seemed to know exactly where they were like he'd had it all prepared just in case. For the first time he had sensed it was up to him and he was determined not to fail. "Don't worry, don't worry," Tony had repeated in fending off nervous comments from four of his five passengers.

Lorenzo had remained silent for most of the trip, deep in thought. Occasionally, he had complimented Tony, or sought to reassure his companions.

Forty miles from Hallingford they had found a motel. No sooner had they settled in their rooms than Lorenzo had announced he would return to Melonia the following morning. Frank had been the most vehement in objecting to such a foolhardy proposal. But the decision had been made.

*   *   *

Mars entered his office and closed the door behind him. To his right stood a young police officer. Straight ahead, before a draped wall in two large leather chairs were seated Lorenzo Denecy and his chauffeur. First Denecy, then Tony, rose from their chairs. Mars nodded to the pair, then to his officer who quietly left the room.

"Mister Denecy," Mars began. "I wish I could say it's a pleasure. Frankly, I'm not sure what it is. I will admit, however, your phone call was quite interesting."

"I hoped you would find it so," said Lorenzo respectfully. "Good morning, Chief Mars."

"Please sit down, gentlemen," said Mars, carefully matching the older man's tone.

Denecy and Tony resumed their seats as Mars walked to the front of his desk and sat on it's forward edge looking down at the two men. Denecy's eyes twinkled for a moment as if the bit of choreography was not lost on him.

"I might find it difficult to prove that you were even in town last night, at least without some intensive interrogation of those we presently have under lock and key. I know you were, of course, but I really don't have the time right now and it probably doesn't make much difference anyway. It appears that those with you also managed to remove themselves from the Hallingford. Quite a trick, I might add. There weren't many."

Tony looked intently from Mars to his boss. He had correctly taken it as an honor to have been included in the meeting itself. The protective bond he already felt toward Mister Denecy had increased as a result. He also knew he must remain silent unless addressed directly.

Denecy smiled vaguely. "I trust you have found that I am not wanted in connection with any crime."

Mars hesitated only a moment. "Well, the N.Y.P.D. is amazed that you were not where they thought you were. But they wouldn't divulge exactly why that was important to them."

"In the past, activities wrongly attributed to me have tended to make them quite nervous. This surveillance has been going on for some time. I suspect it is now little more than an exercise and I doubt if anyone could give you a good reason for it."

Mars smiled. "I love your analogy."

Denecy spread his hands, palms up.

"Which brings me to the question of why you chose to show up here this morning. You mentioned some information about those two . . . trophies we found last night. We know their identity, of course. Are they yours?"

Denecy shook his head in denial. "No, they are not . . . . Chief Mars, would it surprise you to learn that the terrorist acts of men such as those could be abhorred even by what you perceive to be men like me? . . . And further, could you visualize that there could be those somewhat outside your normal law enforcement organizations that might have certain advantages in dealing with them?"

Mars got up, walked behind his desk and sat down as if the movement would allow time to consume what he had just heard.

"Somewhat outside law enforcement, you say? Give a cop some consideration, will you Denecy? . . . Alright, for the moment we'll set that aside. And for the moment I'll agree that crime is getting a bad name . . . God! But, you'll have to admit that this is a new approach. And you expect me to believe that you have only some vague knowledge of this?"

Denecy spoke a bit more slowly as he measured his words. "I am not at the forefront of any such operation. Indeed, until quite recently, I did not know of the existence of these . . . trophies, as you call them."

Mars leaned slightly forward and spoke the moment Denecy finished. "Then how about someone who arrived and left last night in an Executive Lear jet under something less than acceptable flying weather?"

Denecy was not ruffled. "Chief Mars, I have no knowledge of anyone's choice of transportation. I have no idea who might have been on such a plane."

Mars settled in his chair. "I see. So, what of this information you mentioned?"

"Only that there may be more trophies, and that I might personally see that you are the first to receive any information I could come by. In the city the police have a name for someone knowledgeable in certain matters not perceived through official channels."

"A snitch. I've heard the term. Go on. I'm about out of time and so are you. So tell me why."

Mars had appeared to be getting somewhat impatient, but Denecy did not vary his delivery. "Chief Mars, I contacted you this morning because I think this is important. Very simply, I wanted to understand that you appreciated that any future deterrent to terrorism depends on such organizations realizing that they and their assorted causes face certain risks from quarters they can not begin to guard against."

"Like the risk of becoming a king size paperweight? Very convincing,"

Mars nodded. "And if I'm not mistaken, a fate much worse than death itself in some ethnic quarters. A fact our mystery executioners may well have taken into account."

There followed a short silence during which the two men looked at each other as if they had suddenly found themselves going the wrong way on a one way street and each waited for the other to state the obvious.

Denecy opened his mouth to speak, but it was Mars that slowly stood behind his desk, a quizzical look on his face.

"Maybe I'm a little slow this morning . . . , then, of course, you could have been a little more direct. With law enforcement presently in this building ranking from local to federal, might you be wondering if maybe these trophies could get mysteriously buried in some basement vault at the Bureau for one reason or another and never see the light of day?"

The question obviously struck a chord with Denecy as he shifted in his chair. Mars held up a hand so as to continue.

"Well, possibly we are of the same mind on this one thing. As it happens, I am one of a handful on this side of the fence that knows they exist. Personally, I've never been one to keep the public uninformed and in about twenty minutes I intend to roll them out in front of the cameras myself. Let the chips fall where they may. I suggest you look at tonight's papers. I'd ask you to stay, but . . ." Mars let his sentence trail off with a smile.

Now it was Denecy's turn to stand, a broad smile on his face. Tony stood also, understandably a bit confused, but clearly content that his boss seemed pleased.

"Excellent, Chief Mars. Excellent," said Lorenzo. "But remember what I said. Any information . . ."

"I won't slam the receiver in your ear," Mars interrupted.

At that moment the phone on the desk buzzed. Mars picked it up.

Yeah, in a minute . . . Send Kelly in here."

Almost immediately, officer Kelly entered the room and closed the door. Mars addressed his young officer.

"First, I want you to go out front and tell Captain Warner to single out a fair representation of the press, the local, of course, and also some of the heavyweights from down south, and bring them to the squad room. Try to keep it under a dozen people. Then I want you to collect Allenson and come back in here. You two are to take Mister Denecy and his chauffeur out the side entrance to their car and escort them south to the town line. Understood?"

"Yes, sir," said Kelly.

The squad room was already crowded with people. Police officers of the city, county and state, along with a curious mix of unidentified, assertive looking men in fine fresh suits, stood in pairs or in groups of their own kind like specimens waiting for a place on the arc. A scattered minority of elected officials, supposedly in constant charge of the former, but now in the lair of their underlings, exuded an air of uncertainty masked by too many smiles, freely given to those they'd never met.

Consumed in fraternal dialogue, the local men were largely unaware of it's existence, but clearly, impatience was at large within the room. Evidenced to a greater degree by those of higher station from plush offices to the south, these same had therefore been inconvenienced the most in simply delivering themselves at this early hour. Such assumed burden thereby indicated their greater potential for personal loss if the political fall-out from the extraordinary events of the evening past failed to caress them in a friendly fashion.

A table offering coffee, donuts and muffins now appeared to have been ravaged by a family of raccoons. Those in the room seemed to be distancing themselves from the immediate area as though not wanting to be associated with the devastation. Dwane Huckins managed to escape the scene with a covered styrofoam cup which he carried along with his own just before a secretary arrived and viewed the mess with stoic control as she began to tidy up.

As Dwane rejoined Walt Conover against the near wall, they were approached by an overly affable suit who extended his hand before he'd even come to a stop.

"Colonel Conover! Colonel, am I glad to meet you. I'm Dale Goodnow," said the suit.

Conover looked questioningly at the man, then awkwardly transferred his cup to his donut holding left in order to take his hand.

"My, you certainly look like you were in a battle last night," said the smiling Goodnow. "And who is this?" Goodnow asked, not waiting for Conover's answer as he turned to Dwane, his hand at the ready.

Dwane pretended not to notice the hand, but finally raised each cup a few inches as his obvious excuse to Goodnow's insistence. "Dwane Huckins," said Dwane in a dull monotone.

"Oh. Oh yes, you must be with Public Works also," Goodnow nodded, then turned back to Conover. "Tell me, Colonel, how did it go last night?"

Conover had apparently gotten his bearings and didn't look impressed with what he saw. "What do you do, Mister . . . Mister Goodno is it?"

"Goodnow. Dale Goodnow, Colonel," Goodnow corrected still with the smile. "I must apologize. I'm administrative assistant to the Governor, but I guess I don't get north of Concord as much as I should, heh, heh."

"Why are you here, may I ask," queried Conover, starting to take the offensive.

"Well . . . , well, of course, the Governor wants to get a clear picture of what happened last night," Goodnow explained.

"I see the State Police are here, among others. I would think you'd . . ."

"Oh yes. Yes, I know," Goodnow interrupted. "But I've got to get a more personal impression of the situation, you see. The press is knocking at the door, heh, heh, and we want to know how all this is going to play out, so to speak. You know what I mean."

"I don't think I do." Conover smiled a bit sweetly. "Why don't we just tell them what happened? We'll tell them the truth. What the hell?"

For the first time, Goodnow's smile dropped from view, until like a pair of pants, he pulled it back into position. Dwane sipped his coffee, looking somewhat amused.

"Why yes, yes. I wholeheartedly agree," nodded Goodnow. "But we've got to . . ."

"Look. Chief Mars will be down any second. You speak to him first and then I'll talk your ears off if you want." Conover smiled more broadly. "But somehow I don't think you're going to find the time."

A few yards away, three more suited strangers were gathered around a vacant desk where one of them was holding a phone receiver to his ear.

"Christ, already?" asked the man, his eyes widening at his companions. "Where are you calling from anyway? . . . Well, get the hell up here! We've got some things to go over and quick." The man slammed the receiver into it's cradle.

"We can forget about dealing with a few regional news departments. We've got at least two network anchors on their way right now. Bill Judd himself may be here before we get through with this!"

"My God," exclaimed the second man, straightening his tie.

The third man looked intently at some papers he held. "We've got to get a better accounting than this or we're going to look like fools. Where the hell is this Chief Mars, anyway?" he asked, looking around.

The second man grasped a Melonia police officer standing nearby by the shoulder. The officer turned, obviously irritated.

"Officer, where is your Chief?"

"He'll be down directly, sir," said the officer coldly before turning away.

A few yards farther on, the County Sheriff and one of his deputies stood talking as a high ranking State Police Officer joined the pair.

"Well Sid, looks like the county has some distinguished guests this morning," remarked the state officer.

The sheriff smiled and nodded. "So does the morgue."

"So I hear. I guess the count is somewhere around a dozen? Must have been something. Mars is one lucky bastard. Damn! I wish we could have made it up here last night. Couldn't get five miles out of Concord. I couldn't see my Goddamned hood ornament it was blowing so hard."

"Hey, don't feel bad. I never got the chance to try. We got in this morning from that New England Law Enforcement conference down in Boston. Heard it on the radio coming into town an hour ago," confessed the sheriff.

A Melonia officer walked up to the group, but his attention was on two dark suited men who were inspecting the large leather case on a table at the head of the room. The older of the men was fingering one of the clasps along its side.

"Hey! Sir! . . . Yes, you," said the officer, loud enough to gather some attention elsewhere in the room.

The two men at the case looked at the officer, the older, obviously perturbed at the interruption.

"Just leave that be sir, if you would," ordered the officer.

"What is this, anyway?" asked the older man.

"I don't know. Something the Chief had brought down here," replied the officer.

The two men backed grudgingly away from the table.

"Who are those two?" asked the Sheriff of the state police officer.

"I'm not sure. F.B.I. probably. Or maybe Justice . . ."

At that moment everyone turned to the hall door of the squad room as it burst open revealing the loud commotion of people outside. First through, were two men carrying an assortment of television video equipment. Next came the remainder of the group of news people, some bearing additional tools of their trade. Others, free handed, hawkish looking individuals scanned the room like animals looking for prey.

Those already ensconced in what they had thought a secure haven reacted with surprise and indignation, though their outward attitude quickly changed to their best public face as microphones appeared and camera lights flicked on. As Chief Mars came into the room to their rear, much of the attention turned back upon him.

"Quiet please! Quiet," said Mars, his arms outstretched.

For a moment the voices subsided to a murmur.

"I know it's crowded in here, but if we can keep some order, we'll get through this. Would you please direct your attention to the front of the room."

Mars started through the crowd in that direction as background conversation again rose. Dwane stepped forward to thrust a cup of coffee in his path which Mars took with a wink. While pausing to take a quick sip of the now cooled liquid, Dale Goodnow appeared before him.

"This is highly irregular," stated Goodnow with concern.

"You're telling me," agreed Mars, pressing on.

Nearly to his destination, John Griffin, head of the State Police, stepped in Mars' path.

"Justin, what are you doing?" Griffin asked with more curiosity than concern. "This isn't what we had in mind."

"John, just bear with me. I've got my reasons," Mars said as he moved past.

Finally, behind the table at the head of the room, Mars set his coffee cup down and rested his forearms atop the leather case. As cameras were being readied to each side, a hastily erected tree holding a few microphones sprouted a foot in front of the leather case. Realizing they were placed before the apparent spot of his choosing, Mars stepped to his right, reached across the table and slid the stand down with him.

Conversation in the room subsided once more.

"Gentlemen, . . . ladies," Mars began, as there were two female reporters among the news people. "Last evening this department received information that placed Bradford Nevis and his associates at the Hallingford Farm Complex located a few miles north of here. That information was uncovered by members of the Melonia Public Works Department . . . , and I'll get into this more later. As you know, a federal warrant had been issued yesterday afternoon, but before we could act to apprehend Mister Nevis, further information indicated that the gathering at Hallingford involved well over a hundred of this country's major organized crime figures in what has been determined was probably the largest such meeting in twenty-five years."

Mars paused for a quick breath and held up a hand to ward off the questions that were about to be asked.

"We were still bound to apprehend Bradford Nevis, however, the operation at that point gained monumental proportions. We dared not wait for outside help as we feared the meeting might break up at any time and because of the storm it was impossible for any help to reach us. At about this time it was determined that the magnitude of the meeting dictated that surely they would have arranged for their own security. Therefore, from that moment the local police radio frequencies were abandoned. Eventually, we would use the Melonia Public Works frequency. I might add here that at the time Public Works was out in force plowing city streets during last night's storm."

Mars reached to take a sip of coffee, half expecting to be interrupted further. However, no questions were forthcoming. Only a slight undertone of conversation was evident. Mars placed his cup back on the table and continued.

"At that point, additional cooperation from the Public Works Department was sought by me and quickly granted by Colonel Walt Conover, Director of Public Works. The heavy snow plows were to perform a road blockade function of the many entrances and exits of the Hallingford property."

Mars slowed his speech somewhat to place emphasis on his next statement.

"Public Works personnel, knowing full well the gravity of the situation, volunteered to bring this equipment into place around Hallingford. Their offer was accepted by Colonel Conover, and in turn, approved by me."

Mars paused only a second to detect any raised eyebrows, then pressed on.

"Shortly thereafter, the Melonia police force, together with the Melonia Public Works Department, members of the Belknap County Sheriff's Office and a few officers from two nearby towns, approached the Hallingford Complex under my direction.

It appeared that minutes before our arrival those at Hallingford were either warned, or suspected our approach because when we got there it was evident that the first members of the group were taking steps to flee the premises, and that plans had been made to accomplish this. At any rate, they attempted to leave and avoid questioning almost to a man and subsequently, we were fired upon many times . . . . An accurate accounting of the action that followed is being prepared in report format at this time and will be released as soon as possible. But for the moment . . ."

Conversation now swelled within the room as it became obvious that Mars was sliding past the details everyone wanted the most. From both right and left, the questions came forth. For the first time Mars looked tired as he gathered himself and picked up where he left off.

"But for the moment," he started again, without the strict attention previously demanded, " . . . I would like to say that the members of this Public Works Department performed in what I can only describe as above and beyond the call of their volunteered duty, and that much of the success of this operation can be attributed to them . . . One final note for now regarding last night is the fact that all information we have at present indicates that Bradford Nevis drowned in the open waters at the north end of the bay shortly after midnight."

During the last thirty seconds, Mars had again secured the attention of almost everyone. However, as he finished, and for the moment appeared to have nothing further to say, the voices of the press erupted as if on cue.

For a few long moments, Mars stared ahead, oblivious to the rising disorder before him. Out of town police officials and political types began to exchange questioning looks at Mars' performance until they themselves began to be targeted by some members of the press. The persistent young lady who had challenged Captain Warner at the front door now parked herself in front of Walt Conover. But Conover's eyes, as well as Dwane's, were on Mars. As if sensing their attention, Mars' gaze drifted across the room to where they stood.

"Quiet!" Mars bellowed at the top of his lungs.

Everyone in the room was riveted to attention by the sudden, one word outburst. Silence followed almost immediately.

"Before . . . , before we wade into some of the details of the operation itself," Mars began slowly. "There is something else. Something, that as of this moment, only three of us in this room know about . . . Something of extreme importance."

Mars paused, but the silence endured. He had them now and he knew it. At the rear of the room Conover and Dwane exchanged a quick glance.

"And it has to do with the reason," Mars continued, "or at least a primary reason, for the meeting of every major old line underworld figure at the Hallingford Farm Complex last night . . . I will attempt to tell you what little we know about it at present, but before that . . . I will show you the main exhibit."

His gestures deliberate, Mars stepped back behind the leather case, his hands drifting down each side to the release mechanisms near it's base. Hushed murmurs floated, then died about the room as many realized that what they had perceived as just another object in this unfamiliar setting was suddenly of paramount significance. Mars' expression was stern and taut, but strangely, his demeanor suggested he was enjoying himself immensely.

Mars slowly lifted the hood. As the contents of the case were revealed, he discarded the cover roughly to one side where it bounced into an unoccupied chair, knocking it over on the floor. The flourish of movement was not unlike that exhibited by Carl Endicott only hours before.

# chapter 19

Plow truck fifteen slowed almost to a stop, then pulled tightly around the corner, burying it's snow filled plows into the windrow. Custer pulled three levers in succession and the plows rose into the air. Bill Board maneuvered the shift lever into reverse, then stopped to look over at his wingman. A soft rock tune at moderate volume emanated from the cassette player mounted under the dash.

"What's the matter anyway? You've been awful quiet lately. You ain't said nothing since we left the garage."

"Yeah . . . , I know. I . . ." Custer acknowledged in a weak raspy voice.

Bill leaned closer to Custer, his eyebrows almost touching each other. "What's this? You can hardly talk, can you? Ha, ha . . . Well, I'll be Goddamned!"

"I . . . certainly can . . ." Custer struggled to get out.

Bill Board continued to laugh. "You screamed so much over that damned loudspeaker last night you lost your voice. You got laryngitis! If that don't beat all. Ha, ha . . ."

Bill was still laughing as he guided the truck back around the corner for a second pass. Custer looked at his driver, displeasure showing plainly on face. Taking a cassette from his shirt pocket, he quickly exchanged it for the one in the player. Custer altered a couple controls on the machine and suddenly, the crashing sound of a guitar gone wild filled the truck cab at tremendous volume. Custer smiled and leaned back in his seat.

Outside, the guitar was also on the loose as the truck jerked awkwardly to a stop. Through the windshield, Bill could be seen angrily mouthing objections to his wingman who remained oblivious or uncaring or both. With the truck in the middle of the intersection, Board reached over to quell the onslaught only to be pushed away. Driver and wingman wrestled for control of the cassette player.

Truck number twenty-two struggled to hold speed up the slight grade, snow streaming from it's plows. Behind the wheel, Roland Powell forcefully shook his head back and forth and exercised his facial muscles.

"You're going to have to drive this thing. I can't keep my eyes open."

"Yeah . . . , sure," intoned Richard Wright, continuing his attention on the magazine in his lap.

"We got anything left to drink?" asked Roland.

"No. All gone," came the simple answer.

After a few seconds, Roland glanced over at his wingman. "What the hell is that you're looking at?"

"Guy gave it to me at the garage just before we left," announced Richard, his eyes still on the page. "Big dude. Never saw him before. Had that military look about him. Know what I mean? Calls me son. Here son, he says. Take a look at this. We're all proud of you. I'll be talking to you later, he says."

"Well, what the hell is it?" Roland asked impatiently.

"Mercenaries Monthly," said Richard, displaying the magazine cover. "Hey, there's some good stuff in here," he added in response to Roland's changing expression.

"Mercenaries Monthly? And this guy says he'll be talking to you later? You? Ha, haaa . . . Get away from me!"

"No shit! Look, did you know there's at least a dozen full scale wars going on around the world on any given day, but you never hear about most of 'em. Just pick a cause and make big bucks. It gives you the whole dope right here."

Roland finally collected himself. "You're the fucking dope, you fucking nitwit!"

"So you think this is all crap, huh?" said Richard, waving the magazine. "Well, just listen to this . . . , and I quote." Richard looked back at the text to find his place. "'Such is the life and times of civilized man that he seldom understands the faint tug of the primitive warrior within him, nor the rising emotion which occasionally will drive him to risk all to experience that inner smile of courageous worth.' There! What do you think of that? I'm telling ya, I just go berserk when I read that stuff. I just wanna go find a bunch of slimes in some two bit scumbag country and beat the piss out of 'em. Don't you?"

Roland was shaking his head again, but not in an effort to stay awake. "I swear, you get a little crazier every week. Eventually, I'm going to have to get another wingman what with you being in a straightjacket up at the Fuzzy Fern."

Richard threw the magazine in the air inside the cab, it's pages fluttered askew. Laughing wildly, he grabbed Roland by the shoulder and shook him roughly back and forth as Roland held onto the big steering wheel with both hands.

"Alright, alright!" yelled Roland. "Cut it out, will ya? I'm awake now! You don't have to drive. Hell, I wouldn't let you drive if you begged me! Jesus Christ!"

Richard immediately released Roland and settled back in his seat.

"Good, I didn't want to anyway," he intoned, and closed his eyes.

Truck twenty-two proceeded down the boulevard. From the opposite direction, a local car approached. As it neared the truck, the horn started to blare. From opened windows, it's mostly female occupants waved wildly as they passed.

Truck nineteen accelerated down the long hill on Willow Road. Snow cascading off the front plow reached out into the trees crowding the ditch line along the west side. From his passenger seat, Dean Smith leaned forward trying to get a view to the rear through the big door mounted mirror. Blowing snow in the wake of the truck presented only a swirling sea of white.

"They still behind us?" asked Dean. "I can't see anything from here."

"Hell, no," answered Pat Gant. "They turned off. I think it was channel nine."

Dean sat back, a worried look on his face. "Man, I don't want to talk to anybody until I find out what's going on . . . Christ, we just blew them guys off the road!"

"So what? They were trying to kill us at the time in case you didn't notice. We still got these bullet holes in the windshield and another one in the air cleaner to prove it. Hell, don't worry about it. You're a fucking hero."

"Yeah . . . , maybe so," said Dean, his expression unimproved. "I just want to make sure. I don't shoot people every day you know."

"For God's sake! This is going to be the biggest thing that ever happened around here and you're still moping around like Mister Gloom and Doom."

"You mean Oscar?" asked Dean, looking over at his driver.

"Hell yes, I mean Oscar . . . Christ, can you believe he drove that damned Bombardier all the way up to Hallingford last night just to run smack into that police cruiser? Smashed his puss all over again," Pat laughed. "What a fucking mess! Did you see him in the garage this morning?"

"No."

"Well, I got him off to the side, real serious like, and told him that the cops were going to hang his ass for that. He turned white as a sheet, went into the shithouse and puked his guts out. Ha haa . . ."

"Hey, everybody knows his brain just vapor locks every once in a while. Thanks mostly to you, probably."

"Did you hear about his nephew? You know, the goofy one that thought he was going to get a job with us last year?'

"Yeah, I know who you mean. What about him?"

"You ain't going to believe this shit," Pat warned. "Dennis was telling me about it the other day after the kid's old man was talking to him over at the Legion. I guess he was half shitfaced . . . Anyway, it seems the old man goes up in the attic a couple weeks ago and finds all these plants growing up there in pots and you know what they were . . . ? No, it wasn't what you think. You won't believe this, but it was poison ivy."

"Poison ivy?"

"See? What did I tell ya? Poison ivy. Anyway, Dennis says that last summer the kid was playing with the dog out in the field just wearing his swimsuit and I guess he comes down with a wicked case of the shit. It got real bad. The kid swelled all up and they finally had to take him to the hospital. Hell, he was all pussey and bleeding and dripping all over the place."

"Jesus Christ," uttered Dean, wrinkling his face.

Yeah. Well, the kid was in the hospital for a week and when he comes home it wasn't a day or two until he had it all over again and this goes on the rest of the summer. His old man and his mother are going bullshit and by this time the kid's got scabs on top of scabs and he's turning into a real loon. Well, you know what . . . ? Somehow, he'd gotten hooked on the damn stuff. Just loved to scratch the shit. So last fall he sneaks some plants up in the attic to tide him over the winter. I guess he'd go up there and rub the stuff all over him. Hell, he had those purple grow lights up there and everything."

"Jesus Christ," Dean repeated.

"Yeah! And you know what else . . . ? The kid was drippin' all his pus in a cup and then drinking it!"

"Jesus Christ, Pat," exclaimed Dean in almost a pleading tone as he turned to his driver.

"No Shit! Goddamn near died! So now he's in the hospital again, but this time it's at the Loon Corral down in Concord. Can you imagine that? Fucking unbelievable!"

"Well, I ain't feeling that great myself."

"Hey, I'm just trying to take your mind off the fact that you're probably going to fucking jail."

"Will you just shut the fuck up?"

"Ha, haaa . . ."

The truck slowed as it neared the state highway intersection. Turning the corner, the plows held tightly against the high snowbank, the rising temperature allowing the snow to curl up, stick and hold like frosting around the side of a fancy white cake. On the highway, the salt cleared blacktop glistened in the sun. The truck accelerated out of first gear. First the front plow, then the wing, emptied of snow along the windrow and rose into the air where they'd probably stay until the next storm.

Truck nineteen headed home.